REAR WINDOW

I finally settled in my overstuffed living room chair, and looked out over the street. After a few minutes, I noticed a black Volvo, inching past like an out-of-towner looking for a parking space. I could feel the eyes of its driver on my window.

So powerful was the sensation that I shrank back against my chair, not convinced I couldn't be seen, even though there was no light on.

It's terrible when your heart starts to thump against your ribs and your breath comes in shallow, panicky gasps.

As the Volvo turned the corner, I heaved a small sigh of relief. I was about to get up when I felt a cool breath on the back of my neck and heard a cry of silent warning inside my head. I sat frozen, unable to move. Three or four minutes later, the Volvo reappeared, cruising past my window like a shark circling its prey.

"I couldn't put *Homebody* down."

—Barbara D'Amato

HOMEBODY

LOUISE TITCHENER

HarperPaperbacks
A Division of HarperCollinsPublishers

This is a work of fiction. The characters, incidents, and dialogues are products of the author's imagination and are not to be construed as real. Any resemblance to actual events or persons, living or dead, is entirely coincidental.

HarperPaperbacks   *A Division of* HarperCollins*Publishers*
10 East 53rd Street, New York, N.Y. 10022

Copyright © 1993 by Louise Titchener
All rights reserved. No part of this book may be used or reproduced in any manner whatsoever without written permission of the publisher, except in the case of brief quotations embodied in critical articles and reviews. For information address HarperCollins*Publishers,*
10 East 53rd Street, New York, N.Y. 10022.

Cover illustration by Jim Griffin

First printing: August 1993

Printed in the United States of America

HarperPaperbacks, HarperMonogram, and colophon are trademarks of HarperCollins*Publishers*

❖ 10 9 8 7 6 5 4 3 2 1

1

Before I try to tell you what happened when I moved into a murdered woman's apartment, I'd better explain about me. My name is Antoinette Credella, and I live in Baltimore. I'm a widow, twenty-eight years old. My husband, Nick, was a cop. Three years ago I shot and killed him with his service revolver. At the time he'd drunk himself into a rage and beaten me half-dead.

Okay, now if you're still with me, I'll tell you about the apartment. The morning it all started, I staggered into my kitchen in a lousy mood. There it was, lying next to the coffeemaker like a coiled rattler, my landlord's billet-doux. It informed me that he intended raising my rent another fifty bucks.

"Time to move," I muttered. Slightly nauseated because I'm not the adventurous type and change of any kind stirs up my bottomless pit of insecurities, I settled down with the *City Paper* to start looking.

Two hours later I stood in the living room of a one-bedroom apartment in a stately old brick Charles Village corner row house, listening to the eager absentee owner, Mr. Arnold Aronchick, tout his rental property's virtues.

"It's got a new coat of paint and new carpet. Three years ago I had the kitchen remodeled, all new appliances. At three hundred and fifty, this place is a steal."

I couldn't argue. Though Mr. Aronchick's property didn't have the raffish charm of Mt. Vernon, where I'd been living for the past three years, it beat by $200 the rent I would be paying after the last price hike.

"Neighborhood's great, too," Mr. Aronchick was going on. "You a college student?"

When I shook my head, he shrugged. "Well, you're young and pretty, and I don't see a ring. You'll like living close to Johns Hopkins. Lots of people your own age, lots of activities. Where do you work, by the way?"

"I'm self-employed."

"Self-employed?"

I watched Mr. Aronchick's reaction. He was somewhere in his sixties, with a face that had begun to sag like a basset hound's. Either he was shy or something else bothered him because since the moment we'd met outside on the doorstep he'd been avoiding my eyes and talking too quickly. Now, for the first time, he looked at me directly for more than five seconds.

"I run a business called Fresh Features. It's basically wallpapering and faux finishes and reupholstery. Any objections?" I tried to ask it in a way that didn't sound seriously defensive.

He shook his head so the loose skin draping his jaw wobbled. "Sounds clean and respectable. Why should I fuss? What about you? Have I made a sale?"

Stalling for time, I glanced around, taking in the smell of new white paint. The living room was small but had two big double-hung windows with a view of the tree-shaded street. The kitchen off the hall, though tiny, was perfectly acceptable. Yet I hated the thought of moving, and something about Mr. Aronchick wasn't hitting me right.

"Maybe I'm stupid for asking, but why haven't you set the rent a little higher? With the location and all, I'd think you could command more money."

Under his pale yellow golfing jacket he rolled his shoulders, and again I sensed that uneasiness in him that I'd been tuning in to all along. "I just want to get the place rented. Money isn't a high priority. What about it?"

"I'd like to give it some thought."

"I've got two more people coming to look this afternoon. One of them's going to snap it up."

He was right, of course. At $350 it had to go fast, and I'd be kicking myself. "Let me just take a walk around the block and think about it, okay?"

He shuffled his feet. "Okay, but don't take too long." Giving the empty living room a quick, nervous glance, he added, "I'll be out in my car."

Something was wrong, I knew it. Five minutes later I stopped into a corner grocery and had my worst fears confirmed. "Yeah, sure," said the well-padded woman behind the counter cluttered with wire snack racks, "everybody around here knows about that college girl getting murdered there. No wonder the landlord's lowered the rent."

"College girl?" As I studied the letters on the clerk's badge, which read Hi, I'm Kate, I sifted through my memory bank. "Are you talking about Rebecca Kelso, by any chance?"

"That's the one, poor little thing. What's this world coming to?"

I watch the nightly news on channel thirteen and take a powerful interest in all violent happenings within a mile radius of my twelve-inch black-and-white. However, though my memory's pretty good, I might not have been able to come up with Rebecca Kelso's name if she hadn't been unusual. It's common for black teenagers and homeless bums to get shot on the streets of west Baltimore. It's not common for pretty, white Hopkins graduate students to get knifed in their living rooms.

The grocery store lady had settled into dirge mode. "Such a nice young girl. Came in here a lot to buy milk and stuff. Never had a mean word to say. If you ask me, it must have been somebody she was dating. Men these days, I'll tell you! I heard when they found her body there was blood everywhere."

No wonder Mr. Aronchick had sprung for new carpeting and a paint job.

Kate made a jabbing motion at the street, where half a block away he waited for me. "I ask you, who'd want to live in a place where a thing like that happened only two months ago?"

Well, it's not something I fantasize about. On the other hand, the wheeler-dealer in me had sniffed opportunity. A quarter of an hour later I was peering into the open window of Arnold Aronchick's off-white American sedan.

"You drive a hard bargain, young lady," he was saying. "Two-fifty hardly covers my taxes."

"Yes, but I know the truth about your place, and the other people who've answered your ad don't. There's a disclosure law about this sort of thing, you know. How are they going to react when they hear Rebecca Kelso's blood spattered your apartment's walls?"

He'd already blanched at the mention of blood. "Okay, okay! I said okay, didn't I? You've got a deal."

It never fails that every time after I've put on my tough-lady act and driven a bargain, I start wishing I'd kept my big mouth shut. Waiting for the bus and then all the way home on it, I grew steadily more insecure about the lease I'd signed. As I stepped off and headed across the park to my brownstone, cold shivers tap danced up my spine.

I lived on Mt. Vernon Square. It's an area of the city where the Victorian equivalent of the jet set once resided. Lavish Italianate town houses frame a park decorated by the first Washington monument ever built in this country.

Since the days when the society ladies who lived here thought nothing of taking a footman and carriage to church—one block away—the square has fallen on harder times. Now drug dealers, art students, and Baltimore's gay community call it home.

Instead of unlocking my own door, I knocked on my across-the-hall neighbor's. "Toni, sweetie!" Randall cried after he'd peered out. "I've just made a double-chocolate cheesecake. Haul yourself in and have a taste."

Lest you get the wrong idea, let me explain right away that Randall Howarth and I are just good friends. Randall was my lawyer when I was on trial for Nick's murder. Though he's a partner in a fancy law firm, he does a lot of pro bono work in connection with the Rape Crisis Center. Randall is tall, always elegantly dressed, black as midnight, and extremely good-looking. Jonathan, his beautiful boyfriend, is a musician.

Whenever I walk through Randall's door I feel proprietary. This, even though I've furnished my place in early Goodwill while his teems with Victorian splendor. Everywhere you look, crystal chandeliers, Tiffany lamps, mahogany couches upholstered in needlepoint, and Oriental rugs stagger the eye with pattern. Since I hung all Randall's wallpaper, faux-finished his woodwork in malachite, and reupholstered just about every other antique he owns, his quarters feel almost like home.

"I don't believe what I'm hearing. You're seriously contemplating moving into the joint where Rebecca Kelso got hacked to pieces!"

We were standing in Randall's kitchen. It's a gourmet's wonderland, with gleaming copper pots hanging from a brass ceiling rack, hand-painted tiles on the countertops, and a butcher-block chopping island. Randall had just cut an enormous chunk of chocolate cheesecake and plopped it on a cut-glass plate.

"I can't afford the rent here anymore."

Randall, who has an income in six digits, said, "The rent is incredibly cheap!"

"It was when you first talked me into coming. Then you were an urban pioneer. The yuppie types who followed your lead are jacking up property values."

"Which is all to the good." Randall pushed the plate at me, and I stared down at it with a mixture of longing and revulsion. I have never been the sort of woman who forgets to eat when she's unhappy. After my trial, my weight ballooned. I've got it back under control, but if I ate Randall's cheesecake, I'd have to skip dinner. Who wanted dinner, anyway?

"Good for fat cats like you, maybe, not for me," I replied as I slipped the first divine forkful into my mouth. It went down like silk. "Besides, what's the big deal about living where someone got killed? If we refused to live in rooms where others breathed their last, the city would be a ghost town." Ignoring my accidental pun, I plunged on. "It's a fact of life that people die all the time."

"Not the way Rebecca Kelso did." Randall patted my shoulder. "Her murderer is still running around loose. He could live in her neighborhood. Toni, doesn't that bother you just a teensy bit?"

"Why should it?" I said nonchalantly. "I'm probably safer in her place than anywhere else. I mean, he's not likely to hit the same spot twice."

Brave talk, but I'd have been crazy not to worry about that young woman's killer still on the loose. I should have backed off then. But I'm stubborn. Uncertain as my minuscule income is, I couldn't turn my back on bargain basement rent. And there was something else, something buried so deep I couldn't acknowledge it yet. Later on it would surface and get me in a whole lot of trouble.

* * *

Despite Randall's warnings and my own instincts, I kept the deal with Aronchick and moved in. Randall and Jonathan, who drives one of those macho minipickups, helped me. I don't own much furniture, but I'd gained lots of odds and ends over the last three years. Moving them turned out to be a sizable job. When I was finally more or less settled, the guys stayed for dinner.

"You sure you really want to do this?" Jonathan asked.

Randall's lover is my height with a wreath of blond curls, eyes a misty shade of slate blue, and a body-builder physique. He's always been polite to me, but I have to admit I'm not comfortable with him. Perhaps it's just his divine beauty.

"No, I'm not sure," I admitted.

The flash of comprehension I saw in Jonathan's face unsettled me. "Vibes getting to you already, huh?"

"What vibes?" Randall demanded. He bore a freshly tossed Bibb salad to the table. The tiny kitchen looked like east Beirut with all my stuff still lying around in heaps, but he'd managed to put together a gourmet repast.

"This place," Jonathan retorted conversationally. "Sure, it's been prettified with the fresh paint and carpet, but underneath it's screaming with pain. Man, there's blood beneath that paint."

Deep grooves appeared in Randall's high forehead. "The poor girl just moves into her new home, and you try to give her the creeps. Stop with that shit!"

Jonathan shrugged and dug into his plate of linguine. "Hey, I've got to be honest."

"I seem to remember someone pointing out once

that honesty is a highly overrated virtue." Randall turned from Jonathan and gave me a concerned look. "If you think this is a mistake, Toni, I'll help you break your lease so you can move back. You know how I feel about losing you as a neighbor."

The forkful of pasta that had been hot and flavorful when I'd put it in my mouth had turned to tepid glue. I swallowed with an effort. "No, I can't. I changed my mind this morning. But when I called our landlord, he'd already rented my place. So here I am."

Actually, after Randall and Jonathan took off, I began to feel better. There's something soothing about getting your nest in order, and I had a lot of that to do. It was late before I finally climbed into bed. I have no explanation for what happened next. All I can say is that as far as I'm concerned, it really did happen.

For the next full hour I lay in bed unable to shut my eyes. Of course, I was thinking about the last person who'd slept in this bedroom. Had Rebecca Kelso been a nice person? Or had she in some way deserved to die young and violently? Naturally I wanted to believe the latter. It's painful to contemplate a slaughtered innocent. It makes evil and our helplessness in the face of it too real.

Finally I switched on my bedside lamp, swung my feet over the edge, and massaged my aching temples. That's when I felt it, a cool breath on the back of my neck, the feather-light touch of a finger grazing the top of my hair. Spooked, I stiffened and whirled. Out of the corner of my eye, I glimpsed a face in the mirror opposite. It was the face of a pretty young woman with tear-filled eyes. Then it was gone.

I sat blinking at the mirror atop the old-fashioned bureau across from my bed. Shivering, I finally forced my trembling legs to support my weight and made an uneasy circuit of the apartment. I guess I knew I wouldn't find anything, but I had to be sure that what had just happened had been my imagination. Or maybe it hadn't even been that. Maybe I'd been sitting there asleep and dreaming. I didn't feel sure of anything except that I was scared and confused.

"You're one crazy lady, Credella," I muttered to myself when I finally made my way back to the bedroom. "As if you didn't already have enough to worry about, now you're seeing ghosts."

I didn't sleep so good that night, or the next couple of nights, either. Fortunately the days went a little better. I filled them arranging my medicine cabinet, cupboards, and closet, and putting my books on the shelf. Shelving books wasn't a big job, as I don't have many. The reason for this is that until recently I didn't know how to read. I'm severely dyslexic and somehow managed to get through half of high school without ever learning. It caught up with me in tenth grade, though, and I dropped out.

My dyslexia was part of the trouble between me and Nick. He didn't discover that I couldn't read until after we'd married. It really pissed him off that I'd kept this, along with all my many other deficiencies, hidden. Of course, just my luck he found out in the worst possible way. One of our wedding presents had been a fancy set of spices with labels printed in curlicues. Even an Oxford Ph.D. might not have been able to decipher them. In a fit of bridal housewifery, I confused the red pepper with the paprika when I whipped up my first tuna casserole. I'll never forget the expression on Nick's face after he took that first head-clearing bite. That's when he started knocking me around, and I traded in starry eyes for black ones.

Despite the sleeplessness, the day after my move I took my little wire shopping cart down to Eddie's grocery and filled it to the brim. I was just hauling the last two paper bags up the steps when I ran into a fellow tenant.

"Hi," she said, pausing on the steps to watch as I unlocked. "Just move in?"

"Yep, yesterday." I straightened and looked her over. She was somewhere around five eight and slim in faded jeans and a loose denim shirt. Her face was pretty in a horsy sort of way that was emphasized by the off-center ponytail sprouting from one side of her head. As she returned my curious stare, she wore a wary expression mixed with curiosity.

"My name's Susie Zillig."

"How do you do, Susie. I'm Toni Credella. I gather we're neighbors?"

"Yes." She pointed to the ceiling, indicating the apartment upstairs. "I don't want to ruin your day or anything, but did Aronchick level with you about what happened in your place?"

I set down the grocery bags inside the door. "I know about Rebecca Kelso."

"God, then you've got more guts than I do. It happened four months ago, and I still get the heebie-jeebies every time I walk down these stairs. Most of the time I go out the back, actually."

I leaned against the door frame and folded my arms across my chest, a posture I heard somewhere is one of self-protection. "Then why'd you stay on here?"

"Probably for the same reason you moved in. Aronchick cut the rent to nothing. Besides, I am moving. I'm a nurse, and I've just accepted a job in Chicago. A couple more months and I'm outta here. Hey, I was just getting the mail. After you put your stuff away, would you like to come up and have a cup of coffee or something?"

"Sure." I flashed her a big smile. Socially I'm more like a pathetic little puppy than the grown-up and sophisticated woman I'd like to pretend. It always thrills me when people I might want to be friendly with are friendly first to me. Despite what she'd said about getting the heebie-jeebies, I started to feel better about my move.

Susie's apartment turned out to be similar to mine, only maybe a couple feet shorter in the living room and painted a pale yellow. Like me, she'd furnished it in castoffs. Instead of new gray carpeting, however, hers was beige and spotted by several years' accumulation of spilled coffee and assorted grime. Susie was no great shakes as a housekeeper. I like that in a woman.

"Hey, nice art," I said, eyeing a giant painting of a winged man zooming over a line of skyscrapers. He was naked, with a pink penis that dangled in dangerous invitation, I should think, to passing birds in quest of their morning worm.

"That was done by the guy who lives in the studio upstairs. An artist named Damon Wilkes."

"Oh." I cocked my head, still studying the painting.

It was erotic, even despite the winged man's limp apparatus. And it gave me a different idea about Susie. She seemed to have unconventional tastes. "Did he know Rebecca Kelso?"

Susie had gone through to the railroad kitchen off the living room. I heard her turn on a tap. "Oh, we all knew each other here. We're all a bunch of homebodies, so we saw a lot of each other. It was a real friendly place before this awful thing happened and scared the shit out of us all. I know what you're thinking. Damon didn't kill Rebbie. He and I were together when it happened."

"Got any theories who did kill her?"

"I can't imagine who would want to hurt her, except maybe some nutburger."

"The lady down at the corner grocery thinks it must have been a boyfriend."

By this time I had followed Susie into the kitchen. I stood leaning against the counter, watching as she switched on her coffeepot. She was in really good shape, with well-muscled forearms and a trim backside that made me feel a twinge of envy. I have always admired women with boyish figures. Mine is and ever will be, no matter how many desserts I deny myself, aggressively curvy.

"Rebbie was going out with a college professor at Hopkins named Parham. I met him once. Believe me, he wouldn't hurt a fly." She turned to face me, her hazel eyes troubled and her lower lip quivering slightly. "Rebbie was a wonderful person. She was doing graduate work in philosophy, and pretty brilliant, I guess. Would you like to see a picture of her?"

"Sure."

While Susie walked into the other room, I studied the coffee dripping into the glass pot. Did I really want a clear impression of Rebecca Kelso in my mind? Too late to decide I didn't, for Susie was back handing me a snapshot. While she filled mugs for each of us, I studied it.

Rebecca Kelso had had one of those gentle female faces, rounded, with large, soft dark eyes and a sweet smile. Wearing jeans and sweatshirts, their hair hanging limp in what had obviously been one of Baltimore's drizzly spring days, she and Susie stood in front of one of the buildings on the Hopkins campus. They'd draped their arms on each other's shoulders and smiled into the camera as if they never expected to have a care in the world.

That was disturbing enough. What really bothered me was that hers was the face I'd seen in the mirror that first night in her apartment. Maybe I'd just hallucinated it from a suppressed memory of a newspaper photo. I hoped that was the explanation.

"That snap was taken last year at the Hopkins fair. Rebbie and I worked in one of the booths together." Susie handed me my cup, and I returned the photo.

"Who took it?"

"The college professor I was telling you about." She wrinkled her nose. "I see the look on your face. No, Don Parham didn't kill Rebbie, honest. Don't you think the police would have picked him up by now if there was a chance? No, it was someone else, someone who's still out there prowling around, maybe thinking about doing more murders." She shuddered. "Gives me the creeps."

As I sipped my coffee, it gave me the creeps, too. More than I wanted to admit aloud.

Happily for my starving checking account, I'd just got a big job repapering a dentist's office. Randall entertains a lot, and whenever a guest admires his clever use of wall coverings or faux surfaces, he recommends me and my trusty glue pot and paintbrushes. Really, I doubt I would have been able to feed my face these past three years without his having taken me under his wing. With his encouragement, I started reading classes once a week at the library. Now I can sound my way through a simple newspaper article. But when I shot Nick, I was illiterate and unemployable. If I hadn't been able to make my way as a decorator, what would I have done? Nobody wants to hire an unlettered husband-killer.

Anyhow, that weekend I settled in at the dentist's office with my ruler, my glue brush, and several dozen rolls of floral stripe wall covering. It was mostly straight work with very little cutting, so I could go into paperhanging trance while I thought of other things. The other things, naturally, being Rebecca Kelso. I couldn't help it. The more I told myself not to think about her, the more I did. I hadn't imagined her image in the mirror since that first night. Still, she was all around me in that apartment, and I couldn't get her out of my head.

Finally, my fixation drove me to the library. In the old days I used to visit the Pratt to pick up books on tape. Now, being able to use microfilm to lift back newspaper stories on Rebecca Kelso's murder made me proud. I didn't try to read them in the library. Instead I forked over a quarter a page to get them copied and then carted them back home. That evening, after I'd fixed myself a tuna-salad sandwich, I settled down to figure them out.

Reading with me really is a process of deciphering. It takes me three times as long as it would a normal person. Even if I could afford to own a car, I wouldn't. I'm afraid I would have too much trouble with road signs, and maps are way beyond me. As you might imagine, this limits my business. If a potential customer isn't within range of my bike or on a busline, I just can't get there to do the job.

It was after midnight before I finished slogging through the articles. They were not all that informative. Rebecca's mother had found her body when she'd stopped by to take her daughter out for a birthday dinner. What a horrible discovery it must have been! No one had heard screams because Rebecca's mouth had been stuffed with rags. She had been raped and then her throat cut.

Another interesting fact—all the pictures in the paper were college graduation portraits, which showed her smiling. The face I'd seen in the mirror had been wet with tears.

As I sat there in the space where Rebecca had been murdered, with just a pale ring of lamplight between me and the dark, I asked myself why I had agreed to live here. It wasn't just the money, though that had certainly been a big factor. Ever since a jury believed my story about self-defense, I've been eaten by guilt. Randall says I still haven't acquitted myself of Nick's murder. Maybe he's right. I know I've tried punishing myself in lots of ways. Was this a new one?

If I had any sense, I thought, crossing my arms over my chest, I'd call Randall and be out of this hole by dawn's early light. Apparently I didn't have any sense, because instead of placing a call I went out to the kitchen and uncorked a bottle of cheap Chablis. I don't usually drink wine. It's too expensive, and I'm afraid of turning into a drunk. But on the way home from the library I'd stopped at the liquor store and indulged.

Now I poured myself a big glass and padded back out front. I turned off the light I'd been reading by and pushed my overstuffed chair around so it faced the window that looked out on the street. Then I sat there in the dark sipping Chablis and gazing out, as perhaps Rebecca had done when she'd lived here.

It was a chilly night in early April. Through the closed window I could hear the muted *whoosh* of cars barreling past. As I sipped, I began to study them the way I had on other solitary nights when I'd sat up late. Idly I noticed the makes and wondered about the people inside, where they were bound so late and what their lives were like. It was almost two when I finally finished the wine. Still I sat there, hypnotized by the night and my isolation, feeling the loneliness that still closes around me so often and so hard.

Traffic had thinned to an occasional car every four or five minutes. Even if the street hadn't been nearly deserted, the black Volvo would have caught my eye. It inched past like an out-of-towner looking for a parking spot. Through the windows I could feel the eyes of its driver on my window.

So powerful was the sensation that I shrank back against my chair. I was thankful that I'd long ago turned off the light, but not convinced that I couldn't be seen.

It's terrible when your heart starts to thump against your ribs and your breath comes in shallow, panicky gasps. Fear gripped me in its iron claw, fear triggered by the Volvo but that had to be the residue of other nights and other frights when I'd huddled in bed waiting for Nick. This is ridiculous, I told myself. The driver out there had to be somebody looking for an address or trying to find a street to turn on.

As I watched, it did turn right at the end of the block. When it had disappeared, I heaved a small sigh. Ridiculous, I told myself, ridiculous to panic like that. I was about to get up and walk away from the window when I felt a cool breath on the back of my neck and heard a cry of silent warning inside my head. I sat frozen, unable to move. Three or four minutes later the Volvo reappeared and cruised past my window like a bulky shark circling prey.

2

When I *woke up* the next morning I felt sluggish and jumpy all at the same time, and my eyes ached from staring through the dark while I jumped at shadows half the night. As I lingered over bran flakes and coffee, I kicked myself for not getting the Volvo's license plate number. Actually, I probably couldn't have even if I'd thought to try. Supposing I had been able to see well enough in the dark and from that distance, I have a harder time reading and remembering a sequence of numbers than I do letters.

Dyslexic people aren't stupid. Some of the most creative people in history have been dyslexic—even Einstein. It's just that Mother Nature wired our brains differently, and certain messages get garbled in transmission. That's what I learned in my adult education class and what I have to keep reminding myself.

My second cup of coffee shot me into squirrel cage mentality. I wandered around my apartment telling myself to tackle one of my stacks of craft projects, but

I was unable to settle down. Finally I took a long shower and washed my hair. With it trailing down my back in wet strings, I spent the next hour doing t'ai chi.

A guy who used to live in my building in Mt. Vernon taught me t'ai chi. He said it was the best way in the world to deal with tension, and if I did it every day all my life, I'd grow old gracefully. I don't know about the growing old part, but the discipline's slow, dancelike movements do help soothe jumpy nerves. Mostly I do just the short form. This morning I was extra antsy, so I tried the long form. I was just searching my memory for a midpoint move called "waving hands like clouds" when the phone rang.

"Toni?" My sister's voice exploded out of the receiver like the high whine of a bullet.

"Hi, Sandy. How're you doing?"

"Fine. How come when I dialed I got a recorded message with a new number?"

When I explained that I had moved, Sandy approved. "Good. I hated you living with all those faggots and drug dealers."

"The real estate agents and plumbing contractors in your neighborhood scare me even more," I replied sweetly.

Sandy, who's totally under her husband Al's influence, only laughed in disbelief. Al Pennak is the stereotypical chauvinist redneck cop. Given a choice between shooting a drug dealer or an innocent homosexual, he'd probably short-circuit from indecision. Al really hates drug dealers.

"C'mon now, I hope your new neighborhood's an improvement," Sandy was saying.

"It's close to Hopkins, full of clean-cut student types." I could guess what she'd think if she knew the bloody history of my new dwelling.

"Listen, can we get together today, maybe down at the harbor for lunch or something?"

"Sure, what's up?"

"Oh, it's Mom. She worries about you."

"Tell her I'm fine."

"You know how she is, Toni. It's not good enough to tell her that. I have to see you in person and then describe your condition in detail."

I grimaced, but really I was glad to have Sandy's invitation. I needed something to do with myself. I'd finished the job at the dentist's office and didn't have anything scheduled for a couple of days.

"I don't suppose you'd want to eat in the neighborhood. I don't mean the folks' place. We could go to Sabatino's or Mama Cellina's."

"You're joking, aren't you?"

Sandy sighed and named a Greek restaurant in Harborplace. To that I agreed.

Baltimore's Inner Harbor is really beautiful, with a brick promenade, an aquarium, a concert pavilion, and tons of shops. Unfortunately it's also spitting distance from my old neighborhood. Little Italy, where I grew up, is a tiny enclave of brick-and-Formstone-covered row houses sandwiched between restaurants. On hot summer nights the place positively reeks of tomato sauce. Of course, if you like garlic and tomatoes as much as I do, that's not bad.

One of Little Italy's most renowned eateries, Credella's, belongs to my parents. Since the harbor started bringing in so many hungry tourists, most of their competitors in the neighborhood have spent big bucks upgrading to a classier decor. Tablecloths, muted color schemes, black outfits for the waiters and waitresses. My parents haven't spent a dime. Their place is still fitted out pretty much as it was when my grandparents ran it. Yet despite the ancient indoor-outdoor carpet, wrought-iron sprouting plastic grapevines, and smeary paintings of gondolas, patrons from WASP suburbs jam the tables and cheerfully tear open their wallets. It must be my mother's cooking.

When I lived in Mt. Vernon I could walk down to the harbor. Charles Village is enough farther north that I have to ride my bike. Still, I made good time. After I'd locked up at a rack on Pratt, I glanced east toward Little Italy and then headed inside the glass-and-steel sanctuary of the Pratt Street Pavilion. Sandy showed up about ten minutes after me.

"Sorry. Late baby-sitter."

"It's okay. I like watching the boats."

Sandy pulled out a chair. My sister's two years older than me. We both have brown eyes, but Sandy's a brunette and my hair is reddish mahogany. Like me, Sandy's short with a busty figure. Her waist and hips, however, are beginning to square her off. Kids and housewifery will do that to you, I guess. The shapeless jacket and full denim skirt she wore didn't help.

As if she could hear my catty thoughts, she made me feel guilty by saying, "So how's life treating you? You're looking great."

"Thanks."

"Really, you look like you're working out in a gym or something."

"There are certain advantages to not owning a car. I get a lot of exercise."

"Exercise and poverty are the tickets to a divine body, huh? Well, I'm not about to give up my van, so I guess I'd better look around for a health club."

The waiter came and Sandy ordered a beer while I ordered a diet Coke. After he brought our drinks, she said, "You know, all this time I've never asked about how your sex life's coming along. Seeing how great you're looking, I can't help wonder. Are you dating?"

"Not at the moment."

She cocked her head, the expression in her eyes wise. She knew me too well to let me kid her. "I bet you haven't been to bed with a man since Nick died."

"You'd win your bet."

"Jeez, Toni, how do you stand it?"

"I don't know. I seem to be doing okay. You just said I looked great."

"What's the point if you're not getting anything for it? A woman your age shouldn't be living like a hermit with only a couple of faggots for friends. You should be out trying to find yourself another husband."

"I don't want another husband. Even if I did, candidates tend to bolt for the street when they hear I gunned down my last one."

"It's a handicap," my sister admitted. She sipped her beer. "I bet men come on to you all the time, though. I know they used to."

"I've changed from the way I was before. I'm sort of gruff and unfriendly these days. Now it's my turn to quiz you about your sex life. How's Al treating you in the sack? Still the hottest rod since they retired that Corvette on Route 66?"

Sandy looked flustered. "For Christ's sake, lower your voice. What's got into you, talking like that? You never used to talk tough before."

"I told you I'd changed." I'd been deliberately crude, but why did Sandy think she could barge into my private life whenever the mood struck her?

"Not for the better."

The waiter brought our Greek salads, and we dug in. As we ate in the silence of mutual resentment, I studied Sandy. Actually, I was surprised she'd flared up at me so self-righteously. She never used to be a prig. In fact, in the early days of their marriage Al's prowess in bed used to be one of her favorite topics. Maybe he'd become impotent. I savored the thought. Of the people who'd dumped on me after what happened with Nick, and that included most of my friends and all of my relatives, Al had been the worst.

Al and Nick had been pals in high school and attended police academy together. After they'd each married a Credella sister, they'd been drinking buddies. Al refused to believe that Nick had abused me.

"Al would split his pants if he knew you were here speaking to the reincarnation of Lizzie Borden, wouldn't he?"

Sandy shifted uncomfortably. "I'm sorry I brought up the subject of sex. Let's not talk about men, let's talk about Mom."

"Okay."

"Actually, on the way here I stopped in to see her."

"I can still smell the oregano on you." Ever since I can remember, my mother has been slaving over the cauldrons in the family restaurant's kitchen. Pop, on the other hand, likes to dress in immaculate silk shirts and strut around, alternately scowling and snapping at the help while playing Mr. Genial for the benefit of diners.

Sandy and I grew up working like deckhands in that restaurant. We spent our youth with our father growling at our heels and our mother playing martyr of the tomato sauce—sighing and stirring, sighing and stirring. That's what Sandy and I would both be doing now if we hadn't married as soon as we could to get out.

"You could stop in and see her, too, you know."

"Not with Pop there, and he's always there. Have you forgotten he told me never to darken his door again?"

"You know he didn't really mean it."

"Sounded pretty convincing at the time."

Sandy threw down her fork. "Ever since it happened you've been hard as a rock. Don't you think it's time to forgive and forget?"

"We've hashed this over before, Sandy. I can't ever forget. During the trial Pop abandoned me. He said I belonged in hell along with Delilah, Mata Hari, and Madonna. Mom just caved in and went along with him."

"She's always done that. She doesn't know how to do anything else. Toni, you've got to forgive her."

"I have forgiven her. How can I blame her for not being able to have a personality change? If she ever got up the courage to disagree with Pop, she'd probably self-destruct. That doesn't mean I want to see her. I just don't, not yet. It rakes up too much ugly feeling inside me. I want those feelings to sink into the ooze and stay put."

Sandy gave one of her all-suffering sighs and sipped the last of her beer. "Ready or not, you're going to have to see her. She's sick."

"What's wrong with her?"

"She's got a lump in her breast."

I almost choked on the tiny sliver of ice that had started to slide down my throat. For the next hour our conversation read like something out of a medical soap opera and ended with my agreeing to go see Mom. It wasn't until we'd finished our coffee and shared the bill that I remembered to ask the favor I'd had in mind when I first arrived.

"Next time Al's in a good mood, if it's not ten years from now, that is, would you do something for me?"

"What's that?"

"Ask him about the Rebecca Kelso case."

"Rebecca Kelso? Who's that?"

When I explained, her suspicion deepened. "Why would you want to know about a murder victim?"

"I'm just interested, that's all. I'm sure Al has heard stuff about the case that hasn't been in the newspapers."

"Al doesn't usually talk to me about what goes on at work."

"I know, detecting murder isn't woman's work. Women just usually get the privilege of being the ones in the body bags. But maybe if you used your feminine wiles, he'd unbend. It's important to me, Sandy."

"Why is it important to you?"

"I'm not exactly sure. It just is."

* * *

The rest of the day the news about Mom pushed everything else out of my mind. I biked home and fretted about it while I worked on faux-finishing picture frames for a booth I planned to operate at the Artscape Festival that summer. Around six the doorbell rang. I squinted through the glass in the top half of the door. Randall stood on the porch. He's educated me about men's fashion, so I knew the double-breasted suit he wore was a classic Prince of Wales plaid with Italian styling. Though he must have come directly from the office, he carried a bottle of wine and a bag of what I suspected was Tony Cheng's Chinese carryout.

As I threw open the door, tears sprang into my eyes. "Oh, Randall, I'm so glad to see you!"

"Well, of course you are. No other feeling is open to the rational mind."

"You're such a fine and gentle person, and you've been so good to me!"

"That too. Hey, what's wrong, honeybunch?"

"The last twenty-four hours have been a real bummer."

While we sat at my kitchen table forking up the carryout, I told Randall about the Volvo. Of course, I left out the part about Rebecca Kelso's ghost blowing on the back of my neck to clue me in to its evil nature. I didn't want him to think I was ready for the squirrel farm—a notion that had begun to worry me. Even without the ghostly warning, my funny feeling about the Volvo intrigued him. When we finally tired of talking about that, I sighed and described my lunch with Sandy. The news about my mother made him frown.

"Listen, Antoinette, you know I don't like to pry."

"No, of course not." I made my tone wry, and his brown eyes twinkled as he caught the intonation.

"Gossip and kvetch, whine and snoop, kibitz and interfere, yes. But pry, never anything so low class. Anyhow, I've never really understood your attitude toward her."

"I've told you, when I shot Nick, my father wouldn't even listen to the reason why it happened. He cursed me and threw me out. My mother went along with him."

"Not because she wanted to, only because she didn't have the guts to stand up to him."

"That's exactly right."

Randall lifted his wineglass to the light and studied it. "Why are you still so mad when you know she's sorry?"

"I'm not mad at her so much as I'm mad at myself."

"I await the development of this fascinating thesis with bated breath."

Maybe I would have laughed or at least smiled if I hadn't been so caught up in my own emotional whirlpool. "I'm mad because I patterned myself on her. I hate her weakness because it's mine, too. It's why I married Nick in the first place, really. It's why, time after time, I let him come home drunk and rough me up, without telling a soul. It's why he's dead now, and I'm the one who shot him."

"And you blame that on your mother's weakness?"

"All her life she's been a victim. I grew up thinking that was how I should be, too. My reading problem made it worse. I grew up thinking something was terribly wrong with me. I felt I really deserved Nick's punishment. It's why I took it all those years, why I let the anger and resentment build up into something that cost him his life and made me into his executioner."

"Toni, you're not what you were."

"I hope I'm not. I've been trying very hard to be strong, to stand on my own feet."

"I know you have, sweetie. I remember what a crushed little waif you were when you first asked me to defend you. You've been through hell." He nodded his understanding, his eyes gentle on my face. Randall's gentleness is what I love most about him. He doesn't have a violent bone in his body. Moving in next door to him had made me feel safe. Why had I ever moved away? "But," he went on, "your mom's still a victim, hon. Only this time it's not her fault. It's just life."

"Yes, just life." Tears filled my eyes again and overflowed down my cheeks. I grabbed for a paper napkin, hating it that after all this talk about being strong, I was crying like a baby.

Randall, the sainted diplomat, only patted my shoulder and waited until I'd finished snuffling.

"You *have* been through hell," he finally said. "Living in this place, getting scared because you think sinister Volvos are circling your block—honey, what's the point? C'mon back to Mt. Vernon where I can take care of you."

"How can I do that? My place has been rented."

"A couple of jerks moved in. I'll get rid of them."

"How?" Through my red eyes, I focused on him with interest.

He merely smiled like the Cheshire cat lawyer he actually was. "I'll think of something. Trust me."

I gazed at him, bemused. Then I started to laugh, weak with relief. "You will, won't you."

"Count on it, babe." He pinched my cheek. "Give me a month and you're outta here, back home where you belong."

"Okay, okay, it's a deal."

* * *

After Randall left, I felt good enough to get some work done on the frames. At nine-thirty, when I knew my father would be in Credella's dining room charming patrons out of big tips, I called my mother on the kitchen line.

"Antoinette?" She sounded tentative, a little breathless, her voice edged with the thread of anxiety that always runs through her speech. "It's good to hear from you."

"It's good to hear you, too, Mom. Listen, if it's okay, I thought I'd come around tomorrow morning and see you."

"Of course it's okay. Your father has a meeting at St. Leo's, so morning's good." Another pause. "I've been dreaming about you."

"Oh?" Warily. "What kind of dreams?"

"Bad ones." I could hear her voice tighten up. "When I wake up, I don't remember exactly, but I know it's bad. You're not in some kind of trouble?"

"No, I'm fine."

"Still, I worry. It worries me that I'm getting these dreams. I was having bad dreams before Nick died, too."

I didn't know what to say. My mother is convinced she's psychic. Sometimes I even believe her.

After an awkward silence, she exhaled dolorously and said, "I'm glad you're coming. Don't worry about your father. He's gonna be out, so the coast will be clear."

"That's a relief. See you."

I hung up and dithered around in the kitchen, not

sure what to do with myself. It bothered me that I'd been thinking and talking about Nick so much lately and that my mother had been dreaming about me in the negative. Maybe it's my Italian genes, but I have a superstitious nature. I think when you're headed for trouble you can feel it thickening around you. Since moving into Rebecca Kelso's apartment, I'd smelled trouble in the very air I had to breathe. And it didn't help that I was imagining her ghost looking at me with imploring eyes and giving me warnings. For all that had to be my imagination, didn't it?

I watched the evening news on my little black-and-white. After the closing credits, I switched it off along with all the other lights in the living room and worked on t'ai chi some more, another bad sign. I was doing a lot of t'ai chi lately, soothing myself, calming myself down.

Midnight found me sitting by the window with a mug of herb tea, watching the street. Of course, I told myself I was just relaxing before going to bed, that I wasn't really on the lookout for a big bad car. Just the same, with every passing automobile I tensed up like piano wire. Sure enough, the Volvo from the night before came along, cruising slowly past before turning the corner.

I jumped up so fast that I overturned my tea. Ignoring the fallen mug, I grabbed the pad, pencil, and flashlight I'd laid to one side, just in case, and barreled out the front door and down the steps. Outside, the night was chill, and I had on only sweat pants and my T-shirt. My adrenaline was up, my heart pumping away frenetically, so I hardly noticed the shivers setting in. If that car came around the block again, I'd get its license number.

I felt scared silly lurking in the bushes waiting for it. After five or six minutes crawled past, I began to think my four-wheeled bogey wasn't going to circle around again the way it had before. What if the driver had spotted me in his rearview mirror? Comforting to think he'd just driven away. But what if he'd decided to park and come back on foot? For all I knew he could be sneaking up on me now.

You're one crazy bitch, Toni, I told myself. Imagining ghosts, hallucinating the cautioning touch of cool fingers. Just because the same car rolls past every now and then doesn't mean its driver is a killer drawn back to the scene of his crime in search of fresh blood. It'd be more logical to think the Volvo belonged to someone who lived nearby and worked the three to eleven shift. Unfortunately, talking to myself like that didn't dispel the gut feeling I had that the car harbored evil. Superstition, thy name is Toni.

When I decided the Volvo wasn't coming back, the unlikely theory that its driver might be peering at me from behind a bush took hold. I flipped on my flashlight and then, feeling silly about the anemic beam it sent skittering over the grass, flipped it back off.

With no better weapon, I wanted to go inside and lock the door. But that seemed cowardly, and I wasn't going to be a coward. Never again would Toni Credella not stand up for herself. So, mentally beating my chest like Tarzan pumping up courage to face a hungry lion, I began to circle the house. I wanted to be sure that no one had decided to hide in the backyard or along the bushes by the side windows. Not that I had any reason to think someone might. I was just going on a crazy instinct.

Standing shivering in the tiny postage stamp of a weedy backyard, I had about decided to give up and go in before a neighbor noticed my weird nocturnal perambulations and called the cops. That's when my ears picked up stealthy footsteps. Someone was climbing down the fire escape.

Going against my instinct to get the hell out of there, I aimed my flash at the muted scuffles and flicked the switch. Caught in the watery beam of yellow light, a guy in jeans and a ragged T blinked and then scowled. He had obviously just climbed out of Susie Zillig's open window.

"What the hell!" he cried out.

My heart was doing flip-flops so fast that I felt nauseated. I pictured Susie lying upstairs in a pool of blood. Maybe she was half off her bed or sprawled on the kitchen floor. Maybe she was naked, her body still warm, her eyes open and sightless, a rag stuffed in her mouth.

3

Clutching the flashlight with both hands and trembling like a leaf in a wind tunnel, I moved in closer. "Who are you and what were you doing in Susie's place?"

"Turn that fucking thing off before I break it!"

Sweeping the flashlight's beam across his hands in case he was carrying a knife, I repeated my question.

"I live here, for Christ's sake. What's it to you?"

Suspiciously, I studied him. With his long, thin body, profuse, dark curls, and slanted eyebrows he looked more like a satyr than a murderer. Even as I demanded again, "What were you doing in Susie Zillig's apartment?" an answer other than raping and killing her dawned on me.

"Actually, we were playing a game, if you must know," he snapped. "I'm climbing out her window because she got tired and wanted to knock off, and it's easier to get to my place on the fire escape than it is to go all the way down and around."

I glanced up at Susie's window. The light went on and she stuck her head out. "Damon, you okay out there?" she called out in a perfectly healthy-sounding voice.

"I'm fine. Everything's cool."

"Who are you talking to?"

"Nobody, just a neighbor. Don't worry about it."

"Okay." She yawned. "G'night. See you tomorrow."

"Right. 'Night, Suze."

She shut the window. Her light went off, and Damon and I were alone. "So," he said, "now that I've answered your question, answer mine. Who the hell are you?"

Barefoot and slightly bowlegged, he padded down the metal steps toward me. I lowered my flash, took a deep breath, and willed my heart to stop racing. Obviously this must be the artist upstairs that Susie had mentioned and whose innocence she'd vouched for. He looked like someone who would paint a naked winged man with a dangling penis.

"You must be the little gal who moved in on the ground floor."

"I'm not a little gal. I'm a grown woman." Because I was having trouble getting hold of my breathing, my voice sounded as high and thin as a nine-year-old's.

"You don't look all that grown to me," he responded, his gaze traveling over me and his teeth flashing in the moonlight. "Except in the right places. What are you doing prowling around in the middle of the night? Bogeyman scare you?"

"I heard a noise, so I thought I'd check it out."

"You must have very sensitive ears. Or maybe you

heard what happened to the previous tenant of your sweet little abode. That's it, isn't it?"

"I know Rebecca Kelso was killed."

"What would you do if I whipped out a butcher knife?" he asked sarcastically. "Do you have a gun tucked away someplace, or were you planning to fend me off with your trusty Eveready batteries?"

He had a point. I was beginning to feel like an idiot, freezing my tail off in the dark, playing twenty questions with a barefoot stranger.

"Listen, it's cold out here. Since we're neighbors and you don't have to worry that I've been drinking Susie's blood, how about coming up to my place and getting acquainted? I've got some cheap wine and half a bottle of brandy. If you want, I can even heat some cider and doctor it with hooch. What do you say?"

"Sure." I surprised myself when I agreed. Guess I must be more devil-may-care than I realized. Really, I wasn't ready to go back to my place yet. I was afraid to be alone. Rebecca's ghost and that Volvo had scared me more than I wanted to admit.

"Name's Damon Wilkes, by the way." He turned and began climbing up.

As I followed behind, I told him my name and admired the view from eye level. Not that he wore tight jeans. His were a size large, which underlined for me his roguish-artist image.

"I know who you are. I met Susie the other day. She invited me up to her place for coffee, and I saw your painting."

"That's my winged David. Beautiful, but no threat to chastity. I guess that's why Susie bought him." Chuckling softly, Damon climbed through an open window just below the roofline and motioned me to join him.

By the time I'd scrambled in, he'd sprawled on a tubular metal chair that had to be a relic of the fifties. He'd bent his knee up so he could examine his left big toe, which he was doing with intensity.

"Damn! I picked up a splinter out there."

"Serves you right for playing Don Juan in bare feet."

"I wasn't playing Don Juan. I told you, Susie and I were gaming."

"You're serious?"

"Serious as shit. I design games for a living. Besides, where do you get off being so critical? I notice your feet are bare, too."

He was right. No wonder I'd been cold outside. When I looked up again he'd shifted his attention from his toe to me. In the light I could see gray silvering his dark curls. They trailed in a rattail down his back, a style I loathe, but on him it looked right. He had an upturned nose to match his eyebrows, and his mouth looked fashioned for bitter humor. He wore a black T-shirt and well-washed charcoal jeans. A Civil War Rebel jacket had been slung over one of his kitchen chairs. Only it wasn't any scruffy antique. It looked brand-new and possibly custom-made. As his gaze traveled over me, a slow smile lit his puckish face.

"Blimey, look at those curls. A flaming black-eyed redhead. You're even cuter than I thought, Toni. Welcome to my digs. Care to see my etchings?"

"Sure," I said, uncomfortable at the intimacy he was establishing between us but intrigued, "and I'd appreciate that hot cider you mentioned."

While he filled mugs and then stuck them in a

microwave, I glanced around. Maybe he wasn't the starving artist I'd originally supposed. His kitchen was all done in fifties. It included a clunky Formica table, rounded metal toaster with cloth-wrapped cord, and real honest-to-God linoleum on the floor. Ironic that my mother's taste in decor is now considered chic. Either Damon Wilkes was masterful at scavenging dumps or he had money. Retro is pricey these days.

Most striking, however, were the paintings and sketches tacked to the walls. I'm not exactly an art connoisseur, but I've peered into gallery windows on Charles Street. I've got an idea of what passes under the name of art these days. Mostly, it's blotches of muddy color on large squares of overpriced canvas. The painting of the winged man I'd seen in Susie's place had been almost photographic. That's part of what had made it so striking. Damon's other paintings were equally representational. But the subjects they depicted were out of this world.

I gazed at a small canvas. On it two merpeople in luminous shades of blue, green, and gray were mating. Around their beautiful faces their hair swirled in wild abandon. Below their fused torsos their long silver-scaled tails arched in ecstasy. "You have quite an imagination." Quite an erotic imagination.

"You can't write and illustrate fantasy games without generating brain waves that are just a wee bit kinky." Damon turned the dial on his microwave. "Go ahead, feel free to cruise through my gallery. Most of my stuff's down the hall."

I took him up on it, wondering all the while just how kinky Damon really was. After I'd examined the pictures in the kitchen, I wandered out to the main room. All the interior walls had been ripped out to create a large space accented by dormer windows. The attic had also been opened up, and skylights pierced the roof. Even at night the effect was airy and spacious.

"Did Aronchick have this done?" I asked, gazing around at the color-swirled canvases propped against every surface and stacked in heaps on the bare wood floor. Fluorescent trolls and bodybuilder women in breastplates jumped out at me. Unicorns and dragons flashed through improbable purple skies. Monsters and heroes dueled atop craggy mountains.

"Are you kidding?" Damon came in carrying two cups fragrant with hot brandy. "Why would Aronchick accommodate a crazy artist with an expensive renovation? I paid for this myself, and I had a hell of a time convincing him to let me do it."

I accepted a mug and sipped from it gratefully. The sweet apple flavor mixed with more than a dollop of brandy tasted delicious. "That explains why you didn't move after Rebecca Kelso's murder. You had too big an investment in this place to pull up stakes."

"Why should I move? Whoever killed Rebecca goes after women, not guys," he said matter-of-factly. "Besides, it's not so easy to uproot an entire company and change its address, you know. Especially when you're running it by mail."

The remark about being safe because he was a guy didn't exactly endear him to me. "That's what you've got here, a mail-order company?"

"I own Otherworld Inc., which is a play-by-mail fantasy-game company." He walked me over to a large table where he'd set up a miniature landscape complete with rivers, mountains, a cardboard castle, and tiny opposing armies. "This is a game called Dragon Maid. It's going into production next week. I wrote the book for it and designed all the pieces."

I picked up a tiny cast-metal-painted goblin. The detail on it, from the warty skin to the fangs and evil leer, impressed me.

"Susie and I were up here play-testing Dragon Maid the night some creep murdered Rebbie," Damon said. "We never heard a thing."

The demon in my hand took on a sinister personality. I put it back. "God!"

"Yeah, I know. With the associations and all, it's been real hard for me to finish work on the game. But I have too much invested in it not to see it through to the bitter end."

"Did Rebbie ever play-test your games?"

"No. You're either a gamer or you're not. She tried a couple of times, but couldn't work up any interest."

"Susie likes to play, though?"

"Yeah, she's been a big help." He caught me looking at him and added, "We're just friends, by the way—not lovers."

I concentrated on my cider and wondered why not. Damon had a raffish appeal that lots of women would find irresistible. Susie was surely attractive enough to snag most men's interest.

My host moved a step closer. "That doesn't mean I'm not open to boy-girl possibilities. I know I'm awfully pretty, but that doesn't mean I don't like the opposite sex. How are you in the boyfriend department? Is your dance card filled?"

In days past I would either have taken a step backward or started flirting. Now I stood my ground. "I don't have a dance card."

He rolled his eyes. "Let me rephrase that. I don't see a ring on your finger, so you're not married. Are you living down there alone, or do you have a boyfriend?"

"I'm a widow."

"How long?"

"Three years."

"Long enough, and since I'm obviously lusting after your body, I won't say I'm sorry."

All at once I could have spread the sexual tension on a cracker. I suppose I'd known it would come to this when I'd agreed to trot up here in the first place. It almost always does when you're with a man who's not gay. So, why had I accepted his invitation? "Time to go," I said, setting down my mug.

"Hey"—he frowned and looked contrite—"I didn't mean to scare you off. Forget the pheromones and finish your cider."

"It's late. Time I got to bed—alone," I added, and headed for the door.

I walked down the four flights of steps from Damon's place to mine and thought about him and Susie. I pictured them playing games with leering plastic trolls while a murderer raped and stabbed Rebecca. I thought about Rebecca, a rag stuffed in her mouth as she was being savaged. It would make it all the worse if you couldn't scream.

How had it happened? Had an intruder been hiding in her apartment? Had she come home late and gone to the kitchen to get a cup of coffee when suddenly he'd come up behind? I imagined an arm clamped to my waist so I couldn't turn and kick out, a merciless hand stuffing a dirty handkerchief between my teeth, perhaps even holding my nose and choking me so I'd open my lips. All the while he'd be whispering obscenities, telling me the hideous things he planned doing to me. Maybe he'd even be laughing.

By the time I got to my door I was hyperventilating. I put my hand on the knob and then froze. Had I even bothered to lock up when I'd rocketed out into the front yard? Obviously not, since I wasn't carrying my key. What if the man in the Volvo waited inside, rag in hand?

Oh, God, Toni, how could you be so stupid?

I jerked the knob and gave the door a shove. It swung open on darkness. The lights had been off when I'd left. I'd been sitting in the dark watching that Volvo. Taking a deep breath, I reached around the door frame and flicked on the overhead. The room looked empty, but there was still the bathroom, kitchen, and bedroom offering excellent lurking possibilities to mad-dog murderers.

When I finally got up the courage to check all three out, I found everything okay. Still, it took a while to get to sleep that night. As I lay wide-eyed, I rehashed the scene with Damon. I hadn't experienced sexual interest in a man since before that final terrible night with Nick. Yet Damon's overture had stirred up something. So maybe that part of me wasn't completely dead after all. Was that good or bad?

Unable to answer my own question, I focused on the mirror opposite. Ever since that first night I'd been waiting for a face to appear in it. None had. "Rebecca, are you here?" I whispered. There was only silence, and I felt silly. But when I turned my face into the pillows, I imagined the faintest of whispers.

The next morning I pulled a sweatshirt over black spandex pedal pushers, strapped on my helmet, and pedaled up St. Paul to the harbor. As I crossed Pratt I caught sight of a panhandler shuffling along. A lot of them hang out around the harbor, cadging nickels from tourists. I've often wondered what I would do if I were homeless. I've even played the game of picking out the best spots to stand with a paper cup begging change.

On this unsettling thought, I headed toward Little Italy and shifted my wondering to Damon Wilkes and Susie Zillig. He'd insisted they weren't lovers, yet judging from his art and the way he'd come on to me, Damon had a well-primed libido. He and Susie were both young, healthy, attractive, and they liked each other. If Damon was hetero and so was Susie, why not? I don't believe that under ordinary circumstances men and women who are physically attracted to each other can be friends. Friendship just isn't what our hormones program. It's only when the chance of sex has been edited out for some reason or other that friendship happens. Like with Randall and me.

Downtown sunshine warmed the tops of the skyscrapers, and the truck traffic at their feet flowed in fast, formidable currents. Little Italy lay like a midget island assaulted by a sea of noisy giants.

A block east on Albermarle, where Little Italy really starts, I caught my first whiff of fresh-baked bread and closed my eyes, savoring. I hadn't been on these streets since my flight to Mt. Vernon. As I wheeled my bike past Vaccaro's *pasticceria*, I looked around. Things were the same, yet there'd been changes.

I caught sight of a revision in the skyline and smiled. Lately some of the more affluent restaurant owners who moved to the suburbs after making their bundle have moved back. The one whose roof I was eyeing had built a palazzo with a statue of the little mermaid on top of the chimney. The story Sandy gave me is that when Lenny Fiorelli's grandma came out of St. Leo's and caught sight of it, she mistook it for the Virgin Mary and fell to her knees on the sidewalk.

On the corner of Fawn, new restaurant owners had spiffed up a Formstone facade with buff paint. Formstone is the curse of Baltimore. In the fifties hucksters went through and persuaded half the city to smother itself in the bogus stuff. There are still people around who actually think it's attractive.

Behind the windows of a house down from the new restaurant I saw lace curtains quiver. Probably Mrs. Cosimano. If she'd seen me, she was already on the phone spreading the word. Toni-the-killer is back roaming the neighborhood. Lock your doors and windows.

My folks haven't done a thing to their Formstone. It still covers their restaurant and their rooms upstairs. I chained my bike to a spindly tree and, figuring my mother would be gearing up for lunch, went around back to the kitchen.

As I'd expected, I found Mom at her station, stirring soup. Predictably, she wore a shapeless housedress swathed in a spotted apron. Upstairs in our living room, there's a silver-framed photograph of my parents on their wedding day. My father in his cutaway was a dashing fellow, and he doesn't look that much different now. My mother, who's that rarity, a Sicilian blond, could have doubled for a young Ingrid Bergman. Anyone meeting her these days who'd known her then wouldn't recognize her. I'm not sure why that stirs up such resentment in me.

Sandy was there with her three kids, seven-year-old Billy, six-year-old Matt, and Alex, the three-year-old baby. They all looked like miniversions of her husband. They had brown hair mowed so short it stood on end, long eyelashes, chunky shoulders, belligerent expressions, and argumentative manners.

"This is a surprise," I said as I unstrapped my helmet and took in the situation. I felt a little like the prodigal, a lot like an outsider wondering how to appease a village of hostile natives.

Above the din of the boys, who were playing a game on the gray tile floor, Sandy said, "Mom called to say you were coming, so I thought I'd join the party. Welcome home."

At that point my mother, who'd been pretending she didn't know I was there, burst into tears. "Antoinette," she wailed. Flinging aside her spoon, she pivoted and collapsed into my arms. "Toni, my baby! Finally, you've come back."

All my piled-up anger and resentment slid away. I made comforting noises and patted the bun at the nape of Mama's bent neck. She's shorter than me. I could look down and see the pink scalp under her thinning hair. Suddenly I felt like weeping, too.

Things got back to normal when Billy yanked a red plastic water pistol away from Matt and he screamed bloody murder. After Sandy silenced them, temporarily,

Mom pulled away and swiped the back of her hand at her teary eyes. "You shouldn't stay away like you do. It's not right."

"Pop threw me out, Mom."

"He didn't mean it."

"That's not the way I remember it."

"You can't blame your father for the things he said." She sniffed and then wiped her eyes on the corner of her apron. "He can't help the way he is. He doesn't know how to think about what you did. Me, I don't care anymore. What's past is past, and I want to forget. I want to have my baby back."

"I want to forget, too, Mom." I looked around for something to sit down on. The restaurant's kitchen is in the basement. Though it's a fairly large space, it has a low ceiling and small windows placed high up, which gives it a dark, claustrophobic feel. Its walls are lined with a mishmash of equipment, some of it stainless-steel restaurant-grade, some of it odds and ends picked up over the years.

I sank onto an old wooden chair that was probably a relic from my grandmother's days. My legs felt weak and my stomach queasy, as if someone had fed me a bad egg. "Tell me about your trouble, Mom," I said. "Sandy says you've got a lump in your breast."

Mama pressed her left hand to her heart. "Mother of God, I'll know next week. Next week the doctor, he cuts me open and looks inside me to see. I only hope the knife doesn't slip and cut open my heart."

"It won't."

"Who knows what will happen. These doctors, they're only butchers with fancy degrees and big paychecks."

"Mom's got an appointment at Hopkins to have a

biopsy," Sandy chimed in. "I'm going with her. You'll come, too, won't you, Toni?"

"Of course," I said. "Of course I will."

I didn't stay much longer. Though my mother and I hadn't really spoken in three years, there wasn't much we could say. We were like two mountain climbers looking at each other across a very wide gap. We were both too busy trying to hang on to spend much energy on yodeling.

She asked me how I was living, and I tried to explain. Sandy had been reporting back to her, so nothing I added came as real news. I told her my new apartment was nice and in a safer neighborhood. She said that was good. I didn't say anything about Rebecca Kelso.

It wasn't long before we both reached an emotional and chitchat saturation point. When I made an excuse to leave, Mom looked relieved. In lots of ways, we're alike. Maybe that's why it makes me so angry to see what life has done to her. Or, rather, what she's let it do to her.

On the sidewalk, I'd squatted to unlock my bike when Sandy hurried out. "That was good, Toni," she said earnestly. "You made Mom happy today."

"You think so? Well, I'm glad for that."

"I bet you feel a lot better, too. Don't you?"

"I don't know. Yes, I guess so." While I strapped on my helmet, she was studying me. Not wanting to burst into tears, I avoided her eyes. I hate showing weakness in front of my sister. I've hated it ever since I was a little kid tagging after her and begging her to pay attention to me. Suddenly I felt the same way about her that I'd felt about Mama. She was somebody on the other side of a gulf I could never again fully bridge. From here on out, Sandy and I would always be eyeing each other across distances.

"Listen," she said, "about that favor you asked me. Last night I got Al to talk about the Kelso case."

I forgot about crying. "Yes?"

"He says the police are really stumped. And they've got all their big guns working on it, too."

"What do you mean, big guns?"

"Everyone from Detective O'Dell to Jeff Simpler."

The last name rang a bell, but I couldn't place it. "Who's Simpler?"

"You remember Jeff, don't you? He's a psychological profiler. We heard him speak about serial killers at a police wives luncheon."

Now I remembered. "That was a long time ago, Sandy. Four years, at least."

"Yeah, but he made a big impression on you. You talked about his lecture for days."

She was raking up history. I had been a different person then. Still, I did remember him. A short, thin guy with blond hair and steely blue eyes. He taught psychology at Towson State and worked part-time for the BPD. His job was to be on hand at murder sites to work up a psychological profile of the killer.

Serial killers who commit crimes against women were his specialty. I remember how his talk to our women's group gave me the willies. It's depressing to think of men out there stalking women for the pleasure of killing them. At the time, however, all that had seemed remote. Now, living in Rebecca Kelso's apartment, it had become too real.

After thanking my sister for the info, I walked my bike out to the street. Instead of heading it west to the harbor, I turned straight north down President toward Baltimore Street. I had made a snap decision. Like most snap decisions, it had probably been rattling around in the back of my mind for a lot longer than I realized.

Given my history, I guess it's pretty strange I would try buying a gun at the Cop Shop. It's the place where Baltimore police buy their professional goodies—handcuffs, shoulder holsters, billy clubs, etc., etc. But it was only a couple blocks from Little Italy, and convenient. After I'd parked my bike, I peered in to make sure no one I knew was there. Except for the counterman, a heavyset guy with a jaw like a pit bull, it was empty.

"Looking for something, little lady?"

"Umm, yes, a gun."

I glanced around at all the stuff on the racks. The average citizen would probably be pretty surprised by this place. Not only can you buy all sorts of official-looking police equipment, including badges from the various jurisdictions, you can look up and admire walls lined with giant posters of snarling, big-breasted women wielding Uzis and wearing nothing but police hats. The counterman appeared relaxed and genial. I guess he had no idea that a female customer might possibly find his wallpaper offensive, even threatening.

"What type of gun?" He slouched down to the firearms display area and leaned his paunch on top of the glass case.

"Umm, I don't know. Something to keep at home for self-protection." I gazed at his wares. I'd had no idea there were so many different types of pistols or that they were so expensive. Almost everything cost over $200.

"Have you ever fired a gun before?"

"Only once." That was the time I'd shot Nick, but I didn't mention this fact.

"Then you'd better not look at the Berettas, too complicated. What you want is a revolver. They're simple. Just put the bullets in and pull the trigger." He cocked a thumb at a case full of what looked like cap guns. I leaned over and studied them. A small one called the Titan Tigress, which had an ivory handle etched with a rose, caught my eye. It was only $169.95.

"That's cute."

He guffawed. "Sweetheart, you don't buy a gun because it's cute. You buy one that'll be there for you when you need it."

"What's wrong with the little one?"

"Shoot somebody with it, he'll just keep coming, only he'll be a hell of a lot madder."

"Which would you recommend?"

"Smith and Wesson is the best."

"I can't afford those." The least of them were in the $350 range.

"Try a Taurus 85."

That was only sixty dollars less, but it had a business-like look that appealed to me. I'd just realized how scared I really was. Of what? I asked myself. Of the Volvo? That was silly. Of Rebecca's ghost? Even sillier. Nevertheless, my fear was real. Even if I had to fork over a month's rent, I wanted protection.

"Okay, how do I go about buying it?"

"That's the fun part," he said, winking knowingly. "You got to fill out one of these things and then wait while they check you out." He plunked down a pad of gun registration forms. "I don't guess a little gal like you has anything to worry about. You don't look like the type to have robbed a bank."

Like they say in the romance novels, my heart plummeted. I was going to have a heck of a time deciphering those itty-bitty letters. Even now, filling out forms takes me twice as long as it would a normal person. And it might all be for nothing. Maybe, since I'd been tried for murder, I couldn't legally own a gun. But a jury had acquitted me. That ought to count for something.

The salesman misinterpreted the scowl puckering my forehead. "Hey, it only takes a week. You need protection sooner than that? Someone bothering you?"

"A woman was murdered near where I live, and it's making me nervous," I murmured as I self-consciously printed out my name. Fortunately, the form really didn't ask for too much of my shaky reading skills.

"Hey, every woman in this city should carry Pro-Stun."

"Pro-Stun, what's that?"

He reached under the counter and produced a key chain. Attached to it was a finger-size aerosol in a black leather case. "My daughter carries this, and so does my wife."

"Mace? Can't you get sued for spraying somebody with that stuff?"

"No mace in it whatsoever, honey." Emphatically, he shook his heavy jaw. "It's a concentrate of the stuff in cayenne peppers. All natural ingredients. You get out of your car or walk out your door and you've got this in your hand with your thumb on the button. Anybody bothers you, you give him a snoutsnocker full. He'll open his mouth to yell. You spray it down his throat and give him a knee where it counts." He winked. "Then you're outta there and he's rolling around on the ground with his eyes swole shut and his face on fire."

I blinked, liking the scenario but also entertaining a doubt or two. What if the wind blew in the wrong direction? What if my assailant didn't succumb quite so easily? What if I fumbled the spray and he used it on me? Still, maybe it was worth the $14.95. Sometimes when I pedal out as far as Roland Park for a customer, dogs chase my bike. There might come a day when I'd need to use it on one of them. "Okay, I'll take it."

I had just paid for it and stuck it in the pouch on my hip when, just my luck, my sister's husband walked in.

Al Pennak looks like he belongs in one of those old John Wayne movies. He's got a muscular build and a square, meaty face that some might consider handsome. But in my book he's as mean and nasty-mouthed as the law allows. My sister fell in love with his shoulders, which, admittedly, are splendid. Now she has to live with his lousy personality. Maybe that accounts for the sour lines she's starting to get around the mouth.

"Well, if it isn't the husband killer," he snarled. He'd obviously spotted me through the window and come in loaded for bear. Guess he'd had a bad day on the beat.

"Hey, long time no see, Al," I said, striking a cocky pose. It was either that or run out the back way, and I wasn't going to run from him or anybody. "What are you doing wasting taxpayers' money in here? From the looks of you, you're on duty. Shouldn't you be out arresting innocent bystanders?"

He wore full cop regalia, including half a dozen weapons of destruction dangling from the black leather belt that rode low on his developing beer belly. One of them, I noticed, was an aerosol that had to be mace. A big, tough Baltimore police guy wasn't going to fool around with sissy stuff like the hot pepper I'd just bought.

"Innocent bystander, that's one thing you aren't!" He turned to the salesman. "I hope you're not selling this bitch anything, Barney. She's a cop killer. Murdered a pal of mine, one of the straightest guys on the force."

Amazed, Barney looked from me to Al and then back. "You kidding or what?"

"It's no joke. She's a shooter." Al caught sight of the handgun permit I'd just filled out. "Hey, what's that?"

While he scanned it, I heard his teeth click. Then he tore the form in half. All my work pretending to be literate for nothing. Now that really made me mad.

"If you think I'm going to sit by and let you get your hands on another gun, lady, you've got another think coming."

I was so angry that I was shaking. "You've got no right, Al Pennak! I was acquitted, remember?"

"Yeah, well, you may have bamboozled that jury. You didn't fool anybody else. Just try and buy a gun in this town, baby! I'll make you eat it."

I guess it's good I didn't have a gun in my hand. At that point I might have relieved my sister of her burden in life and really gotten myself a reputation as a cop killer. My fingers itched to use the spray in my pouch. But I didn't need to be arrested for assaulting an officer, either. Fuming, I turned on my heel and marched out the door. My insides churned and my hands shook so badly that I barely managed to get my bike unlocked and ride away on it without falling on my head.

4

After the scene with Al, I wanted to talk to Randall. But, dressed the way I was, I couldn't barge in on him at his high-class office. Anyway, by this time he'd probably be in court. So I pedaled on back to the apartment.

My answering machine's red light eyed me stolidly, so even though I'd put an ad in this week's *City Paper*, no one had called to demand my professional services. I could stay home and make pillows out of Oriental rug fragments, something I do to pick up spare cash. But that sounded too tame for my ruffled spirits. I needed action. I just wasn't sure what it should be.

While I pondered this I wolfed down some jelly graham cracker sandwiches and a glass of milk. By the time I'd swabbed all the crumbs and gobs of grape jelly off the countertop, I had a plan. After making a phone call to the JHU administration building, I showered and changed into sandals, khaki slacks, and a pale yellow T-shirt. Armed with a notebook and pencil, I left the house and walked five blocks to the Homewood campus.

Baltimore is a city of neighborhoods with sharp boundaries. Step over the line that sets off Federal Hill or Little Italy or Highlandtown, and abruptly the whole atmosphere changes. Hopkins is like that. Once inside its iron gates, you've slipped past the city's hurly-burly to the dreamland of academia. Gray-bearded professors toting overflowing briefcases strolled down shady paths. Brick buildings, some of them actually ivy-covered, nestled among old trees. They lined grassy squares where bespectacled students who looked like future rocket scientists played Frisbee.

Semiilliterate that I am, in my L. L. Bean disguise, I felt like the spy from Planet LoIQ. This was a world closed to the likes of me. But no question, I could see its charm.

It would be great to fit in here. From everything people had said about her, Rebecca Kelso had. For a flash of time I could almost see her hurrying down the path ahead of me. She'd be clutching a stack of books, and her shiny brown hair would swing around her shoulders. I swallowed hard and climbed the steps to Krieger Hall, where Professor Donald Parham taught his two o'clock class on poetry.

For some reason my subconscious had engineered these ghostly encounters with Rebecca Kelso. I knew she couldn't really be asking me to find her killer. I mean, why would she ask me, of all people? Even so, I'd decided to play girl detective.

According to Susie, this Parham guy had been dating Rebecca. What if Parham's relationship with

Rebecca had been a threat to him in some way? I pictured a faceless professorial type tapping at her door that night. She'd let him in without a second thought. Maybe she'd go to the kitchen to get him a drink. What a shock it would be when he came up behind her and held a knife to her throat. I wanted to see him, hear his voice, maybe even talk to him.

Sure, I knew I was building castles in the air and behaving irrationally, but I couldn't rest until I'd satisfied my curiosity.

Parham's class turned out to be in the basement of the cavernous old building. By the time I found it, I was several minutes late. Self-consciously, I slipped in and took a seat in the back row. None of the dozen other students sprawled at various desks paid any attention. Parham, who was writing on the blackboard, didn't turn around until two or three minutes later. When he finally faced the class, I could see why Rebecca had liked him.

He was cut from a different mold from guys like Nick and Al. Parham was tall, six feet two, maybe. He had the kind of long, angular body you see on basketball players. An Ivy League Beau Brummell he wasn't. His khaki slacks, smudged at the knees, hung low on his spare hips, and the navy blue open-throated shirt he wore displayed smudges of chalk dust. He had sandy hair that brushed his high forehead in an overlong sweep. Behind his horn-rims, his eyebrows were furry as caterpillars in fall and scrunched into a permanent arch. The earnestness in his voice struck a positive chord in me. He was deep into his subject of Victorian poetry and excited about it.

I had expected his class to baffle and bore me. Perhaps because his excitement sprang out and surprised me, I enjoyed his lecture. After it ended, I waited while he talked to other students. When he gathered up his briefcase and shambled out, I followed. In the hall, I hurried up behind and cleared my throat.

"Professor Parham."

"Yes?" He stopped and gazed down at me with mild interest.

"I wonder if I could speak to you for a few minutes."

"Sure. I'm going to my office now. We can talk there. Do you want to discuss an assignment?"

"Not exactly."

When we got to his office, a cubbyhole overflowing with books and paper, I stood in the doorway, clutched my notebook tighter, and told him what I'd come to speak to him about.

At the mention of Rebecca's name, his whole demeanor changed. His long face twisted into a pained mask, and he sank onto the chair behind his littered desk. "Were you a friend of hers?"

"No. I never met her. But I feel almost as if I know her. You see, I'm living in her apartment."

He stared at me.

"I moved in just a few days ago."

"Why?"

"It's sort of complicated." I tried to explain, but he just continued staring at me as if I'd sprouted feelers.

Finally he shifted on his chair. "I've told everything I know to the police. In case you're wondering, I was out of town at a professional meeting the night she was killed."

"I didn't come here to accuse you of anything, Professor Parham."

"Then why did you come?"

"I just—it's hard to explain. Ever since I moved into Rebecca's place I've had this feeling about her, that she's still there," I finally blurted out.

Now he really stared. "Excuse me?"

I felt myself flush. "I guess I sound like a real kook. You're probably about to pick up your phone and dial the campus police."

He'd been sitting very stiff on his chair. Now he leaned his elbows forward on the table. "No, this I want to hear. Why don't you sit down and tell me?"

I'd moved in front of the door. At his invitation, I took the seat across from him. I'd surprised myself with what I'd just said. It hadn't been what I'd intended at all. Admittedly, my plan in coming here had been sketchy. Yet now that I'd told somebody about Rebecca, I wanted to make it sound less cuckoo.

"It's just that I can't stop thinking about her," I babbled. "Every time I walk into the kitchen I picture her there making a sandwich or fixing herself a cup of coffee. When I brush my teeth in the morning it really hits me. I know she must have stood in that exact spot doing that exact thing. I can almost feel her image recorded behind the mirror. I can't explain why I need to know more about her and understand why what happened, happened. But I do."

He rubbed the high bridge of his nose. An expression of such bone weariness crept over his face that I felt sorry for him.

"You've got quite an imagination, haven't you? Okay, ask a question and I'll see if I can answer it."

"What was she like?"

"Funny, sweet, full of hope about the future. She was a lovely young girl."

Pain roughened his voice, and hearing it didn't make me feel any better about intruding on him. But as long as I was here, I might as well try to get what I'd come for.

"Was she happy living on Charles Street?"

"Oh, yes, she really liked that place."

"Why? Was it because of her neighbors?"

"You mean Susie Zillig and Damon Wilkes?"

When I nodded, he answered, "Partly, I guess. They were great friends, used to order pizza together and that sort of thing. Have you met Susie and Damon?"

"Yes. Did Rebecca talk about them to you?"

"Occasionally. It's not that she was gossiping, exactly. It's just that they fascinated her. Maybe you already know about Damon's business?"

"I've seen his paintings and the games he designs."

"Pretty intriguing stuff. From what I gather, these gamers live in their own world. I mean that literally. They create their own private cosmos and then move in. Rebecca was tantalized by that."

"Did she and Damon Wilkes see a lot of each other?"

"She and Susie spent a certain amount of time up in his place. Susie a lot more than Rebecca, though. You aren't thinking Damon could have anything to do with Rebecca's murder, are you?"

"I don't know what to think. I'm just trying to understand."

He shook his head. "Well, I can see where you'd be worried if you thought you had a murderer living a couple floors above you. Relax. Damon may be a ladykiller, but that's strictly in the time-honored sense. He and Rebecca were just pals, that is once she made it clear to him that that's how she wanted it."

"Damon came on to her?"

"At first, sure." He cocked his head and studied me. "Damon comes on to every pretty girl he sees, usually successfully from what I've heard. Maybe Rebecca would have been interested in him that way if she hadn't been seeing me. But she wasn't, and when she made that clear Damon accepted it." Parham seemed absolutely confident of Rebecca's loyalty to him. Male arrogance? Women aren't always true blue.

"Apparently Damon and Susie are just friends, too," I pressed. "Is that for the same reason? Is Susie involved with another man?"

Parham grimaced. "No, that's a whole other story. From what Rebecca told me, men don't interest Susie Zillig."

"You mean she's lesbian?"

"I asked Rebecca the same question, but she said no. Susie just isn't interested in sex. She doesn't climb between the sheets with anybody but herself."

I blinked. Maybe Susie and I had more in common than I'd realized. I didn't entertain company in bed, either. But my marriage to Nick and its violent ending had given me good reasons to want to abstain. The passion I'd labeled love had turned into a nightmare. Now intimacy terrified me. What was Susie Zillig's reason? I passed a hand over my forehead. "What a god-awful mess."

Parham studied me. "Are you thinking about Susie Zillig's nonexistent sex life, or Rebecca?"

"Both, but it's Rebecca and what happened to her that I can't let go of."

He nodded. "I can imagine what's going through

your mind. If you're like me, you're wondering why someone like her, someone sweet and innocent and fine and intelligent—and she was all those things— why she was murdered so cruelly, terrorized and then slaughtered like a dumb animal. God knows, Ms. Credella. It's the wolves."

"Wolves?"

"People like us, ordinary people who buy into all the ordinary values, we're like a flock of sheep huddled together in the night," he said bitterly. "There are hungry wolves circling us, waiting to tear out our throats if we're unwary enough to stray. Some of them have managed to disguise themselves so well that we don't recognize the smell of blood on their breath. They mix in with us, waiting to bring us down and eat our hearts when we least expect it."

I stared at him, seeing the barbed edge of his pain and his terrible cynicism and knowing that he could not have been the one who hurt Rebecca Kelso.

"I loved her," he said baldly. His long, bony fingers clenched and unclenched. "If only I knew who did it. But I'll never know, because I'm just another one of those damn bewildered sheep."

That evening I called Randall and told him what happened at the Cop Shop. I didn't get the sympathy I'd expected.

"What the hell did you go there for? Doesn't the name tell you it's where Baltimore's finest hang out?" In place of the friendly drawl I'd grown accustomed to, he used his steely lawyer's voice. When he wishes, Randall can be very intimidating.

"It's close to Little Italy, where I happened to be this morning. I went to the Cop Shop on impulse."

"Bad impulse. Next time you want to buy a firearm, try a gun show. According to my sources, you can get anything you want at one of those without applying for a permit."

"Are you serious?"

"Not where you're concerned. In fact, I'm sorry I mentioned that. Do us both a favor and forget it. Listen, Toni, you were tried for murder with a handgun. The jury acquitted you, but as we both vividly remember, it was closer than bad breath in a crowded elevator. The last thing you should be doing now is buying yourself another handgun."

"The revolver I used on Nick was his, not mine."

"Right, and that made it easier for me to defend you. It also helped that you were young and pretty and had a spotless record. What if you shot someone now with a firearm you'd gained illegally? You could claim self-defense, but if you didn't have a credible witness, who'd believe you? Remember the boy who cried wolf?"

That made me think of what Parham had said about the wolves among us. Maybe some of their victims are men, but most are women. Females are the sheep in this world—aiming their round, helpless butts at danger and hoping for the best. "Randall, I'm a woman alone. I want to be able to defend myself if I have to."

He swore softly. "Damn that apartment! You should never have moved into it."

"No," I agreed meekly. "I should have taken your advice and stayed put. You were absolutely right."

"We'll do something about your situation as soon as possible. You may not be able to get your old place back, but rumor has it that the couple upstairs could be moving in a month or two. I'll let you know the minute I hear."

"Thanks, Randall, but I need you to tell me one thing now. Am I legally entitled to own a gun?"

He hesitated. "Yes, you are. But it's not wise."

There are situations where you can be wise or you can be dead. "Thanks, Randall." After I ended the conversation I opened the phone book and looked for gun shops. I found one down in Fells Point. I'd check it out tomorrow. After jotting down the address, I thought a moment. Then I flipped to the White Pages and looked up the name *Simpler*.

Since Sandy had mentioned Jeff Simpler was on the Kelso case, he'd been at the back of my mind. Bits of his talk at that luncheon kept coming back to me, and I didn't like what I was remembering. He'd said that serial killers got more pleasure out of the hunt than out of the actual murder. They liked to think about what they would do, a hideous sort of mental masturbation. That fit right in with the black Volvo I had such an eerie feeling about. What if it held a killer circling his prey while he worked himself up into a feeding frenzy? What if that prey were me, or any other woman dumb enough to live in this building?

I wanted to talk to Simpler about the Kelso case and about my fears, too. But I wasn't sure how to approach him. If he knew that I'd shot my husband, he might not be too friendly. He also might not want to talk to me about a case under investigation. Maybe the thing to do was take the lay of the land first. On impulse, I dialed his number. A woman answered.

"Is this the Simpler residence?"

"Yes, it is."

"Is this Mrs. Simpler I'm speaking to?"

"Yes." Her voice took on the wary edge of a woman preparing to fend off the horror of telephone solicitation.

I hurried on. "I represent Fresh Features, Mrs. Simpler. We're custom decorators and we're offering a special on wallpapering. For the next ten days we'll custom wallpaper the bathroom of your choice in one of a wide selection of high-quality coverings for a figure you can't beat anywhere else in the area." I quoted a price that was ridiculously low. If she took me up on it, I'd just barely break even.

To my surprise, after only a moment's hesitation, she agreed. She lived within my limited travel range. Mt. Washington wasn't more than five miles from Charles Village. I could put a sample book in my backpack and hop a bus. Or I could load up the carrying baskets on my bike and pedal north. Since it was a sunny afternoon and I still felt antsy, I decided on the latter.

Mt. Washington is a neighborhood of charming older homes nestled in the hills on either side of Falls Road. The Simplers' white frame bungalow stood at the top of a steep bank planted with ivy and azaleas. The white Camry station wagon parked on the almost vertical drive must have a good emergency brake, I thought as I hiked past it. Mrs. Simpler opened the door as I arrived on the porch. She was a small, pretty woman with a brunette bob and Irish blue eyes.

"You actually rode here on a bike?" she questioned, glancing down at where I'd chained mine to a tree.

"Yes, that's how I get around in the city. It's good

exercise, and it's cheap. When traffic is bad I sometimes make better time than I would in a car."

"I can believe it," she said with an amused laugh. She
asked my name again and told me to call her Gloria.

As she walked me through the living room, I
glanced around. It was a tribute to Ethan Allen, everything new and spotless. The kitchen had been remodeled
recently. Everything in it either gleamed or exuded
bogus country warmth.

She offered me a cup of tea, which I accepted. I'd
packed sample books into my bike's carry baskets.
Now I spread them out at the Colonial pine kitchen
table and sat down with the tea while she looked
through them. Like all women preparing to decorate,
she took on the focused absorption of a brain surgeon
operating on a head of state.

"I love these flowers. So cheerful." She pointed at a
pattern of daisies against an electric yellow background.
A person who's been introduced to Randall's idea of
decorating is not going to get excited about daisies. I
nodded and smiled. At least they'd be easy to match.

She went through the sample book twice before
deciding on them. "Jeff would probably like this mattress
ticking stripe," she said, gazing at it with a little frown.
"He likes plainer things than I do."

That's one advantage of shooting your husband, I
thought. Maybe you don't get to live in an Ethan Allen
cottage, but you don't have to kowtow to his notions
about decor anymore, either.

"Perhaps you should consult him," I said sweetly. "I
could leave the book if you'd like."

"Oh, no. He's here. He's out in the garden, actually."
She got up, opened a back door, and called out, "Jeff,

Jeff. Could you come in here and look at something for me?" A couple of minutes later Simpler walked into the kitchen, wearing jeans and a sweatshirt.

Plainly, he'd been working pretty hard. Sweat sheened his skin. Dirt streaked his forehead where he must have swiped at it with one of his gardening gloves. He was medium height with a lean build and the air of quiet intensity that I'd remembered. He, too, had blue eyes, but his were keen and speculative. I suppose in his line of work he'd learned to wonder perpetually what weirdo thing people might do next.

"Fine," he said when his wife showed him the daisies. "Sweetie, whatever you want is fine."

As I took out an order form, he turned to go. I cleared my throat. "You probably don't remember me, Doctor Simpler, but my name is Toni Credella. I heard you speak a few years back."

"Oh?" He glanced back over his shoulder. "Where was this?"

"At a police wives luncheon." I prayed he wouldn't ask me about my husband. He didn't, just stood very still gazing back at me while he shuffled through some sort of interior mental file. "Your talk about serial killers was very interesting. Lately I've been thinking about it a lot. There are a couple of questions I'd like to ask. I wonder if I could come around and talk to you sometime?"

"About serial killers?"

"Sort of. I guess that sounds strange, but—"

He cut off my lame attempt to explain. "How about now? I'll be in the backyard. Come out whenever you're ready."

When he was gone, Gloria gazed at me curiously.

"Why didn't you say you knew my husband when you called?"

"I didn't realize it was the same Simpler until I saw him," I lied. I would have told her the truth, but I sensed that it would make wallpapering her bathroom awkward.

Out back a few minutes later I found Simpler kneeling in front of a neat line of rosebushes. "Looks like you've been working hard."

"Just doing a little pruning and weeding. I get a lot of satisfaction out of gardening." He rocked back on his haunches and squinted up at me. His blue eyes were very bright in the late afternoon sun. He was attractive in an understated way. "I remember you, actually."

"Oh?"

"That head of hair isn't easy to forget."

I pushed a wad of it behind my ears. "I know it's wild. I'd wear it short if haircuts weren't so expensive."

"In my opinion, cutting off glorious stuff like that at all is a sin against Mother Nature. I followed your trial with interest."

"Oh." My stomach dropped. I'd hoped he wouldn't know anything about that.

"As a matter of fact, after I read that you were acquitted, I even thought about calling and offering my services. I figured that after so much trauma you might need some therapy."

"I did, actually. I sort of got it from my lawyer. After the trial he stuck with me, helped me get resettled and stuff."

"I'm glad to hear that, and I'm glad to see you're doing okay." His face relaxed into a smile that must warm the cockles of his patients' hearts. "What did you want to talk to me about? Was it something about your husband's death?"

"Oh no." I'd been afraid he wouldn't want anything to do with me once he knew my history. That's a fear I have with everybody I meet. His friendliness encouraged me. "I heard you were working on the Rebecca Kelso case."

"That's right." His eyes narrowed, and the speculative light came into them again.

"I was wondering if you could tell me anything about it."

"How do you mean, and why are you interested?"

When I explained to him that I lived in the murdered girl's apartment, he looked astounded.

"I know it's pretty weird," I said as he gaped at me, "but the landlord offered me a real deal on the rent."

"It's quite a coincidence," he finally murmured, and gave his head a little shake. "What did you want to ask me, specifically? Do you have some theory about who murdered her?"

"I was hoping you would."

He shook his head again. "No, and even if I did, I'm afraid I wouldn't be at liberty to talk about it."

"If there's anything at all you could tell me, I'd appreciate it."

He regarded me. "All I can give you is guesswork."

"Your guesswork is bound to be a lot better than mine. I'd really like to hear it."

He shrugged. "Okay, about her murderer. He was probably white, probably in his thirties, probably either someone she knew and trusted or someone who looked harmless."

"What makes you think all that?"

"'This was all in the papers, so it's not confidential. Rebecca's assailant didn't rob her, and he didn't break in. He entered through the front door, which means she must have opened it to him. As far as his age and race, that just fits the pattern with this type of crime. Serial killers tend to be white, you know."

I did know because I remembered him saying that at the talk he'd given. "What gives you the idea this is a serial killing?"

"Maybe it's not, but it has the earmarks." He stood and stuffed some withered rose canes into a green plastic bag. "Why are you asking? Are you scared living in that apartment?"

Reluctantly, I nodded.

"Why don't you move?"

"Right now I can't afford to."

"Wallpaper business slow?"

"Very."

He pursed his lips. "I wish I could tell you that we're about to nab the killer. But so far the police haven't made much progress with this case. That doesn't mean they won't. It's still open."

I hunched my shoulders. "If I get any ideas about the murderer, can I call you and talk to you about them?"

"Sure. I'd be glad for any help you can offer."

"Assuming, of course, that her killer doesn't plan a return engagement in the same setting."

He laughed at the expression that must have crossed my face and patted me on the back. "You're probably perfectly safe, Miss Credella. Just don't open your door to any harmless-looking strangers. They're the worst kind."

5

Back at the apartment that evening, I found a paying job on my answering machine. Sonia Litchfield, another friend of Randall's, was restoring her eighteenth-century town house in Fells Point. She wanted me to put a faux black marble finish on her baseboards, which would actually be in keeping with the decorative style of the period. I called to negotiate a price and agreed to start in early the next morning.

The job kept me busy for the next four days, but it didn't keep my mind off Rebecca Kelso or my family problems. I'd had a couple of brief phone conversations with my mother. Naturally she'd sounded depressed. Not wanting to think about that, I concentrated on Rebecca. What had I found out so far?

Not much, really. I'd met her boyfriend, Don Parham, and her housemates, Susie and Damon. Simpler had speculated that her killer had been either someone she knew or a man who looked so unthreatening that she'd invited him into her apartment. That could be anyone—another student in one of her classes, one of her teachers, the paper boy, Damon or Parham, even Mr. Aronchick. Parham had convinced me that he never could have killed her. But that must have been Rebecca's reaction to whomever she'd made the fatal mistake of opening her door to.

After dead-ending on this train of thought, I switched over to my neighbors, Susie and Damon. They were a pretty strange pair. Several times since our first meeting I'd run into Susie on the stairs. Twice she'd been dressed in white and on her way to work. Last night she'd been coming down from Damon's apartment.

"I've been helping him think about a new game," she'd told me. "It's easier when several people brainstorm ideas, fun, too. Listen, why don't you come up tomorrow night? We'll order pizza and have a ball."

I wanted to say no. Rebecca must have accepted invitations such as this, and I didn't like the idea of stepping into her shoes. "Maybe. I'll see how things go at work tomorrow."

Now, as I aimed a last swipe at the marbleized baseboard in Sonia Litchfield's pale green dining room, I decided to take Susie up on it. Just how weird were the games she and Damon played? I knew they had names like "Invaders from the Blue Planet" and "Witches and Goblins." Did they ever get past the plastic-model stage and involve the sacrifice of young virgins? That's really a crazy idea, I thought disgustedly. Well, at least if my spacey neighbors liked to sacrifice virgins, I wouldn't qualify—that is, unless my hymen had grown back after three years of disuse.

That evening I kept an ear out for Susie's footsteps and caught her as she came home from work. "Hey," I said, poking my head around my door, "if the invitation still stands, I think I will come up and watch you and Damon in action tonight."

"Great," she answered gaily. "He's been after me to invite you. You really made a big impression on him. In fact, I think you've been giving him wet dreams, so watch out."

While Susie went on up to her place to change out of her uniform, I slipped back inside and eyed my reflection in the bathroom mirror. I used to spend a lot of time and money dolling myself up. Since the trial I haven't bothered with makeup, and I spend most of my time in jeans and an old shirt and sweater. That's one of the advantages of the paint-and-wallpaper biz. You have a perfect excuse to look like a slob.

Now, I exchanged my paint-spotted flannel shirt for a pink turtleneck pullover and slipped on a pair of gold hoop earrings. Other than running a comb through my hair and making a pass over my cheeks with a blusher brush, I left my face unvarnished. Even the thought of ever again playing girl-sugarbun gives me the shivers.

"So how's that, Rebecca?" I asked just before I turned away from my image. "Think I'll pass muster?"

I hadn't had any further visitations from my ghost. Yet there were times when I still imagined I felt her presence. So, out of some oddball form of self-defense, I'd taken to talking to her. Of course, she never answered back.

When I met Susie on the stairs, I felt overdressed.

She wore jeans and a faded cotton shirt. Her face bore not a smidge of makeup, and she'd skinned her hair back with a rubber band.

"You must have a lot of energy," I said. "If I'd just spent eight hours on my feet in a hospital ward, I'd be too beat to do anything but crash."

"Gaming is my form of relaxation."

"You'll miss it, then, when you move to Chicago."

"Like crazy. Fortunately, Damon's already put me in touch with some gaming groups there."

"Are you moving because of Rebecca Kelso?"

She paled and nodded tightly. "One reason, anyway. That was too close for comfort. How you can live in that place is beyond me."

"I didn't know her." It was a lie, for I now felt I did know her.

A square of light appeared at the top of the stairs. Framed in it, Damon Wilkes stood hipshot, grinning down at us. "Greetings, ladies. Ready for an evening of mystery and enchantment?"

"We're ready for an evening of beer and pizza," Susie snapped back smartly. "I hope you've already ordered. I'm starved."

Damon had ordered. The food arrived about twenty minutes after we did. While we waited, he poured us drinks and introduced us to the game he was developing. "It's something new for me," he explained, "something, uh, more topical than my usual fantasy, science-fiction stuff. I'm calling it 'City Streets.'"

"Will it be a role-playing game?" Susie asked.

Damon nodded. "A role-playing game of urban horror."

I stood blinking at them, not sure I wanted any part

of this. When you've lived in the city all your life, you don't want to hear about urban horror. Yet, as I listened, I became intrigued.

"We'll have street gangs," he explained, "and each of them will defend a turf and try to invade the turf of others. Sorcerers, witches, vampires, and werewolves will lead these gangs."

"How about something a little more inventive," Susie countered. "How about a monster that emerges from the sewers at night."

"Beauty and the Beast and Ninja Turtles have already been done." Damon looked scornful.

"I mean like a real monster. Maybe he gobbles up bag ladies."

"That might have some possibilities." Damon jotted a note on a pad of yellow paper.

"If you're setting it in Baltimore, you could have something hideous emerge from that old chrome plant on the harbor. You know, the one they're sup-posed to have detoxified so they can make it into a park," I suggested.

Damon grinned. "Now we're cooking. The creature from the poisoned harbor slime rears its scaly head up during a fireworks display and swallows Harbor-place. As high sorceress of the Federal Hill Magicks, it's your task to produce the buried potion that will quell his appetite for conventioneers."

For the next couple of hours we scarfed pizza and tossed screwy ideas around. Once I got into the swing of it, I enjoyed myself. It was like being a kid again. I glanced from Susie to Damon. They really were like a couple of twelve-year-olds dreaming up adolescent schemes in their secret clubhouse. The world outside, the complicated and dangerous empire of the evil grown-ups, receded. Of course, the world we were creating was equally dangerous with its monsters and magicians. It was also a lot more fun, and we were in charge of it. That made all the difference—control.

Finally we began to run out of steam, and I felt the effects of two and a half cans of beer. "Bathroom back that way?" I asked, pointing at a likely-looking hall. Damon nodded, so I pushed myself off the nest of cushions where I'd been sitting cross-legged and moseyed off. When I got back Damon was alone in the living room. Reclining on the heap of cushions I'd vacated, he saluted me with his beer can.

I glanced behind him to see if there was a light in the kitchen. "What happened to Susie?"

"Went home."

"Went home? You mean, she just left?"

"Susie's a funny girl. One minute she's the life of the party, the next she's flatter than a leaky balloon. When that happens, she splits. Or if you're at her place, she tells you to get lost." He took a final swig from his can and then pushed himself to his feet. "Hey, stop looking at the door like there's something you want on the other side. You're not planning to leave, too, are you?"

"Might as well. The party's over."

"Who says?" I was afraid he would hand me that line about having our own party and I'd puke. Instead he gave me a searching look. "This is our chance to get better acquainted, Toni."

"We've been talking all night."

"Not about anything that matters."

"I thought witches and demons were your life's blood."

"They are, but they're not yours. I'd like to hear about what's important to you." He'd glued his gaze to my face. I had the feeling he was humoring me, the way you might a mental patient you intended to persuade into a straitjacket.

"Staying healthy and paying the rent. Listen, I've got to go."

"Not quite yet." He held up a pacifying palm. "Don't look so worried. I'm not going to lay a hand on you. Give me ten minutes, okay?"

"For what? What are you doing?" I watched him set a pad on an easel and then rummage through a messy box of pencils. All the while he kept shooting me intent looks.

"I'd like to draw you, okay? I've been wanting to get you on paper since I met you." His hand made several quick pencil strokes. "Some guys when they see a beautiful woman can't wait to get her into bed. Me, I can't wait to draw her. After that, of course, I'd like to take her to bed."

"Forget it, Damon, I'm not interested."

"I'm only asking you to sit still for the drawing part. After that you can strap on your chastity belt."

Much as I wanted to walk out, I didn't. He was right, I told myself. What could it hurt to let him draw my picture? Besides, I'd never had an artist want to put me on paper. I was flattered and curious.

Damon worked quickly, changing pencils now and then and rubbing at the marks he'd made with the pad of his thumb. "You know," he said, "I've been keeping an eye on you."

"Oh?" I didn't like that. "How do you mean?"

"That window over there has a good view of the street. I see you come and go on your bike. When you get a visitor, I see that, too."

"I haven't had any visitors."

"You've had one. A guy in a fancy suit."

I realized he must be talking about Randall. "He's just a friend."

"Not your boyfriend?"

"I don't have any boyfriends."

"So I've noticed. Nor many friends, either. You pedal off on that bike. You get home before dark, and you stay in like a good little homebody. At your young and vibrant stage of life, Toni me beauty, that's not healthy."

"Who are you to talk about healthy? Some people might consider your life-style a little strange."

"Most people would. Maybe on that basis alone we should get together, form a mutual peculiarity pact." He grinned at me, his curls framing his puckish face like a halo.

"I'm not that peculiar," I lied. Actually, I was probably stranger than he'd ever be. Imagining ghosts, talking to departed murder victims. The thought depressed me. "I've got to go." I left my post and walked around in back of him to have a look at his work. "That's not me!"

"Oh, yes. It's you to a T."

The angry face glaring out of the white paper startled me. It impressed me that Damon had put it together so quickly, but I didn't like what he'd created. "Why did you draw me looking so . . . so . . ."

"Beautiful and wild and tormented? Because that's

the way I see you, dearie. You're an elven princess on crusade, and you're mad as hell. I just wish I knew what's got you so riled."

I continued staring at the drawing. He'd penciled a silver band around my forehead and let my hair stream out around my face as if it were caught in a high wind. My eyes stretched wide, and I'd gritted my mouth in a snarl that could represent either fear or fury.

"Well, you're very imaginative," I murmured. I had a thought. "Did you ever draw Rebecca Kelso?"

"Sure I did."

"Do you have the drawings, or did you give them to the police?"

"Why should I give my work to the cops? Here, you want to see?" He riffled through a stack of notebooks. It took him several minutes to find the one he wanted. While I waited, I felt my stomach knot up. For a crazy second I felt as if he were going to pull out Rebecca's corpse.

"Ah," he finally exclaimed as he flipped open a pad of drawing paper. Almost fearfully, I studied the images it contained. There were several pencil sketches of Rebecca, some of them quite detailed. It seemed to me that they caught her character better than the snapshot I'd seen.

It was obvious that Damon had liked his subject. He'd sketched her with a winsome lightness. There were views of her as a princess on a prancing horse and several of her dressed like Robin Hood with a bow. One where she was bewinged like a fairy and kneeling by a woodland pool to study her reflection caught my attention. She looked so ethereal, so otherworldly. Then it struck me. That was the way I'd seen her face in the mirror, only she'd had tears in her eyes.

In the final sketch he'd penciled her stretched out on some sort of altar with her eyes closed and her hands crossed over her breasts.

I held it up. "She looks like a corpse or a sacrifice. Why did you draw her like this?"

Suddenly, in the artificial light, Damon was haggard, all the flirtatiousness drained away from his expression like water in sand. "I don't know. I've wondered about that myself."

"Did you draw it after she was killed?"

"No, before, just a few days before. Weird, huh? All I can tell you is that when I looked at her, that's what I saw. Maybe I had a premonition."

We stared at each other without speaking. Finally I handed back the sketch pad. "Do me a favor, will you?"

"What's that?"

"If you ever feel the urge to draw me in my coffin, let me know."

I left Damon's place and stood on the landing outside his door, pondering. After spending the evening with Susie and him, I no longer thought they might have arranged to murder Rebecca in some kind of bizarro ceremony. They were too playful together, like a couple of puppies. Anything truly evil coming from them just didn't seem possible. After talking to Don Parham, I'd reached a similar conclusion. Terrific lady detective I was, eliminating all my suspects. Yet Simpler had said it was the innocent-looking ones you should be most suspicious of.

I went on down the stairs. When I got to Susie's landing I noticed a thread of light under her door. On impulse, I knocked. I haven't taken an assertiveness course, but I've given the subject a lot of thought. When something somebody does bothers you, you should let them know. And you shouldn't save it up for later. Too much acid collects over time.

"Who's there?"

"Hey, don't sound so scared. It's just me, Toni."

"What do you want?" Susie cracked the door a couple of inches.

"Could I talk to you a minute?"

"Uh, sure."

When she stood aside so I could come in, I saw empty boxes scattered around the living room. "Packing up for your move?"

"Thinking about it, anyway. I haven't really started yet."

She wore pajamas and a pink terrycloth robe. "Sorry if I'm keeping you up," I said.

"It's okay. I was fixing myself a cup of tea before I went to bed, anyway. Care for some?"

"Sure."

I waited on the couch until she came back with a mug for each of us. "So, what's on your mind?" She looked at me with impersonal curiosity, and I knew what it must be like to have her for a nurse. She'd be cool, calm, competent, and remote. Come to think of it, there was something remote about her all the time, as if she wasn't quite connected to reality. Maybe that explained why she liked Damon and his games so much.

I took a sip of the tea and then set it down. "Listen, Susie, I just want to know why you left like that."

"What do you mean? Like what?"

"I mean, you invited me to spend the evening with you and Damon. The three of us were getting along fine. Then I go to the john for five minutes, and when I come out you're gone. What did you do that for?"

She colored. "What's the big deal? I got tired, so I left."

"Well, I can't accept any more invitations from you if you're going to practice your disappearing act like that. I enjoyed being one of a threesome. I didn't enjoy you leaving me alone in Damon's apartment."

"Don't tell me you haven't been there alone before."

"Once, but it's not something I intend making into a habit. I'm not interested in joining his harem."

"Harem? Who said anything about a harem? Hey, that's not my role in life, either." Her flush deepened. "Listen," she said tightly, "I thought you and Damon liked each other, and that you'd appreciate being left alone. I guess I misunderstood."

"Yes, you did. I like him all right. Fighting him off, I don't like."

"Fight him off? C'mon, Damon didn't attack you or anything, did he? Before you answer, I wouldn't believe you even if you said he did. He and I have been friends for a long time, so I think I know him pretty well. He can have a girl whenever he wants. There's a whole troop of gamer groupies who idolize him. Why should he go out of his way to hassle someone who's unwilling?"

"Okay, he didn't attack me. He only wanted to flirt. I'm just not up for that these days. In fact, I'd like to avoid it. That's why I decided to bring this up with you. I used to be the silent, brooding type. No more. I thought it would be best to make things clear."

She gazed at me, thoughts and questions clearly ticking away behind her hazel eyes. Her long face settled into a mask of suspicion. "I have to admit I'm a little puzzled," she finally said. "Someone with your looks shouldn't be trying to avoid guys. Damon mentioned that you were a widow." She glanced at my bare ring finger. "Still grieving?"

"Hardly." At her inquiring look, I added, "My husband was a police officer. He died of a gunshot wound. I'm the one who shot him."

Telling her was a snap decision. Sometimes the only way to get a thing is to give something first. I was bargaining that my revelation might drag one of equal value out of her. Also, I sensed she wouldn't condemn me. There was something of the walking wounded about her. That remote, self-contained manner of hers hid something, and I wanted to know what it was.

I was right in thinking she wouldn't put me down. Oh, sure, when I described what happened with Nick, she looked a little shocked. But that quickly changed into raw curiosity. I didn't hold much back, which is strange, I guess, since there aren't many people I've told the whole story to. Somehow, telling Susie about Nick's abuse, my violent reaction, and the awfulness of the trial felt right.

"Well, now I see why jumping into bed with Damon doesn't capture your interest," she finally allowed.

"I haven't wanted a man's hands on me since before it happened. The sexual part of me got turned off completely."

"I know what you mean."

"You do?"

She had the look of someone weighing a possibility.

I hoped it was telling me her story. "You know," she said, "I've been wondering about you. You don't seem to have boyfriends, and then your attitude tonight toward Damon—I'm glad you told me about all this. It explains a lot."

"Actually, I've been wondering about you, too."

When her eyes grew wary, I added, "You don't appear to have boyfriends, either. And your relationship with Damon seems strictly platonic."

"It is," she answered quickly.

"That's a little strange considering his many boyish charms and that the two of you get along so well."

"It's because I don't want to go to bed with him that we get along so well."

"I can understand that. Still, it makes me wonder why he doesn't turn you on." True, it was rude the way I pressed. But I'd told her my secret. Now it was time she let me in on hers.

"Men don't turn me on, period."

She spat it out as if it had a bad taste, and it gave me a bad taste, too. My thoughts must have shown on my face because Susie started to laugh. "Don't worry, I'm not about to come on to you. Women don't light my Bunsen burner, either."

"You're not attracted to anybody?"

"Not sexually, no."

"Not even kittens, puppies, and bunny rabbits." I'd meant it as a feeble joke. Instead, the minute it came out of my mouth, Susie started to cry. They weren't gentle tears, either, but loud, racking sobs that had burst through from some giant reservoir of misery. I stared at her, horrified. "Susie, what did I say? I'm sorry, I'm sorry!"

She doubled over with her face in her hands and her shoulders shaking. I'd never heard such anguished cries. They sounded as if they were coming from an animal in one of those traps that gnaw off the leg. I didn't know whether to touch her. She seemed so brittle she'd break if I tried to put my arms around her. Yet she obviously needed comfort. Feeling completely helpless, I patted her shoulders, stroked her hair, and muttered ineffectual little sounds of sympathy.

It must have been a good ten minutes before Susie stopped weeping. Finally, when she began calming down, I put my arm around her shoulders and squeezed. "I'm sorry if I upset you."

"It's not your fault." She lifted her head. Her swollen eyelids and red, puffy face made her a less than appealing sight.

I went into her bathroom and came out with a damp washcloth and a roll of toilet paper. "You look as if you could use these. Sorry I couldn't find any tissue."

"I don't have any." She held the folded cloth up against her eyes and then blew her nose into a crumpled wad of toilet paper. "I haven't cried like that in years. Honestly, not in years."

"I guess you had it stored up."

"Guess so. Flash-frozen for the appropriate occasion." She gave a mirthless little laugh. "Listen, if I tell you what defrosted me like that, will you keep it to yourself?"

"Who would I tell?"

"Damon. I don't want you talking to Damon about me. I like our relationship just the way it is, and I don't want it to change."

"Okay, I won't talk to him."

She wiped her nose again and took a deep breath. As she gazed down at the crumpled tissue in her fist, she said, "When I was nine years old I was raped."

I'd expected something like this. Yet when I heard it I felt as if she'd punched me. "God, Susie, I'm sorry. That must have been so terrible for you!"

"You don't know the half of it." A bitter smile flickered on her mouth. "I wasn't just raped, I was nearly killed, too." She pushed her robe and pajama top to one side and I saw a scar at the top of her breast. "That's a bullet wound. Only it didn't come close enough to my heart to do the job."

"Who shot you?"

"A nasty little creep named Christopher Espey. He's in Maryland State Pen now."

"I certainly hope so."

"Oh, yeah. That was the first thing I wanted to know when Rebecca was killed. Espey's still in jail all right, though he's coming up for parole. Between that and what happened to Rebecca, I figured it was time to move."

We both glanced at the empty boxes. My mouth felt like the inside of a lime kiln. "How did it happen?"

Susie rubbed the flats of her hands together, rolling the tissue between them. I noticed that her knees were trembling and was almost sorry I'd asked. On the other hand, I wasn't going anywhere until she'd told me.

"When I was nine I had a girlfriend who lived a couple houses down from me. We played together all the time—jump rope, dolls, roller skates. We were best pals. Her name was Maryanne Frazier."

"She was the same age as you?"

"Yeah. When we met Espey, we were both nine."

A coldness started in my feet and worked its way up to my stomach. "How did you meet him?"

"We were playing in Maryanne's yard when this van pulled up and a harmless-looking young guy got out with a puppy. Of course, we ran over to pet the puppy. After a couple of minutes, he took it away. He said he had to feed it. He told us if we got into the van we could play with it some more after it ate."

"You got in?"

"Yeah. We were just kids."

I forced myself to ask what happened. "He molested you?"

"He handcuffed us and put tape across our mouths. He drove us to Patapsco State Park, to a wooded place. He raped us in turn and then he shot us. Maryanne was killed. But he'd never bothered to check to make sure we were both dead, and I wasn't. I managed to crawl into the woods and hide. Some campers found me and took me to the hospital. I was able to describe Espey's van and later to identify him."

I sat gaping at her, then asked an inane question, the only thing my frozen brain seemed able to muster. "What happened to the puppy?"

"Oh, he didn't hurt that. He just let it go."

At that moment I felt an icy breath against the back of my neck, and I knew beyond question that I hadn't imagined it. Rebecca was warning me.

6

I *left Susie's with my mind* churning like one of those dough machines. Sickened by what she'd told me, I lay awake picturing those two little girls. I thought of Don Parham. He'd talked about wolves among us. This man Espey hadn't been a wolf. He'd been something far more evil.

Coincidence, I thought. They say coincidences happen in real life that you'd never dare put in a play. Still, was it a coincidence that twenty years later Rebecca Kelso had been raped and murdered at Susie Zillig's address? Susie had escaped this Espey monster, and her testimony had put him in prison. Wouldn't he hate her for that? Wouldn't he want to punish her? Might he not have nursed the idea of tracking her down and getting revenge? Susie had insisted that Christopher Espey was still locked away in jail. Maybe so. But before I finally closed my eyes and went to sleep, I knew I had to check that out for myself.

The next morning I called Jeff Simpler's house. He

wasn't there, but his wife gave me his office number. When I dialed that, Jeff picked up the phone. His voice, crisp and professional, reassured me.

"Dr. Simpler, this is Toni Credella. The wallpaper lady who asked you questions about Rebecca Kelso's murder?"

"Of course I remember you, Toni. My wife is really excited about this wallpaper job you're going to do for her. She talked about it all morning at breakfast." He sounded amused. I pictured him being one of those superior husbands who smile indulgently at their wives' feminine foibles.

"I'll be out slapping glue on your walls as soon as the paper she ordered comes in. That's not what I'm calling about. I wonder if you ever heard of a man named Christopher Espey?"

He hesitated. "The name rings a distant bell, but I can't place it right off. Is this someone who might have been a patient?"

"No, I don't think so. My upstairs neighbor told me something last night that makes me wonder if he might have a connection with the Kelso case."

"What sort of connection?"

"What she told me was in confidence, so I can't really explain. But Espey is a rapist and murderer. She says he's still in prison, where he's been for the last twenty years. I'd just like to make sure."

There was a brief pause, and then Simpler cleared his throat. "If this Espey is in prison, he can't be connected with Rebecca Kelso's murder."

"My neighbor might be mistaken. He might have gotten out on one of those good-conduct things."

"Oh, I don't think so, not a convicted murderer."

"You hear about administrative mistakes like that

all the time. Anyhow, if there's any chance he was out when Rebecca was killed, it could explain a lot." Supposing Espey had gotten out somehow and decided to look up the girl who'd put him in jail? It had been twenty years since he'd seen Susie. He could have looked up the right address and then revenged himself on the wrong girl. Of course, the notion was far-fetched. But I couldn't put the idea out of my head until I'd made sure it was impossible.

"How can I make sure that Espey really was in prison the night Rebecca was murdered?"

"I'm still not sure what this is all about, but I'll check it out for you. If you try, the bureaucracy will give you the runaround for days."

I sighed with gratitude. I hate hanging on phone lines. The thought of tackling the penal system really intimidated me. "Thanks."

"Thank you. If this should turn into a lead you can discuss with me in more detail, I'll be grateful. This case is still open and I'm assigned to it, you know."

"I thought you were just a consultant."

"True, but it would be a feather in my cap to pick up an important lead."

He sounded open to the possibility that I might actually be on to something, which made me feel a lot better about imposing on him.

"How are you?" he asked, his voice warming.

"Um, okay, I guess."

"You can't be all that okay if you're this obsessed about Rebecca Kelso's murder."

I kneaded the telephone cord. "It's hard not to think about a crime like that when you're living where it happened."

"Of course. And I respect the help you're trying to give the police department. But right now I'm concerned about you. Toni, I can appreciate the strain you must have been under since your husband's death."

"Before, too."

There was a blank pause.

"I was under a strain before his death, too. That's why I shot him."

"Oh, of course."

I could imagine him rolling his eyes.

"Toni, what I'm getting at is that living in that apartment is stressful to you. Frankly, my guess is stress is the last thing you need. How about taking some free advice from a professional? You'd be better off moving."

Now, where had I heard that before? "Thanks, doctor, I appreciate your concern. Right now I can't afford to move. As soon as I'm able, I'll give it serious thought. In the meantime, I'm looking forward to wallpapering your bathroom and to hearing from you about Espey."

After I hung up, I sat nursing a cup of coffee. I rehashed my conversation with Simpler and brooded about the victims of this world. Then I started thinking about my mother. At eight-thirty the next morning, Sandy and I had a date to take her to Hopkins. All week I'd avoided thinking about it. When it comes to my family, it's like I have an infected sore. I want to put a bandage over it and never look. This thing with Mom meant I was going to have to tear off the dressing and contemplate the damage.

"Right on the dot," I said when Sandy picked me up in her peanut-butter brown van. When Al's not hotrodding around in a squad car, he drives a souped-up electric blue Camaro.

"I would have been early if Matt hadn't squirted toothpaste all over the upstairs hall," my sister commented through gritted teeth. "The mess was unbelievable. I finally just told the baby-sitter I'd pay her extra if she cleaned it up. Who knows if she will, though."

I started to laugh, but not because of my devilish nephew. "We're wearing the same getup."

Sandy glanced down at her pleated skirt and then over at me. I'd put on an outfit I thought Mama would like, a white silk shirt with a navy blue jacket and skirt. It was a grown-up version of the uniform Sandy and I had worn in Catholic high school.

"Shades of Saint Leo's. I guess we both wanted to feel young and innocent again," she commented dryly.

"Maybe that was it. Now, let me get this straight. Mama's not going to be staying in the hospital overnight."

"No. Are you kidding? I could never have talked her into that. This is what's called a two-step biopsy. It's strictly an outpatient procedure."

"Will we know the score when it's over?"

"I hope so."

"Lucky," I said a few minutes later when Sandy found a parking spot half a block from the restaurant.

"It's early. The tourists aren't out slumming yet."

Inside the kitchen we found Mom sitting at the table. She had her fingers laced together in front of her, and her expression was, as usual, bleak. She wore her Sunday best, a black silk suit with a yellowed lace collar. I recognized the collar. It had been part of her dowry. Back in the old country her mother's family had been lacemakers. Once when I was little and home from school with a bad cold, she took me up to her bedroom.

"Now, *cara mía*, I going to show you something to make you feel better."

Smiling secretly, she lifted down a flowered hatbox from the top of her closet. After placing it on the bed, she reverentially removed the lid. I still remember the smell that wafted up to me, mustiness mixed with dried violets. Under the layers of yellowed paper had been bits of lace. Some of them had been collars and handkerchiefs. Others, I couldn't imagine a use for. Yet to my eight-year-old eyes they had all been wonderful, like intricate spells spun by some ancient and magical spider.

"Someday, *cara*, these will be yours," she'd promised.

I had carried that thrilling secret close to my heart. One day I would own a box full of my mother's gossamer treasure.

Now, as she lifted her eyes to mine, I thought of that box and wondered what I would do with it if I should inherit it. I had no idea, and the backs of my eyes stung.

"Mom, you didn't need to get all dressed up," Sandy said.

"Neither did you need to get dressed up," she said, her gaze going from Sandy to me and then back. Though she was smiling, her skin was sallow and her eyes looked frightened. "All of us look like we're going to a funeral."

"Now, Mom," Sandy cajoled as she took her arm and maneuvered her toward the door. "It's not a funeral. It's just a test. You're going to feel a lot better when it's all over."

"I'm going to feel better when I'm dead, too. There's no pain in the grave." As she bent to get into the back of the van, she glanced at me and her mouth turned down like an inverted U. "I had another bad dream about you, Toni."

"You did?" Just what I needed to hear.

"Something was chasing you, a monster. I tried to call out a warning, but when I opened my mouth, nothing, only a silent scream. It worries me."

It didn't exactly relax me, either. I couldn't think of anything to say on the subject that didn't seem ill timed, so while Sandy chattered about the kids, Mom and I rode the rest of the way to the hospital in morbid silence.

When we finally walked into the Johns Hopkins oncology wing, the three of us with our somber clothes and dejected expressions must have looked like a PR team for the Grim Reaper. After Mom signed the consent form and a nurse took her away, Sandy and I looked at each other. "How long do you think this will take?" I finally said.

"The operation itself probably won't take more than an hour. If they give her general anesthesia, they won't let her go home for two or three hours after that. We're going to be here for a while. Do you want to walk down to the cafeteria and get a cup of coffee?"

"Sure."

When we'd found the automated Formica wasteland that served as the hospital's watering hole, we fed quarters to a machine and settled into an empty corner.

"Pop might come," Sandy said as she gazed into her coffee cup. "He had to stay in the restaurant for a salesman. But he might come afterward."

"Great. Does he know I'm here?"

"Of course he knows. Mom tells him everything." Sandy looked at me sternly. "You can't leave, Toni."

"Did I say I was going to?"

"I know you don't want to see Pop."

"Perceptive of you."

"Maybe it's time you bit the bullet."

I gave her a look, and she crossed her eyes.

"Sorry about that. What I mean is, maybe it's time you stopped acting so damned hypersensitive. So the way he treated you wouldn't get him cast on 'Father Knows Best.' He's still *our* father, and he isn't getting any younger."

"Nobody's getting any younger, Sandy. That includes you and me."

"All the more reason to make peace with the family. What if this thing of Mom's is malignant? What then?"

"It's not," I said fiercely. "She's going to be fine."

Sandy stared. "Well, finally I get a reaction from the Credella sphinx. So, you won't believe she might really be sick because you can't deal with the guilt."

"Guilt, what guilt? Why should I feel guilty about Mom's health?"

"Because you've been ignoring her all this time, punishing her because she didn't give you the support you thought she owed her pretty baby. Christ, Toni, what did you expect? You shot your husband. Italian women just don't do that. If it had happened a few years back in the old country, you might have been stoned."

She was right about that, but it didn't exactly improve my mood. "It was okay for Nick to beat me up? That doesn't have any bearing?"

"The folks couldn't believe it. And why should they? All the time you say Nick was knocking you around at home, you never breathed a word. You never showed us any bruises. Whenever you and Nick were out together you were all smiles. The folks thought he was a great guy. We all thought he was a great guy."

"Tell me something, Sandy. Do you believe me?"

She gazed at me soberly. "I have to, don't I?"

"Thanks a lot."

"Best I can do." She reached out and took my hand. "We're family, and families should take care of each other. Let's try and put it together again."

"Coming from you that has a certain irony. By any chance did your enchanting husband describe our latest meeting?"

Sandy flushed and took her hand away. "He mentioned running into you in the Cop Shop. He didn't repeat the conversation word for word. But I got the idea it wasn't a positive experience."

"Since Al is about as subtle as a load of wet cement, I bet you didn't have to work hard to figure that out."

"Oh, get off it. I apologize for Al. What can I say? Nick was his best friend. He's never going to believe your abuse story."

"No." I toyed with my cup. I'd only had a few sips of the coffee, but it had gone cold and bitter. My stomach churned queasily. I worked hard to keep all the bad feelings inside me hidden. Now they were all stirred up and floating loose.

"What were you doing in the Cop Shop, anyway? Al said you were buying a gun. I told him no way."

"I *was* trying to."

Sandy's jaw dropped. She smacked her forehead with the flat of her palm. "I don't believe what I'm hearing. Why in hell would you try to buy a gun?"

"For the same reason that other women buy them. Protection." I hadn't planned to tell my sister about the Rebecca Kelso business. Now I felt too weary and depressed to keep it to myself. After I'd spilled the main outline, I was sorry.

"I really don't believe you! What, are you crazy, living in a place like that?"

"It's cheap," I offered lamely.

"No wonder! You couldn't pay me to live there!"

I didn't want to hear it. I scraped my chair back and stood. "Time we got back up to that waiting room. Who knows when they'll finish with Mama."

"If she survives this biopsy, I wonder if she'll survive you."

"You aren't going to say anything about this to her, are you?" I tossed my coffee container into a trash can, and Sandy did the same.

"Of course I'm not going to tell her. She'd go through the ceiling if she knew that her darling baby girl, her *bèlla* Toni, is trying to get herself murdered."

Upstairs, the receptionist at the waiting room desk told us Mama was in surgery now, and there wouldn't be any news for another half hour. We settled down to wait. Sandy picked up a *New Yorker*, and I grabbed one, too. But I was too uptight to try to decipher any of the legends on the jokes, so I just flipped through, looking at the pictures.

Well, *The New Yorker* just doesn't have enough pictures for the likes of me, so pretty soon I dumped it for a *Sports Illustrated*. It happened to be the swimsuit issue, which in my current mood was exactly the wrong thing to look at.

As I turned the pages and studied all the scantily clad girls with their toothy smirks, cold shivers snaked down my spine. It wasn't just that all their youth and health seemed out of place when my mother lay behind a door nearby, losing a piece of her breast. The beaming models made me think of that snapshot of Rebecca and Susie smiling sunnily. Rebecca had been young, pretty, and, from what everyone said, smart and nice. She had been the daughter every mother dreamed of, the girl everyone would like for a friend. And then some monster had decided to pleasure himself by cutting her to pieces.

No matter what people kept saying, I couldn't just walk away from such hideous cruelty. He should be caught and punished, this beast who walked the streets lurking behind a human mask. Someone must find him and tear that mask away. I couldn't forget about Rebecca. As long as her killer was on the loose and Susie Zillig might be in some danger, I had to stay and try to do something.

"Here's Pop. Now, don't say anything to upset him," Sandy whispered.

I looked up in time to see my father stride through the double doors and stop to speak with the receptionist. "Well, hooray for Mister Concerned Husband," I wanted to say. Instead I picked up another magazine and pretended to bury myself in it.

My father seems to grow handsomer and more distinguished looking with the years. He's tall for an Italian, with snapping dark eyes and hawkish features. He's a snappy dresser. He wears hand-tailored shirts and buys only the finest shoes imported from Italy. He's one of the few men I know these days who likes to wear a hat. His are always rakish Borsalinos in a touchable gray the color of a dove's breast.

He surveyed the room, which was full of people pretending not to see one another. My father prides himself on his perfect health and claims he hasn't gone to a doctor since the day he was born. This place where we had all been dragged to chew on our mortality would naturally horrify him.

Spotting us, he crossed and spoke sternly to Sandy. "How's your mother?"

"I don't know. They say she's still in surgery."

"*Malandrinos*! I just hope these doctors know what to cut and what not to cut." With that, he sat on a chair and began tapping a staccato rhythm on its arm-rests. So far he hadn't acknowledged my presence. I kept my gaze pinned to the open page of my magazine.

"Papa," Sandy said, "don't you see Toni sitting here next to me?"

Tight silence. "I've got eyes. I see her."

"Well, aren't you going to say something to her?"

He pursed his lips and then blew them out with a little popping sound. "What should I say? Long time no see?"

"That would be better than nothing."

Out of the corner of my eye, I saw him lace his fingers together. "It's not my place to speak to your sister first, Sandra. It's better that she should speak to me."

Sandy poked my forearm with her elbow. "Say something to Pop, Toni."

I closed my magazine and put it down on the empty chair on my right. "Hello, Pop. How's the restaurant biz?"

The finely arched nostrils on his Roman nose flared. "You hear how she talks to me," he said. "This one who was nothing but trouble since the day she was born."

Now that I resented. I had been pretty good as a

kid. It's true that in my teen years I was a little wild, grandstanding to attract the boys. But that was only because I was trying to do what I thought I was supposed to, persuade one of them into marrying me. Until that night with Nick's revolver, I had never disgraced the Credella name. Suddenly I wanted to bawl, to just crumple down on the chair, cover my face with my hands, and scream and wail. Instead I pokered up and stared straight ahead.

"Pop, Toni, have you forgotten Mom's sick and that we're here to try and make some peace in this family," Sandy whispered urgently.

A nurse came out from behind a swinging door and told us that our mother was resting comfortably in recovery. We could see her for five minutes.

We followed her back through the antiseptic tile corridor in single file, no one speaking. Sandy led, and I brought up the rear. Mom lay in a huge rectangular room filled with beds. They were coed, and nothing but a flimsy curtain on a track separated them. My mother is so modest that it's loony. If she'd been anything like her normal self, strange men seeing her in a tissue-paper hospital gown would have sent her into hysterics.

She was still too knocked out by drugs to speak. Her skin was gray, and her face looked older than I'd ever seen it.

"You'll be feeling better in just a little while," Sandy said, giving her hand a squeeze. "I'm going to speak to the doctor," she whispered to me.

When she'd gone, Pop and I stood staring down at Mom. After a minute had ticked past, he took her hand and started to weep. I was already in shock, but that bowled me over more than anything. My father weeping for my mother! I had to grab the rail at the foot of the bed to steady myself.

"Pop, Pop, are you okay?"

His hand tightened on hers, and he turned his head so I couldn't see his wet cheeks. "Your mother is going to die."

"No, we don't know the results of the surgery yet."

"Look at her. Death sits on her shoulder. I see him grinning."

"Pop, be quiet. She can hear you."

"Who are you to tell me be quiet?" From red, wet eyes he shot me a venomous look.

"I'm nobody, just your daughter."

"What daughter would do as you have done? What daughter would walk away from her mother, never calling, never writing? Night after night she prayed for you with tears in her eyes. If she's sick, it's because you made her eat her heart out."

"You threw me out. You cursed me."

"You disgraced us."

"I was defending myself. It was an accident. I didn't mean to kill Nick."

Mom moaned and clutched at his wrist. He turned back to her, patted her shoulder, and then stroked the back of her hand. "Toni," he said in a low, intense voice, "your mother needs you now. You can't stay away from her. You have to come back to us."

"What do you mean, come back? You mean move home?"

"Yes."

"No, Pop, I can't."

"You must. There's a black mark on your soul. If you

want to erase it, you'll come back and be a good daughter to your mother."

"Why aren't you saying this to Sandy?"

"She's married, and you're not," he retorted fiercely. "You killed the husband who would have cared for you and given you children. Because of that there's a curse on your soul."

7

Immediately after I got back from taking my mother home from the hospital with no result yet on her biopsy, Gloria Simpler's wallpaper came in. When I relayed the glad tidings, she screeched like a sweepstakes winner.

"I could come out and get started on it this afternoon," I offered. I was glad of the chance to think about something other than my conversation with my father.

"Oh, could you? That would be so great!"

It's amazing how excited some women get over wallpaper. Maybe that's because they can't govern their lives, so they settle for taking command of a wall. Actually, I can understand my clients' pleasure because when Nick and I first married I suffered through a violent case of nest building. I painted, made curtains, and refinished flea-market furniture like Martha Stewart on speed.

Since I killed Nick, I haven't decorated anything for

myself. As I pedaled south on Falls Road, I mused on this. I had no desire whatsoever to pretty up Rebecca Kelso's place. Even the thought hit me wrong, for in my mind it would always be hers.

At the Simplers' house, I wheeled my bike up their drive and unstrapped my helmet. I was just unloading my baskets when Gloria opened the side door.

"No wonder you look so healthy, pedaling around town all day loaded down like that!"

"No problem. The weather's good today, and the paper's self-pasting and not all that heavy. Your husband isn't around, by any chance?"

"Nope, he teaches a class this afternoon. Why? Did you want to talk to him about something?"

"Nothing that can't wait." I'd had it in mind to tell him my nutty fixation on the black Volvo. Maybe he could counsel me out of my delusion that I was being stalked by an evil car. I also wanted to ask him if he'd learned anything about Christopher Espey.

As if she'd read my mind and wanted to warn me off bugging her husband, Gloria said, "Poor guy, he's really had a lot on his plate lately."

I set down my materials in the kitchen, and she led me to the bathroom-in-waiting. "I bet. It must be tough to hold down a full-time teaching job and work for the police, too." As I commiserated, I sized up the cramped corners around the old-fashioned washbasin and did a mental moan. I'd be cutting to match daisies for hours.

"Jeff's completely dedicated, a real workaholic. And as if working two jobs isn't bad enough, now he's taken on a third. A few months ago his father died."

"Sorry to hear that."

"Don't be. The old man was eighty-nine, deaf as a post, senile, and, from what I hear, cantankerous beyond belief. He left Jeff a ramshackle old barn of a house that he'd let go to rack and ruin. Now Jeff spends every spare minute, including evenings and weekends, trying to fix the place up enough so he can turn it over to a real estate agent."

I felt guilty for asking Jeff a favor. But he'd offered to check out Christopher Espey. Much as I wanted the information, I decided to wait a couple of days before I badgered him for it.

I tuned my portable radio to an easy-listening station and settled in to work. At first Gloria left me alone, which I appreciated. Really, I prefer not to play twenty questions while I'm trying to fit paper around a toilet tank. But she couldn't stay away for long and kept peering in and exclaiming over this and that. "Oh, I worried that I picked the wrong paper. Now I see it's going to be exactly right!"

Finally she carried a kitchen chair from the hall and became a full-time audience.

"You're really good with your hands."

"Thanks. I guess everybody has to be good at something."

She clucked. "Jeff told me about you, about your trial and your dyslexia. He followed your case rather closely and remembered it the instant he saw you."

I almost dropped the large strip of wet daisies I was manhandling. "He did?"

"Please don't feel embarrassed. Believe me, my heart goes out to you. These last years must really have been rough."

"Yeah, but I'm doing okay." I don't like it when people who aren't close friends start sympathizing with me. I don't believe they're really sympathetic, just curious. Besides, it's true I have really bad problems, but so does almost everyone else. I stuck the piece to the wall, carefully matching flower petals.

"I know it's none of my business, but I can't help wondering. Are you making a good living at what you're doing?"

"The decorating business is always chancy, and lately things have been slow."

"Are you doing it because you like to decorate, or because you had trouble getting a job after your trial?"

"A little of both, I guess." Actually, I hadn't even tried to get a real job. As a nonreader, the only employment I could hope for was waitressing, and even that was problematic when it came to writing down orders. Anyhow, growing up in Credella's, I'd had my fill of feeding other people's faces. The piece I'd just applied to the wall had a very stubborn wrinkle. I concentrated on smoothing it.

"Did you work before your husband's accident?"

I loved her delicate euphemism. "Yes, I worked. Believe it or not, I was a singer. Nothing fancy. I sang pop tunes with a little combo called Overnight Leave. We used to get quite a few weekend bookings at clubs around town. Of course, after the trial I had to give that up."

"Did your partners tell you they didn't want you to sing with them anymore?"

"No. They were nice guys. But after I got heckled off the stage a couple of times, they agreed it would be best if I quit. They were right. Professionally speaking,

I was poison for them." Trying to see if I'd really got rid of all the wrinkles, I stood back and caught a glimpse of my pale image in the mirror. With my hair skinned back in a bandanna and my shirt spotted with gluey water, I didn't exactly look my best. Behind me, Gloria Simpler's reflection was fresh and pretty.

"I hope you won't think I'm prying, asking you these questions, but I used to do some counseling. That's how I met Jeff, actually."

"You counseled him?"

"Oh, no." She laughed. "I taught high-school Spanish and did some counseling on the side. Jeff and I met through a mutual acquaintance."

"That sounds nice. Do you still teach Spanish?"

"No, I quit."

"Why?" Since she and Simpler didn't have children, I couldn't see any reason why she'd give up her career. These days I think a woman who gives up a successful career for any reason whatsoever is crazy.

"To stay here and make a real home for Jeff, of course."

"I thought most professional men wanted their wives to work. Did he ask you to quit?"

"Yes, he did, as a matter of fact. You see, Jeff lost his mother at a young age. Having a real, lived-in home is important to him. Besides, I'm really just a homebody at heart. I was tired of teaching and resigned gladly. But now I have to admit that sometimes I miss my old calling—even the counseling end of it." She said that so wistfully, I knew she was putting it mildly. "Maybe I could help you, Toni."

"Oh?" I pricked up my ears. Did she have more rooms she wanted papered or friends she could recommend my decorating services to? Of course, I couldn't go on charging the ridiculous price I'd offered her.

"Let's pretend you're a student of mine who wants advice on picking a career. Tell me about your skills."

My heart didn't exactly sink, but I certainly experienced a stab of disappointment. Work is something I could really use. Advice—I'd already had a belly full. "I have a good eye for color and design, and as you already mentioned, I'm good with my hands."

"Are you mechanical?"

"I don't know how to fix cars or anything, but I can paint and do home repairs. Living alone, I've had to learn how to fix a leaky toilet and change a washer. Basic carpentry isn't beyond me, and I can hang pictures."

"You're way ahead of most women, then."

"They've been conditioned to stay away from those jobs. They're not so hard. Actually, most don't take much strength. Of course, most women also have men around to do for them."

"True. Whenever something goes wrong in the house I just tell Jeff." She gnawed her fingernail. "May I make a suggestion?"

"Sure."

"You're never likely to have a reliable income doing odd jobs. Why don't you think a little bigger?"

"How do you mean?" I turned toward her.

"With your skills and moxie you could tackle rehabbing a house in the city."

I could feel how artificial my smile was. "I have almost no savings and no credit rating. There's no way I could buy a house."

"Your family wouldn't help you out?"

I thought of my father. After the hospital released

Mama, the four of us had walked her out to the parking garage.

"Toni," Pop had said after he'd stowed Mom on the front seat of his Lincoln. He'd straightened and looked me sternly in the eye. "It's good you came today with your mother."

"I came because I was worried about her. And of course I'll come home and care for her if it turns out—"

I couldn't finish the sentence. He nodded, the brim of his hat casting an angular shadow over his shaved cheek. I caught a whiff of his cologne, and it made me ache. On the rare occasions when he'd kissed me as a child, I'd been both frightened and thrilled.

"I don't approve of the way you're leading your life, not at all. But we're still family, and your mother needs you. It's good you recognize you owe her something." He'd dug his hands into his pockets and looked over my right shoulder. "One more thing. If you need some money, you can come to me."

Now I smiled tightly at Gloria Simpler. "No, I could never go to my family for a loan. That's just something I couldn't do."

Nevertheless, what Gloria had suggested intrigued me. As I pedaled back home through evening traffic, I mulled it over. She was right about the wonderful old houses you could buy dirt cheap in Baltimore. A century ago shipping and railroad fortunes had abounded in this city, and domestic architecture had been splendid. Restoring a fabulous old brownstone that had fallen into disrepair would be a joy. As my legs churned up and down, my heart raced. Money, money,

money—if only I had a stake. If only I were a normal person who hadn't messed up her life.

Back home I toasted a bagel and opened a can of hearty beef soup. I put my meal on a tray, carried it into the living room, and flipped on the evening news. As I perched on the edge of the couch I hardly heard the weather and sports. Almost, I wished I hadn't talked to Gloria Simpler. She'd rubbed my nose in all the facts I didn't want to know.

The phone rang, and I almost knocked over my soup.

"Did I get you at a bad time?"

"No, I was just watching television."

"This is Jeff Simpler, by the way."

"I recognized your voice. You've got a great voice, as good as a radio announcer's. Your patients must find it very soothing."

"I'm flattered. Hey, terrific job in the bathroom. Gloria's thrilled."

"I'm happy if she's happy."

"My philosophy exactly. Listen, I called to tell you that I checked on Christopher Espey."

"Yes." I felt my whole body tighten.

"He is still in jail, and he hasn't had any furloughs."

I lifted a hand to massage the crease between my eyebrows. "Are you sure he's never been out for any reason?"

"Absolutely certain. He's been locked away tight and tidy for the last twenty years. He couldn't have had anything to do with Rebecca Kelso's murder."

"No, I guess not."

"Sorry to disappoint you."

"I'm not disappointed, exactly." I was, though.

Espey had been the only hot idea I had. Dispiritedly, I thanked Simpler, hung up, and then wandered back out to the living room. I'd just turned off the television set when someone knocked on my door.

"Who is it?"

"It's your friendly neighborhood cosmic overlord and semiretired ax murderer."

"Damon?"

"You guessed it. Now open the door or live in regret. I bear in my right hand a crusty pizza with all the toppings. In my left I grasp a bottle of Chianti complete with tasteful straw skirt and classy four ninety-nine price sticker."

Of course, I opened the door and there he was, posed with pizza held aloft and a silly grin on his cute-bad-boy face. He wore his usual jeans and a gray T-shirt with a unicorn rampant.

"Thanks," I said with a smile, "but I just ate."

"You call that eating? Baby, that doesn't compare with the offering I bear," he said as he strolled past me. Pushing my cold soup and half-devoured bagel to one side, he set down the pizza carton and opened it. It did look and smell wonderful.

"What are those white lumps?"

"Feta cheese. I find the flavor of Greece adds piquancy to even the most mundane activity."

"Yeah, right. This is really nice of you. I can't think of anything I've done to deserve it."

"Me neither," he said with a cheeky grin, "but when we're through wining and dining, you can make up for your lapse. Simply drag me to your bed and rub your naked body all over mine, concentrating on selected spots."

I gave him a level look. "That's not likely."

"Neither was the sinking of the *Titanic*, but it's history."

"So will you and this pizza be if you brought it to try to separate me from my underpants. Damon, if I haven't already made it clear, let me do so now. I'm not interested in sex with you."

He flattened his right palm on his heart and rolled his eyes. "You wrong me," he said in a wounded-angel voice. "Now let's not waste any more time. The pizza's getting cold and the wine is getting hot. Lead me to your corkscrew." He wiggled his eyebrows. "I want to show you my corkscrewing technique."

I'd been feeling lonely and sorry for myself, and Damon cheered me up. I laughed and then laughed some more as we settled down in front of the coffee table and shared the food and wine. "Thanks," I said at one point. "I needed this."

"Me too. I've been working upstairs since dawn, so a little R and R is in order."

"What do you do up there all by yourself?"

"Create private worlds, sweetheart. No, better than that." He leaned back against the couch with his legs stretched out straight and his moccasined feet crossed at the ankle. He put his hands behind his head and gazed inward for a second or two. "I create whole private universes and then rule them. Upstairs I'm God. No, I'm better than God."

"Why better?"

"Because my game universes make a lot more sense than the lousy one we're stuck in."

I studied him. When we'd first met I'd sized him up as a harmless artist. Now I recalled a point Jeff Simpler had made when I'd heard him lecture on serial killers.

He'd said they were obsessive-compulsives who needed to be in control and who liked to play God. Had I dismissed Damon as a possible murder suspect too casually? He'd said Susie dropped off to sleep easily. What if she'd done that the night Rebecca was killed and he'd slipped downstairs without Susie realizing it? Though the idea lay in my mind, I couldn't take it seriously.

Nevertheless, I asked, "Does it bother you that we're sitting in the room where Rebecca was murdered?"

His eyes widened. "If it doesn't bother you to live here, why should it bother me to spend an hour or two in the place?"

"Yeah. I'm sorry I said that. I don't know what's wrong with me."

"Bad day?" Lazily, he refilled my glass.

"Oh, I don't know. Is spending four hours in a four-by-six bathroom gluing daisies a bad way to make less than minimum wage?"

"I saw you load your bike up with wallpaper. Why do you fuck around with that? There've got to be better ways for a sharp lady like you to earn a buck." He dug around in his pocket and pulled out a business card. "I was thinking about you the other day. I've got a friend who does gold leaf. He says he could use an apprentice. Why don't you give him a call?"

He handed me the card, and I studied it. "Thanks. Maybe I will."

"Not that you couldn't find something that would pay better."

"Sure." I didn't want to explain about my limited employment options. Outside of my family, very few people were aware of my reading difficulties, and that was how I preferred to keep it. Instead I told him about Gloria Simpler's suggestion.

"Well, it's an idea. Restoring an old house in the city would be heavy work. You really think you'd be up to it?"

"I'd love to try. I don't see why I couldn't be up to it. I'm strong and good with my hands. What I don't know, I could learn."

An amused little smile lifted his mouth. He played with a strand of my hair. "You know, I bet you could. So, what's holding you back?"

"Money. I don't have any."

"You could find business partners."

"Business partners?"

"Sure, someone to put up the bucks while you put up the time and effort. Then when you resold, you could split the profit."

"I don't know of anyone who'd be interested in a deal like that."

"I might be. That is, I might be persuaded." He brought his face to within an inch of mine. "Let me kiss you, Toni."

So we were back to that. And here I thought I'd made myself clear. I flattened back against the couch, trying to give myself space. "No."

"Why not?"

As he stared into my eyes, I began to feel dizzy. Panic squeezed at my guts. I pushed myself against the arm of the couch. "Knock it off, Damon! I told you, I don't want this."

Scowling, he drew back and then jumped up. "All right already. Sorry I offended you."

"You didn't offend me. I'm just not interested."

"Jeez, what is it with the ice princesses who live in this building?" He gathered up the remains of the pizza and the half-full wine bottle. "Think I'll retreat to my sanctum."

"You don't have to go."

"Nothing left to do here, is there?" He shot me a derisive look.

For a couple of terrible minutes there, I'd wanted to apologize to him. It was a flashback to the way I'd behaved with Nick—craven, groveling, excusing myself because I was afraid to vent the anger I felt at the way he walked all over me. My panic changed into a hot wave of resentment. I'd warned the guy I wasn't up for a game of hide the sausage. When he'd shown up here uninvited I'd made that crystal clear.

"You're right. We're all done here," I said coldly. "Thanks for the meal."

"Welcome." With the half-empty carton under one arm and the wine bottle swinging jauntily from his free hand, he headed for the door. As he walked through it, he glanced back at me over his shoulder. "Sweet dreams."

That night I dreamed of Nick. I saw him coming at me with his face red and twisted, his fists balled. "Bitch!" he screamed. "Stupid, lazy, good-for-nothing bitch!"

I scrambled to get away, but I wasn't fast enough. He grabbed my shoulders, and I went flying across the room. I tasted blood where he'd already backhanded me. The kitchen chair where I crashed stabbed into my back. In dumb terror, I stared up at my husband. He'd been out drinking, and I'd made the mistake of complaining because he hadn't come home for the special dinner I'd prepared.

"Stupid cunt! I'll teach you to mouth off at me!"

His service revolver lay on the kitchen table where he'd dumped it when he'd come in. I didn't look at it, only at Nick. Yet I knew the gun was there. After he'd started slapping me around, I'd imagined blowing him away more than once—though I'd never in my life even laid a hand on a gun. It had just been imagining.

The funny thing is that when I did do it, it didn't seem any more real than the imagining. Even when I'd snatched it and pulled the trigger, even when I saw Nick clutch his chest and fall on the floor, even when I saw the blood, I couldn't believe it had actually happened.

For the longest time I just sat there staring at him. "Nick? Nick?" I finally heard myself whimper. "Nick, are you all right?

"Nick!"

I woke up drenched in icy sweat, trembling in every part of my body, my heart banging away. I covered my chest with my crossed hands, hoping to still the crazy sledgehammer inside me. It wouldn't slow down. I worried it would tear me open and burst right through my breast. "Oh God, oh God!"

I finally found the strength to push myself into a sitting position against the headboard. Around me the darkness thickened, pressed inward. I heard rustles and creaks, thin whisperings. It was the house settling, the wind and the late night traffic outside. That didn't mean something wasn't in that room with me, some horror. I flashed on an image of Rebecca's body lying drenched in blood, a black shadow standing over her. My trembling fingers switched on the bed-side lamp, and the spidery thing drew back into the murk. But it was still there, very private, very personal.

I found the courage to get out of bed and tiptoe into the kitchen. When I'd flicked on the overhead, I snatched up the phone and punched out Randall's number. He answered on the sixth ring, his sleepy voice thick with outrage.

"Hell in a handbag, who is it?"

"It's Toni."

"Toni? Is something wrong?"

"Yes, no, I don't know. I need a favor."

"A favor? Christ, Toni, do you know what time it is?"

"I know it's late."

"Au *contraire*, it's early." I heard him fumble with something, probably his clock. "Four-fifteen A.M., to be exact."

"I'm sorry. I'll call you later."

"Jesus, don't hang up. As long as you've ruined my beauty sleep, you might as well tell me what's on your mind."

I swallowed. "I need to get into the state penitentiary. There's someone there I need to talk with."

8

It's *a lot more complicated* to visit a person in a penitentiary than you might think. You must write a letter, they have to give permission, and then you have to be put on an approved list. Lucky for me, Randall could hurry the process. Three days later I met him for lunch at Mack's Bookstore Cafe.

After we threaded the book section and chose a table opposite the bar, I thanked him again for his help. He opened the menu. "I'm at the state pen on an appeal anyway, so we might as well go together. That doesn't mean I like any of this. I wish I hadn't let you talk me into it."

He'd already been clear on that, so I didn't answer. I decided on a falafel in a pita and then looked around and drank in the atmosphere. Mack's is within spitting distance of the Walters Art Gallery and my beloved Mt. Vernon Square. It's in a venerable old building with bare wood floors, high ceilings, and uncomfortable bentwood chairs. A rotating gallery of inscrutable paintings decorates its dark green walls. Dabs of color, squiggles and dots, ridiculous prices.

"I love this place," I said, hoping to change the subject.

"Why?" Randall glanced up from the menu, which was still absorbing all his attention.

"I guess it's the atmosphere. Dark and smoky, you know, with student types having intellectual conversations. Look at that black guy sitting at the bar over there. You mentioned that he's reading Nietzsche. Where else would you see that?"

"Don't show your prejudice. We black guys read Nietzsche all over town."

A gangly young man, dyed jet hair moussed into an artful minimountain range, slouched over, and we ordered. After Randall surrendered his menu, he scowled at me. "It's still not too late. Is there any way I can talk you out of this prison visit?"

"Nope."

"I still don't understand why you're so determined to do it."

"It's the only lead I have."

"Toni, you're not a detective."

"I know, but I can't get Rebecca and how she died out of my head, and I can't shake the feeling that Christopher Espey may have had something to do with it. I won't be able to sleep at night until I've talked to him."

"Even if he has nothing useful to say to you?"

"At least I'll know that I tried." I gave him my best gamin grin. "Hey, have I told you how gorgeous you look in your classy threads?" Over his chalk-striped three-piece suit with pleated trousers he wore a black cashmere double-breasted topcoat with a fringed white silk scarf. As I watched him slip it off and drape it over the back of his chair, I thought he'd easily pass as a fugitive from a *GQ* cover.

"You don't need to tell me what I already know. If you'd ever wear something decent, you could apply that compliment to yourself." He gazed critically at my ancient corduroy blazer. "When are you going to stop dressing like a bag lady?"

"Hey, what do you wear to go visiting with a rapist and murderer? I mean, do you try to look your best?" After Randall muttered at the ceiling, I said, "Tell me the truth. Are you ashamed to be seen with me?"

"No, but if we were dating, I'd burn those jeans and shapeless sweaters and drag you to Femme by your gorgeous hair."

"Do you pick out Jonathan's wardrobe?" I was really curious. Randall and Jonathan had totally different styles. Randall was elegance to the hilt. I never saw him in anything that wasn't hand-tailored. Jonathan went in for a different brand of glamor—$300 leather jackets, spotless white T-shirts, sand-washed jeans, glove-soft Italian moccasins. He had his golden hair wedge-cut by the trendiest stylist in town, and when he swaggered down the avenue heads turned, male and female.

"I merely admire the effect, sweets."

"Well, no matter what I wear, you're not likely to throw the divine Jonathan over for me, are you?"

"Not likely, but that doesn't mean I don't love you." He reached across and patted my hand.

The waiter sidled up to us with our order. "Artichoke and feta salad," he declared, gazing with disapproval at our clasped fingers.

Randall released me and sat back. After the guy plunked down our plates and stalked off, we laughed. "I know him, actually," Randall said. "A couple of years back he tried to come home with me."

"That explains why he looked at me as if he'd like to spit in my falafel. Maybe he has." I prodded my sandwich with a fork. I hadn't had much appetite to begin with. Now it was totally gone.

"Forget him. It's you I adore, Toni baby. I mean that. I love every inch of you. I just don't want to have you in bed. Do you understand the difference?"

"Sure."

Randall sighed. "That's the trouble with women. They don't understand sex. They confuse it with love and make messes of their lives. That's what you did, so now you're living like a nun. Very unhealthy." He forked up one of his artichokes and gazed at it critically. "Don't get me wrong, I'm sympathetic to women's problems. That's why I took your case."

"I'll always owe you."

"Then do me a favor and wise up. Stop finding new and ever more bizarre ways to punish yourself for what happened to Nick."

"Is that why you think I want to talk to Christopher Espey, because I'm punishing myself?"

"I think it's connected to this Nancy Drew act you're putting on. You're ashamed you let your husband abuse you all those years and then lashed out, so you're trying to make up for what you see as your weakness by solving a crime against another woman.

Oh, Toni, that's so irrational. Do you think you're the only one with a dirty secret? How many women do you think will be beaten between Thanksgiving and New Year's?"

"How should I know?"

"This morning I did some work for the Rape Crisis Center, so the official guess is fresh in my mind. The number is four hundred and fifty thousand. Last year the number of women abused by their husbands was greater than the number of women who got married."

"If this is patter to convince me I ought to doll myself up to attract a boyfriend, maybe you ought to change a few lines."

Randall shook his head. "Toni, you can't hide from sex. You can only start using your brain and stop letting your emotions choke you. It's time you started living again, and sex is part of life. Handle with care and use a little perspective, yes. Don't get a roll in the hay confused with the meaning of the universe. But don't give up on it altogether, either." He shot me a wicked grin. "You don't need to solve a crime even the police can't get a handle on. You need a good lay."

"Now you sound like my sister, Sandy."

He laughed. "I remember her at the trial. Feisty. I liked her."

"She doesn't like you."

"That's only because she wasted so much energy batting her eyelashes at me."

Sandy had been taken with Randall until she'd figured out he was gay. Now whenever his name came up she spit like a furious cat.

"I like women," he mused. "Sometimes I even love them. But in their hearts that's not what most want."

"I must say, you're in a very philosophical mood this afternoon."

"Aren't I, though? It's positively revolting."

Delicately I rotated my water glass. "So, tell me, Randall, what do women want?"

"They want to be worshiped and kept safe. The poor things think they can get what they want with sex. Trouble is, there are men out there who only worship what they hate and fear and secretly wish to destroy."

"And you're telling me that what I need is a good lay?"

"Sunlight can be lethal, but we turn into slugs if we don't get it. I did say handle with care, remember?"

"Yeah, right."

He examined the bill and then threw down a couple of tens. "On that delightful note, it's time we headed for Maryland State Pen. Ready?"

I reached for my shoulder bag. "Ready as I'll ever be. And I'm not doing this because I want revenge. I'm doing it because . . ."

"Yes?"

"Because Rebecca Kelso's ghost insists," I said lightly.

Randall laughed and turned away. He didn't catch the expression on my face. If he had, he might have guessed that part of me really believed what I'd just said.

*   *   *

We drove to the penitentiary, but since it's only a few blocks to the east on Eager and Greenmount, we could have walked. It's a complex of buildings, old and new. The one that sticks in my mind looks ancient. Its pitched roof and silvery gray spires made me think of a medieval fortress or a very depressing cathedral.

"Good thing I didn't eat much at Mack's," I muttered after Randall and I walked past the barbed-wire fence. Wherever I looked I saw stone or metal. Everything seemed gray. Even the sky had clouded over.

"Nervous?"

"My stomach is jumping around like a break dancer." Actually I felt like puking. The whole idea of this terrified me.

"We could turn around and leave. I could take you home."

I was sorely tempted. "No."

Randall sighed. "All right. You asked for it, and I've already explained why this is a bad idea. Good luck."

I'd seen movies and TV shows where people talked to prisoners through mesh screens. Sometimes they were even behind soundproof Plexiglas so their visitors had to speak to them on a phone. That's not how it is at Maryland. The visiting room is horseshoe-shaped. There's a table all along the wall, divided by partitions. There's nothing between you and the inmate, no screen, no Plexiglas.

As I waited for Espey, I sneaked looks around. I'd expected the prisoners would wear uniforms. But they were dressed like anybody else. The ones I caught sight of looked no different from people you see on the street. Maybe they weren't any different. After all, without my sympathetic jury, I might have wound up in a place like this.

I'd pictured Christopher Espey as squint-eyed and evil. Instead, the prisoner who came in and pulled out a chair opposite me was a pale, balding wisp of a man with exaggerated sideburns and lips that looked too fat for the rest of his face. He wore a navy blue parka. Where it hung open I saw a wrinkled plaid shirt and jeans. His light brown eyebrows straggled across his high, egg-shaped forehead. His eyes kept peeking at me sideways and then darting off to never-never land.

"Mr. Espey?"

"Yeah."

"I'm Toni Credella. Thanks for seeing me."

He shot me an off-center glance that held curiosity and suspicion. "Your letter surprised me. I don't get too many visitors. Not very many letters, either."

What did he expect, a fan club? "I guess you're curious about why I'm here."

"Yeah, you wrote something about asking me a question."

I have no talent for diplomacy, so I plunged right in. "I did some reading up on your crime. It's been twenty years since it happened."

"So? I was just a kid. What are you? A reporter?"

"No. Nothing like that. I hear you're coming up for parole soon."

"A couple of months. I only said I'd see you because I thought maybe you might be one of those writers doing a book. If that's what you're up to, let's get something straight. I'm not going to talk to you unless I get paid. And I'd want to get paid a lot."

I squeezed my hands together. They felt like freezer packs. Obviously this man wasn't going to answer my questions unless I promised him a best-seller. No way could I promise that. So what did I have to lose? As long as I was here, I might as well go ahead and tell him what I thought. "I'm not a reporter, and I can't pay you. About your parole, knowing what you did, I have to say I'm kind of surprised."

That got his attention. Finally he looked directly at me for a full ten seconds. "Why? There are guys here who did a lot worse stuff than me and got out a lot sooner."

"Really?"

"My old cell mate got out after fifteen years, and he did a Girl Scout. Hey, what's this all about, anyway? Why have you been sticking your nose into my business? There's no law says I have to talk to you, and if you're not going to pay me, I won't." He started to stand up.

The phrase *did a Girl Scout* ricocheted around in my mind like a horsefly in a bottle. I blurted, "I know Susie Zillig."

Long pause. "Yeah?" Again his eyes were everywhere but my face. He licked his puffy lips and then sat back down. His hairless fingers began tapping aimlessly at the tabletop. "She send you here?"

"She doesn't know I'm here at all." I felt a sharp twinge of guilt. Susie would be mad as a hornet if she knew what I was doing—and she'd have every right to be. I'd promised to keep her secret. But by mentioning her name to Espey, I wasn't telling him anything he didn't already know. By the time he got out, if his parole was granted, she'd have left town. I told myself that ought to be okay.

"What's little Susie doing now?"

"I'm not going to tell you. She doesn't live in this area anymore."

"Sure." He smirked. "She nervous that I might come after her?"

"Well, naturally she's not anxious to have a reunion."

He eyed me, and I wondered if he was asking himself what it would be like to rape me. Randall had warned me that I might be making myself into a target, but I'd been so bent on seeing Espey that I'd blown off his warning. "Tell her to relax," he said. "I'm not like that."

"Like what?"

"Vindictive. Evil-minded. A lot of the guys in here carry a grudge. Not me. You see, I don't blame her for putting me behind bars. She was just a kid, anyway."

Suddenly I felt such rage that I was almost blinded by it. I was literally seeing red. "She was only nine, and so was her friend."

"I know their ages." His voice choked up. "Look, I'm sorry for what I did, but it was a long time ago. I'm a different person now."

Did we ever really get to be different people? I wondered. For a millisecond I reflected on myself now and three years ago. "What kind of person were you then? Why would you go after nine-year-olds?"

"What's this? Twenty questions? Why should I talk to you if you're not going to pay me?" The tip of his nose had started to quiver. He pushed his chair back. "What business is it of yours?"

"What you did is everybody's business, and I'd really like to know. It doesn't make any sense to me."

"Yeah, well, sex doesn't make much sense to anybody, I guess," he said sullenly.

Though he kept saying he wouldn't talk to me and he was glaring resentfully, he was also still sitting there. He wanted to continue the conversation, I realized. It was like what sometimes happens on long train trips when strangers reveal their most intimate secrets to each other. Maybe Espey was even flattered by my interest in him. Maybe he wanted me to tell him what a shit I thought he was. Maybe nobody else had been interested enough in him to bother doing that for a long time. Whatever it was keeping him there, I decided to cash in on it. "Children turn you on?"

He began rubbing his palms together. "I was nineteen and turned on by anything that moved and had holes, see? I liked pretty girls with long blond hair best. But they weren't attracted back. So I had a problem."

Made sense. Christopher Espey with his sloping shoulders, muddy skin, and shifty, boiled gray eyes sure didn't ring my bell. Twenty years back he'd probably been plagued with acne as well. But it was more than his complexion that made you want to break a record doing the fifty-yard dash in the opposite direction. Something about him made me think of caged weasels with tiny razor-edged teeth.

"I tried to get a college girl first," he said in a whining voice.

"Oh, yeah? What happened?"

"I hid in the bushes over at Goucher and waited until one walked past real late at night." He continued rubbing his palms together with a fleshy scraping noise. "When I grabbed her, she made such a fuss kicking and screaming that I let her go. Scared the shit out of me. Afterward, I didn't leave my place for three whole days. That's when I decided I'd get a kid instead."

I just stared at him. I guess my expression must have said it all, because his Adam's apple started bobbing like a pile driver. "I didn't mean to kill them. I didn't think about killing them until afterward. Then I realized I didn't have any choice."

My bile rose, and I fought to choke it down.

"Listen, to tell you the truth," he babbled on, "I was almost glad when the cops picked me up. In a way, prison was a relief. But now I've paid my debt, see. You're not going to make trouble for me, are you?"

"You mean interfere with your parole? How could I?" If I could, I would. I didn't believe this guy had paid his debt. There were times when I believed drawing and quartering wasn't such a bad idea after all.

"Tell your friend Susie not to worry. I'm not out for revenge." He was pleading with me, as if my opinion mattered. Now I was the one who wanted to end the conversation. But I hadn't yet asked him the question I'd come for.

"Some guys might be out for revenge?"

"Yeah, maybe."

"Have you told this story to anybody else?"

"Lots of people. So what?"

A wary look had come back into his eyes, so I hurried on. "Who, for instance?"

"My lawyer. Why? What do you want to know for?"

"You mentioned your cell mate. Was he a rapist, too?"

"Yeah."

"Did you tell him this story?"

"Sure. What else is there to talk about in this place?"

"And he's out now?"

"Six months ago. Hey, what's this all about? Are you trying to get me in trouble?"

"What was his name?"

"Leo Acker, for Christ's sake!"

"Leo Acker?" Randall said.

"That's the guy's name. Tell me, is there a social committee that pairs cell mates with similar tastes and hobbies? I mean, it makes sense. One child molester is probably going to have more fun swapping shop talk with another child molester than he would with, say, a bank robber." Randall and I were sitting in his Mercedes sport coupe. He'd just pulled up in front of my apartment building and killed the engine so he could listen to me finish my story about Espey.

"Cut the comedy. What's going on in your mixed-up head? Or can I guess?" Randall tapped out a tattoo on his leather-covered steering wheel. "You think Espey told Acker about Susie, and Acker decided to go after her. But he made a mistake and got Rebecca Kelso instead."

"It's not as crazy as you make it sound."

"Toni, my pet, let's be honest here. It's *très* nutso."

"These are very twisted guys, Randall."

"Takes one to know one. You really believe you can second-guess a pair of psychopathic rapist-murderers?"

"I listened to Espey talk, and I watched the expression in his eyes. He's a pathetic creature who probably had a bad time in high school. But that doesn't give him the right to kill people. Randall, he doesn't think of women or little girls as human, and he's mad as hell because they don't invite him to screw them at will. He sees them the way hunters probably see geese and rabbits. Tracking down the one that got away and made trouble might give a guy like that a rush."

Randall just sat there staring at me.

"So, what do you think?"

"Toni, what's going on with you? Why are you doing this? Are you trying to put yourself in danger because of Nick?"

"Of course not. I thought you understood."

"I understand you're a babe in the woods poking around under very creepy rocks. You're deliberately asking for trouble. Back off."

"I have to talk to Leo Acker. I have to find out if he's the one who killed Rebecca."

"Why?"

My mouth hung open. I couldn't tell him how Rebecca's murder haunted me. I couldn't even understand that myself. "I just have to."

"Over my dead body, excuse the pun."

"I only hoped you'd tell me how to get in touch with him."

"Hope away. I'm at the end of the line on this thing."

"You mean you won't help me?" From the set of his jaw, I already knew the answer.

"That's exactly what I mean. Call on me for anything else and I'll be there. But you're not involving me in some self-destructive guilt excursion."

Back in my apartment, I slammed the door behind me. So much for anger and frustration. Truthfully, I was halfway glad Randall wouldn't point me at Acker. Maybe that gave me a good excuse to do what he advised and back off. Tracking down Acker was the last thing I really wanted to do, and my interview with Espey had shaken me badly.

I forced myself to check my answering machine and then dialed Sandy. "Any word on Mom's tests?"

"Nothing yet."

"Did you call and ask what's holding things up?"

"Yes, and they said something about the weekend and their computers being down. These medical labs are beyond belief. I mean, it's only a matter of life and death. When I hear I'll call you."

"Thanks."

"You okay, Toni?"

"Sure, why?"

"I don't know. You sound funny."

"Bad day."

There was a little pause. "Mom told me you said you'd move home and take care of her if it turns out she's sick."

"Yeah, so?"

"You surprise me, that's all. I know how you'd hate moving back in with them. You were so anxious to get out from under their thumb."

"If Mom got really sick, someone would have to take care of her, and you couldn't."

"Pop has enough money to hire a nurse."

"If I were sick like that, I'd want someone who loved me taking care of me. Wouldn't you?"

"Yes." Sandy sighed. "For your sake and her sake, I hope it doesn't come to that."

After I hung up, I gave myself a shake and went upstairs and knocked on Susie's door. I knew I had to tell her about Espey, but I wasn't looking forward to her reaction.

Well, I had that right. I hadn't figured she'd be home. So when she opened the door wearing her bathrobe and with her dirty blond hair hanging in her eyes, my heart dropped. "Did I wake you up?"

"Yeah. Late night at the hospital. What is it, for God's sake?"

I looked down at her toenails, which leaked from stained blue scuffs, and then back up at her face. I could still see the imprint of a wrinkled sheet on one of her cheeks. "Mind if I come in?"

"What is this, Toni?" Her tone was cool. I guessed she regretted telling me her secret and suspected she was about to regret it even more.

"There's something I need to tell you."

"Okay, sure."

A few steps inside her living room I gave her the scoop on my trip to the prison. Her face went into patches of sickly white and livid pink.

"Just what the hell are you saying?"

"I'm saying I talked to him. Listen, Susie, I felt I had to. After what you told me, I kept thinking there might be some connection with Rebecca—"

"I told you that stuff in confidence. Where do you get off spreading it around?"

"I didn't spread it around." I tried to explain why I'd visited the prison and my fears about Acker, but Susie wouldn't listen. She was furious.

"Damn you! Just keep your nose the hell out of my business, or I'll break it for you! Do you hear?"

"Honest, Susie, I don't think you have anything to fear from Espey." I raised my hands imploringly, fully realizing how far out of line I'd stepped.

"That's exactly right, because I'm leaving this burg." She gave me a shove that sent me sprawling against the wall.

"Hey, Susie, c'mon!"

She opened the door and hustled me through it. "Now you've given me another reason to be glad I'm splitting. The last thing I need is a snooping busybody like you! I wish I'd never set eyes on you!"

The rough stuff would've got me mad enough to fight back, except I couldn't blame her. I'd gone to see Espey with tunnel vision. I'd been so obsessed with finding Rebecca's killer that I hadn't considered Susie the way I ought to have.

"Susie, I'm sorry, but—"

"Interfering bitch!" She slammed the door so hard that it shivered the hinges. I stood there feeling icy down to my toes. Then I covered the top of my head with my spread fingers. What a shitty day.

Back downstairs, I really wanted to pull my quilt up over my head and spend the rest of the afternoon hiding in bed. After Nick died, that's how I spent half my time. These days when I get the impulse to retreat to the covers, I try not to give in. Now it was too strong to fight.

I headed for the bedroom. A step past the doorway I kicked off my shoes and pivoted toward my bed. I was preparing to dive in when I saw the bug.

For the longest time I stood petrified, staring at it. Unconsciously I'd crossed my hands over my chest. Against my flattened palm I could feel my heart battering my ribs. I guess I was making little wheezing, whimpering noises. All I knew was a giant insect sat in the middle of my bed, ogling me like some outrunner from hell. Finally I calmed down enough to tell myself it couldn't be real. No living insect was a foot long, with jagged wire legs and bulging, evil eyes. At least, not in these parts.

I couldn't stand there forever, so I approached the mattress. It must have taken me five minutes to cross a space no wider than six feet. The bug had a long, brown body made of some shiny, plastic-looking material. Its eight legs and feelers were thick black wire. It carried a stinger in its tail, so maybe it was a scorpion.

I turned around several times, hugging myself. Then, not wanting to touch it but needing to get it out of my sight, I ran out into the kitchen and grabbed a broom and a paper bag. When I'd poled the bug off my bed and maneuvered it into the sack, I yanked the quilt away from the sheets. The quilt was a pretty patchwork of green and pink with a central pinwheel design. When I'd picked it up at a flea market, I'd regarded it as quite a find. Now I wanted never to see it again.

After I'd bundled the quilt into another bag, I

stuffed that into the garbage can out in the alley. Back in my bedroom, I stood looking around like a junkie in a dead-end alley full of narcs. It didn't take long before I saw other signs that someone had been in my place. The drawers in my bureau were pulled halfway out. I never leave them like that.

Gingerly I walked over and peered into the open part of the middle drawer. I saw bras, panty hose, socks, and nightgowns all stirred together as if a giant hand had paddled through them and then flailed like an angry whirlwind. Two bras had been tied together in an obscene-looking knot. When I undid it, I saw that the cups had been stuffed with my panties to make them bulge.

Carefully I laid out the underwear on top of the bureau. Then, dreading what I might find, I opened the upper drawer where I kept the rest of my panties. They lay in a tangled nest of white cotton and nylon. A bottle of crimson nail polish had been dribbled over them so it looked as if they were spattered with fresh blood. At first I thought they *were* spattered with fresh blood. It was only the smell that finally tipped me off to the nail varnish.

Even so, it was five minutes before I could bring myself to touch them. Then I took each panty out and spread it flat with the others on top of the bureau, just to make sure no more surprises awaited in the drawer. I don't have all that much underwear. I soon realized that an expensive pair of French lace panties that Randall had given me as a gag and that I'd never worn were gone.

When I saw that, I couldn't do anything, couldn't even lift my head. I just stood there shivering. Before I'd moved in, Aronchick had assured me he'd changed all the locks. Whoever had played this sick joke had used a key. How was that possible, since I was supposedly the only person who had one? Who could it have been? Susie? No, she'd only been mad at me for the last fifteen minutes. Damon? Given his crazy imagination, I wouldn't put the bug past him. And he was mad because I'd refused his advances. But I couldn't honestly feature him as the culprit who'd vandalized my panties with nail polish—not unless he was a lot crazier than I thought.

So, who else could it be? Rebecca herself? Surely ghosts could do better in the bug department than plastic and wire. Besides, Rebecca and I were allies, or so I'd been imagining. That left Rebecca's killer.

I considered calling the cops. But aside from my reluctance to deal with them, I figured they wouldn't find the bug and panties menacing. Every night those guys are out scraping bodies off the streets. To them, the bug would seem like an early Halloween prank. It didn't strike me as funny, though.

I made fast time into the kitchen and fumbled the phone book out of a drawer. Locksmith had to start off with an *l*, didn't it?

With new locks in place, I made it through the next day. About eight, Damon came by. I called out a cautious, "Who is it?" and took the time to peer through my peephole before I opened the front door.

"Seen Susie?"

"No."

"We had a date to eat at my place and do some

gaming. The Chinese carryout I ordered has arrived, but she hasn't showed to share it with me."

"Maybe she had to stay late at the hospital for an emergency."

"I called, but they said she left a couple of hours ago."

He shifted his weight, and I noticed that his black T was decorated with a large white spider. In the dim light from the overhead bulb, he looked tired. "Maybe she forgot," I said.

"Yeah. She's a little on the flaky side, so it's possible." He started to turn away.

"Before you go back up, would you look at something for me?"

"What?"

The paper bag with the bug sat on my coffee table. I opened it and beckoned Damon to come in and look.

"Jesus! What's that, a cockroach on growth hormones?"

"It's not real."

"So I see, and a good thing." He picked it out and held it to the light. "Hey, can I borrow it? Next time I take Grandma out to the brunch buffet at Harrison's, I can drop it in the fondue."

I'd been tense since yesterday, but now I laughed and started to relax. Whatever else he was, Damon was amusing, and there were times when that was more than enough. "Great idea!"

"Where'd you get it?"

"Found it."

He shifted his weight again, and his eyes played over me. "Listen, it looks as if you're alone tonight, too. I got a ton of food upstairs. How about you sharing it with me?"

"Did you say Chinese carryout?"

"Szechuan lo mein and sauteed mushrooms and broccoli."

I hadn't eaten yet, and I like Oriental food. After finding the bug, I was also nervous about being alone. "What if Susie arrives after we've scarfed it all up? Won't she be mad?"

"There's plenty. We'll save her some."

This was the first I'd seen of Damon since I'd sent him home with his Chianti bottle. I'd decided then not to give him any more opportunities to proposition me. But time and loneliness and terror have a way of softening hard-edged resolutions. Besides, when I hadn't been searching my apartment for more signs of the intruder and working on getting my locks changed, I'd been mulling over what Randall had said to me. Maybe this antisex thing of mine was getting out of hand.

"Sure."

He brightened. "Great. Come on up whenever you're ready. Now that we're in the age of science, food can be microwaved at will."

"So, what've you been up to?" Damon asked. We'd settled onto pillows in his studio and each wolfed down a plate of steaming noodles and vegetables. I'd brought up a couple bottles of beer I'd had squirreled away.

Since I'd decided not to get myself upset all over again by talking about the intruder with the bug, and I had no intention of betraying Susie further by mentioning Espey, my answer options were limited.

"Remember the gilding guy you recommended to me? I gave him a call."

"Good going. What'd he say?"

"I have an appointment to go see him. Who knows, maybe he might take me on as an apprentice."

"Gilding." He raised his eyebrows. "Does that mean you've given up on the restoring-old-houses idea?"

"It's not a matter of giving up on the idea. It's more closely related to zero cash flow and zilch credit."

"Does that mean if you had the cash and the credit, you'd do it?"

"Maybe."

"Fooling around with crummy plumbing, pulling out old plaster, you'd really like that?"

"Yeah, I think I might."

He looked at me as if I were a refugee from a blanket tent under an overpass. "You poor kid. You really have to scratch to feed your face, don't you?"

"Yeah, I really do. I wouldn't be living here in Murderville otherwise."

"I gather you refer to Rebecca's demise and the rock-bottom rent?"

"Exactly." All day I'd been trying to justify rooming with a ghost, chumming up to rapists, and fencing with crazed break-in artists by telling myself it was cost-effective. "What about you? Don't you have to scratch?"

He took a swallow of wine and shook his head. "Business is going pretty good for me. In fact, I'm thinking of expanding. I might even hire another writer and develop some new lines. Hey, what about you?"

"Me?"

"You've got a good imagination. How'd you like to go to work for me?"

"As a writer, you mean?" I almost laughed in his face. Me a writer, that was a hot one. Why were people accusing me of being a writer? Even Espey had imagined I was interviewing him for a book when I could still barely spell "cat." "No thanks. I get restless if I sit sill too long."

"So you're the physical type?"

"You might say that."

He leaned closer and practiced some heavy eye contact. "You might, I wouldn't."

Here we were, back to the sex issue again. With Damon it never kept its perky little head down for long.

"Let's not do this, Damon."

"Yes, let's. What is it with you, Toni? Are you made of ice, or what?"

"Oh, Jeez, do we have to go this route? Can't you give it a rest?"

"As turned on as I am by you, no, we can't. Now, be honest. You think I'm a cute little sex object, too."

"I'm fascinated to hear how you've come to that conclusion. Is it something in the way I've been turning you down every hour on the hour since the night we met?"

"I'm an intuitive guy. I can sense those things."

"Oh, I see. You're psychic." I wondered if he could sense Rebecca's ghost. I restrained myself from telling him about it and choked back a semihysterical giggle.

He leaned closer, and his voice got all dark and husky. "Admit it, the thought of getting physical with me doesn't make you want to barf."

"Now there's a romantic line. Even if it were so, I wouldn't exactly call it an overwhelming recommendation. You know, Damon, the only reason you're chasing after me like this is that I'm resisting. If I'd jumped into bed with you the first night we met, you'd probably have lost interest by now."

"I doubt it, but you never know. Let's try a controlled experiment. You fuck my brains out for the next couple of weeks. If I'm not speaking to you by the end of that period, you can mail me a postcard with 'I told you so. Nah, nah, nah!' printed on the back in purple ink."

"Don't you ever quit?"

"Never. I'm like a robot programmed for conquest. Every woman I see is an Everest I must melt, mount, and conquer. Take pity on me. Help me deal with my relentless sexual inner directive. Kiss me, Toni."

"Why should I?"

"Who the hell knows. Because I'm here and so are you, that's why."

"You're a fool."

"We're all fools. That doesn't mean we can't don our cap and bells and have a little fun."

He put his hand on the back of my head and drew my face to his. All the time I was thinking about Randall and what he'd said. The way I'd been living, afraid of men, afraid of sex, afraid of everything, really wasn't too healthy. Now I had the example of Susie Zillig before me. I didn't want to be like her, all uptight and antisocial and scared of her own shadow. Maybe Espey had spent the last twenty years behind bars, but the prison he'd locked her into was almost as bad.

Still, you won't believe this, but I was more nervous about being kissed by a man than I was about actually having sex with one. While Damon's face came close to mine, I had to force myself to hold still. It was okay, though. He turned out to be quite an artist in that department, too. It wasn't long before I'd loosened up and started to enjoy myself. He had me flat on my back and definitely warm when the pounding started on his front door.

"Who the hell is that?" he growled.

"Answer it, Damon. It might be Susie."

"I'm busy, and she's not welcome."

"You can't let her stand out there banging on your door. Answer it."

"Oh, hell!"

He got up and padded out through his kitchen. I sat up and tried straightening my clothes. After all the fuss I'd made, I didn't want Susie guessing what we'd been doing. As I combed my fingers through my hair, I tried working out what I would say to her. I really felt bad about my interference with Espey, and I wanted to let her know without spilling her secret to Damon.

He stayed away longer than I expected, and after a while I began to get a funny prickly feeling at the back of my neck.

"Damon?"

He didn't answer, so I came out to see what was going on. There was a cop in uniform and a tall, skinny guy in a raincoat standing inside the door.

"Damon?"

When he turned around and looked at me, his face was white as new snow. "It's Susie. They found her in Druid Hill Park with her throat cut and a rag stuffed in her mouth."

9

All *the worst times* in my life I remember like blurred movies with black-and-white stop-action stills.

Damon tells me the police can't reach Susie's parents, so he and I have to identify her body. I go downstairs and get my coat, and Damon and I get into a cop car. The detective glances at me with iceberg eyes but says nothing.

Blur.

Susie with a sheet pulled back from her still, bloodless face. Her feet cocked up, stiff and white. The polish on her toenails makes obscene spots of color, as if they'd been painted with gore.

Long blur—nanosecond flashes of answering questions and signing papers.

I'm back in Damon's apartment, and he's holding me and stroking my hair.

* * *

"Oh, God! I can't believe it! It's so awful."

"Shhh. Don't think about it."

"How can I not think about it? How can you not think about it? She was your friend."

"I know. But I can't let it get to me. I don't want to remember her the way we saw her tonight."

"I'll always remember her that way."

"Try not to."

"Oh, Damon . . ." I was thinking about the killer, imagining him with the scent of blood on his fingertips. Susie's blood this time, but who would be next?

"I know, I know," Damon was murmuring. "You're freaked out. We both are. That detective didn't help with all his questions. A regular walking refrigerator. Listen, fill your mind up with something else." He rubbed my shoulder blades. When they began to relax, he tipped my face up and kissed away my tears.

It felt good, all those soft little kisses on my wet face, his arms holding me, his hands rubbing and stroking me. It had been a long time since I'd been cuddled and cherished. And he was right. I didn't want to think about what had happened to Susie. I didn't want to think about how she had been killed or who had killed her. It was too late for her now. For her it was all over.

Next to death, sex is cracked up to be the ultimate escape, isn't it? Surrender to your senses and forget the world. That's how it's supposed to go, anyhow, and that's the way it was that night.

I let him lead me into his room, where his bed was a mattress on a shadowy floor. I let him lay me down on it and take off my clothes. All the while he kissed and petted me and murmured soothing words. I wanted a drug to fog the image of Susie's pale, lifeless feet mocked by those crimson toenails. And that's what Damon offered. But maybe there was more to it. Susie was dead, but we were still alive. I think we both wanted to assure ourselves of that.

I don't remember much about the sex, so I guess it must have been okay without going for spectacular. Afterward I fell asleep right away and didn't wake up until dawn crept in and tugged my eyelids open with spidery gray threads.

Except for a battered chest of drawers and the mattress, Damon's bedroom had no furniture. His walls didn't share this spartan decorating scheme. Paintings of monsters, warriors, and sorcerers covered them. I sat up and stared into the baleful red eyes of a fanged griffin. I thought of Susie with her eyes wide and sightless and blood leaking from her throat, and I shuddered.

Beside me, Damon lay with his mouth ajar, dead to the world. Good. I crawled off the mattress and scavenged for my clothes. In his haste to unwrap me, he'd flung them all over the floor. As I retrieved my underpants from the inside of a sneaker, I made a decision. I was getting out of this place. Rebecca and now Susie were dead, and I didn't want to make it a party of three. I would go down to the ghost palace and call Randall. If he couldn't put me on to an apartment in my old building, I might even shlep back to my parents whether Mom needed me or not. That's how desperate and terrified I felt.

"Hey, what're you doing?"

I had just yanked my sweater over my head and was stepping into my jeans. I looked over my shoulder.

Damon, naked above the sheet that draped his narrow waist, had propped himself up on his elbows. His face was a wild aureole of salt-and-pepper frizz around his choirboy-on-the-wrong-side-of-thirteen face.

"I'm getting dressed."

"I can see that. Why? You're not leaving, are you?"

"I'm going downstairs for a bowl of cereal."

"I'll fix breakfast for you. First, come back to bed."

"No offense, Damon, but last night I wasn't myself."

"Me neither, but I can do better. This morning I can definitely do better." He pushed the sheet aside and revealed how well prepared he was to live up to his claim.

Maybe last night's sex had been a good thing. I'd gotten past a milestone. But now, to put it mildly, I just wasn't in the mood. "I appreciate the thought and effort you've put into it, but no thanks. By the way, I was in such bad shape when we went to bed that I didn't even think about birth control. Did you use a condom?"

"I wasn't thinking too logically myself."

"Guess that means no." I was due for a period in three days, so I told myself not to sweat it. I just hoped Damon was as healthy as he looked. Stupid, Toni! I snapped my jeans and bent over to grab my socks. Before I could straighten, I felt something pressing against my rear end.

Damon's naked arms snaked around my waist. "I've got plenty of condoms here. Only take me a minute to scare one up. As you may have noticed, everything else is raring to go." He pulled me hard against his chest so I got the full benefit of his primed male apparatus. It reminded me of scenes with Nick. I always did whatever my husband wanted—half because I was afraid to deny him, half because his aggression turned me on. Oh, yes, there was that element in it, I'm ashamed to say.

"Damon, no."

"C'mon, baby." His hands slipped under my sweater and caressed my breasts. Fingers found my nipples and squeezed. I leaned away, but he yanked me tighter and started dragging me back toward the bed.

At that point I certainly would've given in to Nick. It was so much easier not to resist, to just try to please him. And in bed he usually was pleased—for a little while.

Maybe that spineless response had been ingrained so deep that it would always come first. For a few seconds my body went limp, and I have to admit my lower parts were starting to get fired up for action. Above the neck, however, I felt angry and confused. How could Damon be so intent on sex when Susie was lying in a refrigerator box? Or maybe that was the reason.

Taking full advantage of my moment of weakness, Damon pushed me down flat on the mattress and then landed on top of me. I lay pinned beneath him, staring up into his face. His eyes glittered, taut and triumphant with that fixed expression men get when they're thinking with all the finesse of a bull ramming a gate. I hadn't realized how strong he was. He looked thin, almost slight, but as he held me down, his hands felt like steel claws. I got an adrenaline surge of panic.

"Get off me. I don't want this."

"You know you want it. You know you do." His

hands lifted from my shoulders to fumble at my jeans.

"You want it, but I don't. Stop this." I batted at him and rocked from side to side.

He shut me up by gluing his mouth to mine. He had morning breath. Me too, no doubt. The added element of yuckiness strengthened my resolve.

I twisted my head away. "Damon, for God's sake, Susie was raped and murdered last night! I'm not in the mood for this!"

I could feel the change in his body tension. "This doesn't have anything to do with Susie."

"Last night had everything to do with Susie, and so does this morning. If you force me now, it's rape."

"Rape!"

I glared up at him. "Yes. Now get off!"

Still, he didn't move. "Last night you fucked like a rabbit. You slept with me in my bed. No court in the world would convict me of rape."

"I do not want to have sex with you. Let me up."

His face darkened. He looked so mad that I felt afraid of him the way I'd been afraid of Nick. But I held myself rigid and didn't blink. Maybe I had something to prove, too.

"Jesus H. Christ!" He rolled away and jumped off the mattress. He stalked out of the room, his buns as bunched and hard as twin basketballs.

I felt sick to my stomach. I grabbed my shoes, hurried out to the studio, snatched my coat, and made a beeline through the kitchen to the door.

Downstairs I dropped everything and flopped on the couch with my head between my knees. I must have spent five minutes groaning and thinking seriously about throwing up. I was still a mess from the night before. At the police station I'd been in shock. I couldn't even remember what questions I'd been asked or how I'd answered them. Had I told them what I knew about Susie's childhood or about my intruder? I didn't think so. Then it occurred to me I'd better check around to see if I'd had any return visits from the bug person. I really had to make myself go into the bedroom and eyeball my mattress.

There was no sign my intruder had returned. So either his key didn't fit into my new locks or he'd been too busy raping and murdering Susie last night to bother hassling me. Was it Leo Acker? Was he the man in the black Volvo? Had my visit to Espey had anything to do with Susie's murder? Was I next on the hit list?

I hadn't forgotten my decision to bolt. I went to the kitchen and reached for the phone. My fingers had just closed around the receiver when it rang and I jumped back a foot.

"Hello," I whispered with one hand pressed over my slamming heart.

"Toni?" The voice was Sandy's. "Did I wake you?"

"No."

"Great news! Mom's biopsy came back negative."

It took several seconds for that to sink into the swamp taking up all the room in my braincase. "Negative?"

"Yeah, isn't that great? She's gonna be fine."

"That's terrific. I'm really happy."

"You can imagine how she feels—walking on air."

"What's Pop say?"

"Complaining about the doctor and the lab making us wait so long. But he's real relieved."

"I bet. Saves him from losing an unpaid cook."

"Oh, Toni, c'mon, don't be like that. Be happy."

"I am happy. Honest."

"I thought we could have a little celebration. You know, a family party. Tomorrow night at my place."

"Would you like me to bring something?"

"Just yourself. The parents will pick you up."

"I suppose, since it's at your house, your husband will be present?"

"Of course Al will be there. Toni, let's make this nice for Mom. Forgive and forget."

"Have you discussed this with him?"

"If you'll be civil, he will, too. I'll make sure of it." Sandy's voice went steely.

In my mind's eye, I contemplated my brother-in-law. Maybe it was time to make peace with good ol' Al. Maybe he could even be useful. Last night when the detective had interviewed me about Susie, I hadn't mentioned my visit to Espey or my notion about Acker. My theory seemed so half-baked and I'd been too shocked to answer his questions in anything but monosyllables.

Still, until I'd checked Acker out, I wouldn't be able to stop thinking about him. And until I discovered who'd killed Rebecca and now Susie, I'd never be able to stop thinking about either of them. I pictured that snapshot of Rebecca and Susie arm in arm, laughing into the camera. Lambs torn to bloody pieces by a wolf, I thought. And the wolf was still running loose. I could almost see his yellow eyes leering obscenely at me through the dark.

A few minutes earlier I'd come into the kitchen to call Randall. I'd planned to ask for his help so I could move out of Rebecca Kelso's haunted apartment. Instead I pulled out the phone book and looked up Don Parham's home number. He picked up on the second ring.

"Doctor Parham, this is Toni Credella. I'm sorry to call so early, but I wanted to catch you before you left for work." When he didn't answer immediately, I babbled on. "I'm the woman who came to talk to you about Rebecca Kelso?"

"Yes, I remember you, Ms. Credella."

"Something terrible has happened." I told him about Susie's murder. After he finished expressing shock and horror, I said, "Since you dated Rebecca, I thought you might have met her parents."

"A couple of times," he answered cautiously. "I had dinner with them at their place once. They live out in Greenspring Valley near Rosa Ponselle's place." Everyone who lives in Baltimore knows about Villa Pace, the famous opera singer's fabulous mansion.

"I wonder if you would be willing to call the Kelsos and ask if I could come out and see them?"

"Why don't you call yourself?"

"Well, for one thing their number is unlisted. For another, I think they would be more likely to agree if they got the request from you."

"What is it you want to talk to them about?"

"Just about Rebecca." I wanted to know more about Rebecca. Though she was a devastating presence in my life now, I hungered for the kinds of details that would allow me to see her more clearly. I thought that perhaps if I talked with her parents, I might pick up some clue about the terrible way she and Susie had died and why.

"You mean your fantasy that her ghost still haunts that apartment?"

"No. I just . . . I'd like to talk to them."

There was an uncomfortable pause. "I wish I could help you out, Ms. Credella, but I don't believe I can. This thing hit Rebecca's mother very hard. I don't believe talking to you and hearing about Susie would do her any good."

I didn't beg. I'd called him on impulse, and even to my ears the impulse sounded ill thought out and a little kooky. But once something takes root with me, it's hard to oust. By the time I'd eaten and showered and washed my hair, I knew how I was going to spend the rest of the morning.

Even pumping hard, it's a good two-hour bike ride out Falls Road to Greenspring Valley. After all the traffic and noise in the city, turning left onto the valley road was a little like turning left into paradise. The road is tree-shaded and relatively quiet. It winds and dips past stands of oak and maple and great pillowy stretches of emerald grass. Glance up and you see stone mansions peering down at you from hilly crowns. This is horse country, the neck of the woods where Baltimore's old money fled a century or so ago to escape the hoi polloi. When you're not pedaling in the dust of Jaguars and Beemers, you're being passed by pickups pulling horse trailers.

Luckily for me, the day was fair and mild. I stopped my bike by the side of the road near the Ponselle mansion. I've never seen it up close, but from a distance it looks like a white Italian villa. I've heard it has marble bathrooms with real gold faucets.

The sun warmed my shoulders. I'd dressed for a long ride—spandex pants, lightweight jacket, helmet, and goggles. Beneath my jacket I was sweating, and my muscles felt that pleasant sore glow.

I walked along the side of the road, sounding out the names on mailboxes and noticing signs of spring. Baby green buds showed on most of the trees, and a forsythia looked ready to pop yellow flowers. Parham had said Rebecca's parents lived out here. I figured my chances of spotting their mailbox were less than fifty-fifty. I wasn't even sure why I wanted to talk to them. I guess I wanted to know Rebecca better and hoped I'd see something or hear something that would help me make sense of this business.

It was pure chance that I happened to turn down that little side road and come across their mailbox. Gazing uncertainly down their private lane really brought home how different Rebecca had been from me. The house, what I could see of it, was a sprawling white Colonial with pale blue shutters. It nestled in masses of trees and bushes. Framed by the drive that circled it, a pale pink magnolia had burst into early bloom.

I almost turned back. What if Parham was right and seeing me would hurt Mrs. Kelso? I had no wish to harm Rebecca's mother. Yet I couldn't get it out of my head that I might learn something valuable by speaking with her.

In the end I swung my bike into the lane and plodded down it. My helmet dangled from the handlebars. I wished I wasn't wearing the black cycling pants. Spandex seemed out of place here.

As I drew abreast of the magnolia, a golden retriever rounded the corner of the house, barking furiously. It slid to a stop six feet away and growled low in its throat.

"Hey, guy, don't bite, huh? I swear I'm here on a mission of peace." As I spoke, I alternated nervous looks between the dog and the house. The front door opened and a woman in khaki slacks and a suede jacket came out.

"Daisy! Daisy, stop that noise." She shaded her eyes to get a better look at me and then left the door ajar behind her and stepped off the flagstone porch. As she approached, I panicked. This had to be Rebecca's mother. What would I say to her?

As it turned out, I didn't have to explain who I was, because Don Parham had called after all. "How was Susie killed?" she asked after I'd introduced myself.

I swallowed and then told her. "Raped and her throat cut."

"Oh, God!" Her hand went up to her mouth, and she turned her head away. "Oh, God!"

There's a look people have when they've been beat up so bad they'll probably never get over it. Mrs. Kelso had that look. I saw a quivering tightness to her eyes and mouth. Her rice-paper skin looked as if it might tear away at any instant and show you the raw flesh beneath. When you hear of murders on television or read about them in the papers, you feel sorry for the dead victims. What about the people who loved them?

For the first time I thought about Susie's parents. Though they lived nearby in Catonsville, they were out of town, so the police hadn't been able to reach them last night. They still might not know their daughter was dead. And what about that other little girl Espey murdered? What had her death done to her family? Circles of pain and horror rippled out from these crimes and just kept on spreading. Somehow, somewhere, it had to stop.

Roughly, because my throat ached, I tried to explain why I was there, even though I hardly understood the reason myself and felt like a tactless intruder. I explained how living in Rebecca's apartment had given me a feeling of closeness to her and how I hated it that her—and now Susie's—murderer was still at large. My stumbling, apologetic words must have struck a chord with Mrs. Kelso, because she stopped looking at me so suspiciously. "I'd guess you're about my daughter's age."

"I'm older."

"Yes, Rebecca was very young. Just a child, really." She put a hand on Daisy's burnished head. "This used to be Rebecca's dog."

"She's beautiful."

"She loved Becky. She used to get so excited when Becky came home from school for a visit."

"I bet she did." The dog stopped growling and sat back on her haunches. Her tail thumped. On impulse I patted her head, too. It felt warm and silky and very much alive.

"I hadn't planned on speaking to you, but now that I see you— Would you like to come in the house and have a cup of tea? You must be tired after such a long bike ride."

I accepted her invitation. After leaning my bike against a tree, I followed her and Daisy up the flagstone porch. Inside, the house was a dream. Wide planked floors in a mellow golden oak, walls painted a buttery cream, and comfortable furniture covered in flowered chintz. The kitchen had a wall of old brick and an old-fashioned Colonial-style hearth. The table was antique with ornate claw feet. What would it have been like to grow up in a place like this? I wondered. For a moment I envied Rebecca. Then I remembered why I was here.

"I can't imagine living in that apartment," Mrs. Kelso said. "To me it's the gate of hell."

The gate of hell. Now, that was an interesting idea. "Several times I've thought of moving. This morning I really planned to."

"What stopped you? Why don't you get out of there?"

I really hadn't intended telling her about Rebecca's ghost. I knew how crazy it sounded and that it might only make her feel bad. Nevertheless, the story came spilling out of me. "I guess you must think I'm some kind of a nut," I finished weakly.

She played with her teacup, and I noticed she had long, slim hands with immaculately manicured nails that had been polished pale pink. She wore only her wedding band, no flashy diamonds. Her ear-length brown hair had many streaks of gray, and her fine-featured face looked free of makeup. Excepting her sadness, I wished I could be like her at that age. I knew, however, that I would not be. I would never live in a house like this or dress the way she did. We were formed of different clay.

"I believe, dear," she said carefully, "that you're a very sensitive and imaginative person, and that living in that dangerous place isn't good for you. I'm not surprised you're haunted by Rebecca. I'm haunted by her, too. I can't tell you how terrible these months have been. My dreams are always nightmares. Sometimes I'm afraid to think at all." She hesitated. "I don't understand why you're involving yourself in her murder so personally. Unless it's the reward."

"What reward?"

"Mr. Kelso and I are offering a ten-thousand-dollar reward for information leading to the capture of Rebecca's killer."

"I didn't know anything about that." I was stunned.

DISCOVER A WORLD OF TIMELESS
OMANCE WITHOUT LEAVING HOME

GET

4 FREE

HISTORICAL ROMANCES
FROM HARPER MONOGRAM.

JOIN THE
TIMELESS ROMANCE READER SERVIC
AND GET FOUR OF TODAY'S
MOST EXCITING HISTORICAL
ROMANCES FREE,
WITHOUT OBLIGATION!

*Imagine getting today's very best historical romances sen
directly to your home – at a total savings of at least $2.00
month. Now you can be among the first to be swept awa
by the latest from Candace Camp, Constance O'Banyon,
Patricia Hagan, Parris Afton Bonds or Susan Wiggs. Yo
get all that – and that's just the beginning.*

PREVIEW AT HOME WITHOUT
OBLIGATION AND SAVE.

*Each month, you'll receive four new romances to
preview without obligation for 10 days. You'll pay
the low subscriber price of just $4.00 per title – a
total savings of at least $2.00 a month!*

*Postage and handling is absolutely **free** and there is
no minimum number of books you must buy. You
may cancel your subscription at any time with no
obligation.*

GET YOUR FOUR FREE BOOKS TODAY ($20.49 VALUE)

FILL IN THE ORDER FORM BELOW NOW!

YES! *I want to join the Timeless Romance Reader Service. Please send me my 4 FREE HarperMonogram historical romances. Then each month send me 4 new historical romances to preview without obligation for 10 days. I'll pay the low subscription price of $4.00 for every book I choose to keep – a total savings of at least $2.00 each month – and home delivery is free! I understand that I may return any title within 10 days without obligation and I may cancel this subscription at any time without obligation. There is no minimum number of books to purchase.*

NAME_____

ADDRESS _____

CITY_____STATE_____ZIP_____

TELEPHONE_____

SIGNATURE _____

(If under 18 parent or guardian must sign. Program, price, terms, and conditions subject to cancellation and change. Orders subject to acceptance by HarperMonogram.)

GET
4
FREE
BOOKS
(A $20.49
VALUE)

TIMELESS ROMANCE
READER SERVICE

120 Brighton Road
P.O. Box 5069
Clifton, NJ 07015-5069

Had Susie or Damon known about it? I wondered. They certainly hadn't said anything to me.

"No, I can see you didn't. We intended the reward for a police officer or some informer, not for an innocent bystander like you. I'm sure Rebecca wouldn't want you to risk your life for her."

Though I didn't say so, I believed in my gut that she did. I believed that somehow, somewhere, she was jumping up and down rooting for me to risk my life for her. As much as I'd wanted to call Randall this morning and beg him to move me out, I hadn't been able to. Hearing about the money certainly didn't take away my incentive. There was the little question of how I would pay next month's rent.

It wasn't the ten thousand that made me stay put in Rebecca's apartment. No, it was a crazy feeling I owed it to her, and now to Susie, not to be scared off. And it was hatred. I hated that creep out there who'd murdered them. I wasn't going to let him smoke me out like a rat. Instead I was going to get him. Yet even as I thought this, I knew how loony it was. How could someone like me bring down a violent, insane killer?

I asked, "Did Rebecca and Susie go around a lot together?"

"Yes. Several times Becky brought Susie out here for the weekend. You're thinking the same person who killed our Becky must have killed Susie, aren't you?"

"Anything else would be too much of a coincidence, wouldn't it?"

Her throat worked. Very carefully she said, "Becky was our only child, the dearest thing in our lives. To slaughter her the way he did— How can such a monster live with himself?" She shuddered and hugged her chest. Her eyes looked red and wet again. She covered her face with her hand.

I had considered telling her about Espey and my theory that Leo Acker might have murdered Rebecca by mistaking her for Susie. But the story was such a downer that I knew I couldn't hang it on Mrs. Kelso. I wished I could think of some way to comfort her. But there was no way, so I just waited until she got hold of herself.

She blew her nose and said as she crumpled the tissue, "As long as you're here and so interested in Rebecca, would you like to see her room?"

"Yes, very much."

She led me out into the hall and up a wide, curving staircase. Daisy followed behind us, her sharp nails making staccato clicks on the polished oak treads. Rebecca's room was at the back of the house, overlooking a flagstone patio and keyhole-shaped pool. It was a young girl's dream room, painted pale yellow with matching flowered drapes, bedspread, and slipcovered chair. On shelves, mixed with books and stuffed animals, were silver-framed photographs and ribbons.

I picked up a red one and tried to decipher the gold inscription on its rosette.

"That was for coming in second at a jumping meet when she was fifteen."

"Rebecca rode horses?"

"Oh, yes. In fact, we still have her bay gelding, Cyrano. Nobody ever rides him now, so I suppose we'll have to sell him soon. When you're done here, I'll take you out to meet him if you'd like."

"That would be nice."

"Dear, if you don't mind, I think I'll leave you alone for a bit. There's something I need to do."

I could tell from the way her throat was working again that she needed to get out of the room.

"That's fine. I'll be down in a minute."

Mrs. Kelso walked away down the hall, and after a couple of beats, Daisy followed. I heard both their steps on the staircase. Then Rebecca and I were alone together. Except she wasn't here, at least not the way she was in her apartment. The Rebecca I'd seen in the mirror and felt at the back of my neck had been terrified, anguished. This one felt much younger.

Maybe it was just my imagination. Or maybe it came from the sunny walls and flowered curtains, the dust motes in sunlight, and the stillness. A bitter sweetness lingered in this room. I could taste it on my tongue. Looking at the rows of ribbons and stuffed animals, I could almost hear the tinkle of girls giggling over something harmless.

I leaned forward and studied some of the pictures. One showed a skinny young Rebecca sitting on a dock in a bathing suit. She had her wet hair slicked behind her ears, and her eyes were dazzled by sun. In another she wore one of those black hats with a chin strap and stood next to a horse. She held up a winning ribbon. A silly grin split her face. She couldn't have been more than twelve or thirteen. I stared at that picture a long time and felt a deep anger swell inside me.

I have no idea how long I stayed in Rebecca's room. It must have been too long, because when I came downstairs Mrs. Kelso, whose eyes were now dry, looked at me strangely. We went out back to a pretty little stable and fenced exercise ring. Cyrano looked out from his stall mournfully. I patted his nose.

"I see you're not afraid of horses," Mrs. Kelso remarked.

"No. For a city girl I'm pretty comfortable with them. In Little Italy where I grew up, the cops ride around the neighborhood on horses all the time—real urban cowboys. I remember they used to tie them to a lamppost, and we kids would dare each other to pet them. Then, years ago I spent a summer driving tourists around the harbor in one of those carriages for hire. I had a nag named Bessie, and we got pretty fond of each other."

"Maybe you'd like to come out sometime and ride Cyrano."

"Thanks, but my knowledge of horses doesn't extend to climbing aboard one's back. Mrs. Kelso, before I go I wonder if you'd be willing to look at something?"

"Of course. What is it?"

"It's in one of the baskets on my bike."

Out front, I opened a paper sack and showed her the plastic bug. When I hauled it out, she stared at it and blinked like a turn signal. "I found it. I just wondered if you'd ever seen anything like it?" I said.

She had gone pale. "Becky found something like this on top of her car."

"When?"

"It was . . . it was about two weeks before she died. She laughed about it. She thought it was a joke."

"Did you mention the bug to the police?"

"No, I didn't. I never even thought of it."

"What did she do with it?"

"I have it." She turned and went into her garage through a side door. A moment later she emerged carrying my bug's twin.

10

That night I *lay awake* running it all over in my mind. Mrs. Kelso had given me her bug, and now both plastic insects sat on my bureau giving me the evil eye. Rebecca and I had both been presented with them. Yet so far as I knew, Susie hadn't been. I thought of the red nail polish I'd found on my underwear and suddenly remembered the polish on Susie's toes. She hadn't been wearing polish when I'd had the argument with her. I had no way of comparing, yet the polish I'd seen on her toes in the morgue seemed about the same color as the stuff on my panties.

Were all these things connected somehow? I realized I should have told the police about the vandalism in my apartment. Tomorrow I'd do that. Tiredly I got up and covered the bugs with a pillowcase. Rebecca, I thought, if you're really there, give me a clue.

But she didn't, and finally I slipped into the sleep of the confused, frightened, and exhausted.

The next morning I kept my appointment with Ron

Smith. It was the job lead Damon had steered me onto. Smith's company restored gilded antiques, and he'd agreed to interview me about an apprenticeship.

I wasn't too hopeful. I felt suspicious of anything that came through Damon, and the business sounded strange. I mean—gilding? Pasting gold leaf on plaster Cupids? But I was desperate. Recession had really dried up decorating money. Lately I'd had to scratch so hard for pennies that my fingers were bloody. *Consider the pros and cons of running back to Randall all you want, Toni. You haven't got next month's rent at Charles Village. No way could you swing a place at Mt. Vernon without borrowing from your father.* Now, that was *really* scary.

It's funny how weather affects your spirits. Broke, terrified, handicapped, and unemployed, I certainly didn't have much to cheer about. Yet as I pedaled down Falls Road with the sun on my shoulders, I achieved a little glow of happiness. Maybe it was the conversation I'd had with my mother. I'd called to congratulate her on her good test results. She'd sounded so relieved and happy to be back among the living. I stopped at a florist shop and ordered a dozen red roses to be sent to her. So what if my wallet was thin? Reprieves like Mom's should be celebrated.

The gilding company was in Hampden. It's a neighborhood within blocks of classy Johns Hopkins and the private school set in Roland Park. Yet Hampden, which used to be a mill village, has its own character. As I wheeled my bike along the stretch of sidewalk between Thirty-sixth and Thirty-seventh, I admired the jumbled architecture and pictured a bygone era. The huddled, down-at-heels storefronts made me think of girls in flapper skirts. I pictured speakeasies and gangsters in big, black autos.

Unfortunately, that reminded me of the Volvo. I wasn't in the mood to think about the car of doom now. I hadn't seen it in more than a week. Hadn't been staying up late to look for it, either. Could well be it still circled my block, sniffing for blood. Had it been on the prowl the night Susie died? I grimaced and looked at the address penciled on the slip of paper in my hand. It matched that on a big old brick pile across from the 7-Eleven on the west side of the street.

Fabulous old buildings fill this city. Smith's, I found out later, had been put up in the twenties as a recreation hall. After he buzzed me in, I ambled through a wide, empty, freshly painted hall. Upstairs, the studio where Smith did his work made me stop and stare.

It was like walking into a church, or maybe even like walking into heaven. The ceiling must have been eighteen feet off the whitewashed walls. The space was so enormous that despite the many worktables around the edge, it looked almost empty. Yet it didn't feel cold. The golden art objects that glowed from the walls and stood propped on the bare wood floor gave it warmth. They were all so beautiful—huge gilded mirrors and picture frames, ornate chairs, scrolled columns that looked as if they belonged on the gates to paradise. As I looked around, my heart squeezed tight in my chest, and I inhaled the perfume of turpentine and clay. This was the most wonderful place I'd ever seen. Oh, God, I implored, let him hire me!

Smith came striding out of a back room. A bearded black man wearing a white apron and with his shirtsleeves rolled up to his elbows, he was so tall and lanky he had to have been a basketball player.

Smith gave me a big, friendly smile and took me around and showed me the different workshops and processes that went into restoration and gilding. Despite his gentle, joking manner, as we walked from table to table, he asked a lot of hard-nosed questions about my background and experience.

I racked by brain trying to mention everything artistic I'd ever done. I made faux-finishing sound a lot fancier and more exacting than it really was. I so much wanted him to like me that I practically slobbered on him like an overeager puppy. If only he'd teach me how to do this great stuff. If only I could stay in this lovely, safe, light-filled sanctuary forever.

"How do you happen to know Damon?" I asked after he'd finished the tour and led me back to an office.

"He was a student when I was teaching at the Maryland Institute. Talented guy."

"Oh, yes, Damon's very talented." He was also a jerk, but if his recommendation got me into this studio, I'd forgive him. That didn't mean I'd ever sleep with him again. Once was definitely enough.

"Well, Toni, you think you might like to try this line of work?" Smith's dark eyes crinkled up at the corners and his white teeth flashed.

"Oh, yes. Please."

"While you're learning it pays minimum wage, and I can give you the sack at any time."

"That's fine."

Smith's smile widened, and I could almost see a halo settle into place around his handsome head. If he gave me this job, he'd be my savior almost as much as Randall had been. "Okay. You can start Monday. Eight o'clock sharp, and you can bring a lunch and leave it in our refrigerator if you want."

I didn't ride home, I floated. The sun seemed bright and kindly. I could smell spring, damp rich earth, new buds, fresh juices. Clouds grazed in the sky like fluffy Easter bunnies.

I wheeled my bike into my building's tiny lobby and stopped short. The detective assigned to Susie's case waited at my door. I came back to earth sharply.

"Ms. Credella? I'm Detective O'Dell. We met on the twenty-fourth when I questioned you and your neighbor about the Susan Zillig homicide."

I nodded. I'd been so out of it that night, I hardly remembered the police interrogation. Now, however, I found I recalled Detective O'Dell distinctly.

He looked to be somewhere in his thirties, but it was hard to guess his age, as he had one of those fleshless, close-to-the-bone faces that time doesn't change much. Tall and greyhound lean, he was the jeans-and-sweatshirt type and didn't look right in his rumpled gray suit and shapeless tan raincoat. I could also tell he didn't give a damn how he looked. I guessed no one else did, either. Sometimes you know that about a man. One glance says whether he goes home to a loving wifey or an empty apartment with nothing but a couple of cans of beer and a package of stale lunch meat in the refrigerator. With O'Dell it had to be the latter.

His coffee brown hair had been hacked off short by a barber in need of a refresher course. His lightly freckled skin had seen too much sun and wind, and his calculating hazel eyes were about as congenial as frozen pond scum. Despite all this, he had a kind of I-could-make-you-melt-if-I-wanted-to sex appeal. But maybe that says more about me than it does about him.

"Some new information has come to light. I'd like to ask you a few more questions, if I may."

"Sure." I unlocked my door, wheeled the bike inside, and leaned it against the living room wall. These days I'm not one to take pride in my housekeeping, but I felt glad the place looked uncluttered. Not that it was clean. I'm one of those people who minds mess but doesn't even register fingermarks and dust balls. Another of the grievous sins Nick used to get so mad at me about. Why was my mind running along these pipsqueak lines?

I dropped onto the couch. "Uh, make yourself comfortable."

Disregarding my offer, O'Dell positioned himself in front of me with his long feet planted wide. He clicked the top of a ballpoint as if he were cocking a six-shooter, snapped open a small notebook, then ignored it. "When I questioned you on the twenty-fourth, you stated that you were not a close friend of the deceased. Is that correct?"

"Yes. I just moved in here a few weeks ago. I talked to Susie a couple of times and spent the evening with her and Damon once. But we weren't pals or anything."

"Yet you knew she'd been molested by one Christopher Espey some twenty years earlier."

I took a swallow. "Yes, I knew."

"How did you know?"

"She told me."

"She told you? Mr. Wilkes upstairs claims to have been her good friend, yet he says he didn't know."

"So?"

"So, why would she confide something like that to you when she hadn't mentioned it to him, supposedly her close pal?"

"Look, it was just one of those girl things. She broke down and told me one night."

"When was this?"

"A week ago." My slow-motion brain finally made a few feeble connections. Since the subject of Espey hadn't come up the night Damon and I went down to the station together, he couldn't have denied knowing about it then. O'Dell must have interviewed him again just lately—more than likely only a few minutes before I'd found him staked out at my door. I cast an apprehensive look up at the ceiling.

"Perhaps you'd like to explain why you didn't mention any of this during our first discussion."

"I was in shock."

"In shock? You mean you forgot?"

"Not exactly. I'd just been hit with identifying Susie's body, and I felt sick. At the time, past history didn't seem important." Maybe I'd also been feeling guilty and hadn't wanted to think about it. I don't know. That whole identifying-her-body scene was still a hideous blur.

"It must have seemed fairly important on the sixteenth."

He finally referred to his notebook. "On that date you visited Christopher Espey at the Maryland State

Penitentiary. This was after writing a formal letter requesting visitation privileges."

"Yes."

"Yes what? It seemed important, or you made the visit?"

"Both."

We eyed each other like tomcats staking opposing claims on neighborhood turf. I decided he didn't have sex appeal after all and began to have a very bad feeling about where this gotcha session was headed.

"Ms. Credella, I must warn you that withholding information is an obstruction of justice and could make you an accessory."

"I'm not withholding information." I thought of the bug and knew I should tell him because it might be a significant clue.

I was opening my mouth to do just that when he snapped, "You certainly kept a lot to yourself during our last interview. For instance, you failed to mention that three years ago you were indicted for murdering a police officer."

"That was self-defense, not murder. A jury acquitted me. And it has nothing to do with any of this." How could I have imagined that this man was in any way attractive? He was a an SOB.

"No? Yet it's quite a coincidence, wouldn't you say?"

"What's a coincidence? What are you talking about?" I went stiff.

"You move in here just a few weeks before Susan Zillig is murdered. You know the details of her past and are poking around in her life. Yet Mr. Wilkes, who claims to have been her best friend, says he knows nothing about her being raped as a child. On top of all that, the two of you are giving each other an alibi for the time she was murdered."

"Damon and I were together eating Chinese carry-out when Susie was found."

"Very convenient for you both."

"What are you saying? Are you accusing me of having raped Susie and then slit her throat?" My voice spiraled up to high C.

His eyes slitted. "How do you know she was raped? The autopsy report didn't come in until this morning."

"You said yourself that's how it looked."

Again we measured each other. I saw a man who could be a dangerous enemy and who didn't like me much. God knew what he saw. When neither of us managed to stare the other down, he shrugged. "All right, she was raped."

"Before or after she was killed?"

"Now, what makes you ask a thing like that?"

"I don't know. It just popped into my perverted little head."

"The coroner guesses it was during, and that's the last detail I'm going to give you."

"Why? Because the details are so awful? Or is it because you want to keep the murderer's MO secret in order to catch him?"

"Both."

As the impact of what Susie must have gone through before she died resonated through me, I felt so sick that I put my head between my knees. O'Dell, bless his sensitive soul, waited until I could raise it again.

"Obviously," I said, "I couldn't have raped her while I was slitting her throat."

"No, but your boyfriend could, and you could be giving him an alibi."

"Damon Wilkes is not my boyfriend."

His brows lifted, and I flushed. It's true that Damon and I must have looked pretty lovey-dovey that night. I remembered how I'd wandered into the kitchen with my clothes and hair mussed and my lips puffy from his kisses.

"I'm not lying for him," I said between my teeth. "I'd never give a man an alibi for cutting a woman's throat."

O'Dell switched to another track. "You haven't explained why you went to see Espey."

"You haven't asked."

"I'm asking now, Ms. Credella. Did you do it at Susie Zillig's request?"

"No, but she knew he was coming up for parole. She told me she was nervous about him getting out. In fact, she was planning a move to Chicago soon for that reason."

"Is that why you went to see him? To find out if he'd be a danger to her?"

"Not exactly."

"Why, exactly?"

"I went to see him to check out a theory about Rebecca Kelso's murder."

While O'Dell stared at me as if I were a cockroach in his pitcher of Budweiser, I outlined my theory about mistaken identity and getting the victim who got away. I gotta admit, it sounded pretty weird. When I mentioned Leo Acker's name, O'Dell's eyebrows did a little snake dance.

"Are you claiming Leo Acker got the idea of murdering

Susie Zillig from Espey, that he murdered Rebecca Kelso by mistake and then went after Susie to correct his error?"

"Well, it's a thought."

"A farfetched one."

"It's worth checking, isn't it? Acker is out on parole. You could see if he has an alibi."

"Maybe."

"What do you mean, maybe?" Suddenly I was so steamed I felt as if my hair was on fire. "You let these murdering rapists out and then don't keep tabs to see that they aren't up to their old tricks?"

"Hey, I'm not in charge of the courts or the prison system."

"I thought you guys were paid to protect the public. Women are the public, too, you know." I got up, stomped into my bedroom, and came back with a handful of the panties that had been decorated with nail polish. "See these? Some creep broke into my apartment a few days back and did this. It could be the same guy who murdered Susie giving me fair warning that I'm next. In fact, the polish Susie had on her toes the night she died looked like a match for it."

I described the panty incident in more detail, pointed out that Susie hadn't been wearing polish earlier in the day before she'd been killed, and told him about the bug I'd found in my bed. O'Dell took the underwear out of my hands and examined it.

"I'd like to see this plastic insect."

"Sure."

When I brought it to him, his eyebrows lifted. "I'll have to take it and your underwear in to see if we can come up with anything on them. Do you have anything else you want to tell me about?"

I knew I should mention the bug I'd gotten from Mrs. Kelso. But I didn't want to. That was my clue, one I'd worked damn hard to get. O'Dell already had one insect. Maybe in a couple of days I'd turn the other over to him. But in the meantime, even at the risk of being charged with withholding evidence, I felt I deserved the chance to see if I could figure anything out about it on my own.

I guess the conflict I felt about this must have shown in my face.

"Cool off, Ms. Credella," O'Dell said. "I'll find out about the nail polish and the bug, and I'll look into the Acker thing." He snapped his notebook shut and glanced around my humble abode. "It's kind of strange, isn't it, you living in this place where two women have been killed."

I stood there hugging myself, feeling guilty because I hadn't mentioned the other bug. "I moved in because the rent was low, and only one woman was actually killed in the apartment." Only?

"Yeah, well, you know what they say, don't you?"

"No, what do they say?"

"Bad things come in threes."

After O'Dell left, I sat massaging my temples. Yesterday with Mrs. Kelso I'd been on some kind of Joan of Arc kick. Pumped up on emotion, I'd pictured myself capturing Rebecca's killer and marching him into the police station. That was why I'd held on to the second bug. Who was I kidding? I was no warrior woman. It felt good to have turned the whole business over to the police. Maybe by tomorrow O'Dell would have proved Acker was behind all this and the creep would be off the street and back in prison where he belonged. Meanwhile I could get on with my life. Now that I had a job, even that was beginning to look a little better.

My hopeful thoughts didn't go much farther because a few minutes later Damon hammered on my door. When I opened up, he was standing so stiff and rigid that he looked strung together from broom handles.

"I want to talk to you." He stalked in without being invited and kicked the door shut behind him.

"Hey!"

He rounded on me with clenched fists. "What the hell did you just say to that cop?"

"I answered his questions."

"Well, how about answering some of mine? Why didn't you tell me what happened to Susie when she was a kid?"

"She didn't want me to pass it on. She told me in confidence."

"Yeah, well, after they found her in Druid Hill, you could have mentioned it. When O'Dell dropped it on me, I felt like a damn fool."

"I didn't get much chance to confide all my innermost thoughts to you. If you'll recall, when we got back to your place that night you wanted action, not talk."

His eyes flickered and then narrowed. "So did you, baby."

"All I wanted was a little human comfort. Now,

please leave. I'm tired." I wrapped my arms around my chest. God, how I hate male aggression. I hate having to stand up to it. But when you don't, they roll over you like tanks on Easter chicks. Sometimes they roll over you anyway.

"Not until I mention something else. Susie's past wasn't the only turd O'Dell dropped. He told me you were tried for murder, that you killed your husband."

"Quite the little bringer of tidings, isn't he?" I could just picture O'Dell springing this info on Damon to put him off balance and perhaps get him to say something revealing.

"It's true, then?" For a moment Damon looked deflated.

"It's true."

"Jesus!" Damon ran a nervous hand through his salt-and-pepper curls. "All this time I thought you were putting me off because you were grieving."

"I was, in a way."

"For what? Not for your husband, if you shot the guy."

I started pacing back and forth, still hugging my arms. "Yes, I was in mourning for Nick. I still am. You've never been married, so you wouldn't understand."

"There's a hell of a lot about you I don't understand, Toni. More every day."

"I've been mourning many things—my dream of love, my illusions about romance, my happily-ever-after, my self-respect . . . God, I sound like a yuppie get-well card, don't I?"

"What I want to know is why you were poking around in Susie's life. Why did you go to see this creep Espey?"

"That's my business."

"Did you have some cockamamie idea you were going to solve Rebecca's murder?"

"What's it to you?"

"What do you mean, what's it to me? We're lovers."

I rounded on him. "Why is it that when you let a man take you to dinner, he thinks he's rented you for the night? And if you make the mistake of going to bed with one, he believes he owns you. We are not lovers. We had a one-night stand."

"Come on upstairs with me, Toni."

"What?"

"You'll be safer up there. I worry about you alone down here. I don't want anything bad to happen to you."

I'd be lying if I said I wasn't tempted to take him up on it. I hadn't even admitted to myself how scared I really was. But I guess living with a man again scared me more. "Thanks, Damon, but no."

He didn't give up right away. It took another quarter-hour of wrangling before he finally left. And when he walked out he slammed the door behind him, just in case he hadn't already made his displeasure clear.

I paced around and tried to think. One fact had really floated to the top out of these last two nasty little conversations. I didn't want to get killed by this creep who'd murdered Rebecca and Susie.

For a long time after my trial I'd thought I wanted to die. Several times I came close to making it happen. I remember sitting in the tub with a razor blade once and rubbing the flat of it across my wrist. Then the phone rang, and I'm one of those people who always has to answer a phone. It had been Randall asking me over for dinner and conversation. He'd offered me a lifeline from the side of the mountain where grass grows, and I'd grabbed it.

Still, for a long time death has been at the back of my mind, death where there's no guilt or confusion, no bills to pay, only endless peace. In a way I'd been courting death when I moved in here, daring it, tweaking its nose. So it surprised me a little to realize how much I really didn't want to be Leo Acker's victim.

After I'd told O'Dell about him, I'd figured I was safe. Yet even if O'Dell picked him up tomorrow, there was still tonight to get through. I counted on my fingers to see how long ago I'd applied for my gun license and decided I'd call about it first thing in the morning. Then I hurried around and checked the locks on all my windows. They were far enough off the ground so it wouldn't be easy for someone to break one and jump in. On the other hand, they were within climbing distance for someone athletic, and they didn't have the protection of grates.

I stood in front of the window in the living room, picturing a dark figure flowing in like smoke while I slept in the bedroom. That sent me skittering to the kitchen. I filled a paper sack with glasses, jars, and soup cans, which I then stacked beneath all the sills in little pyramids. At least they'd make a racket if an intruder stumbled over them in the dark. Now my imagination was really revved. I propped a chair under the doorknob the way Nick had once shown me and then looked around for some sort of weapon. Finally I took a hammer into the bedroom and stuck it under my pillow.

I still didn't feel safe. I walked around and around,

needing to hear a reassuring voice but not wanting to bother Randall or go whimpering upstairs to Damon. On an impulse I called Sandy, but when Al answered the phone I hung up. Talking to my brother-in-law wasn't going to soothe and reassure me. Still, I needed to hear a friendly voice. Finally I dialed Jeff Simpler's office number. He answered on the second ring, and instantly I felt better.

"I'm glad I caught you. Do you have a minute? Or do you have to go to class or something?"

"This is my office hour. I was just thinking of you, Toni. How've you been?"

"Not so good."

"That's no surprise. I heard about Susie Zillig. A terrible thing. Has it made you nervous?"

"Terrified is more like it." I described the night Susie was killed, how I'd been with Damon and how we'd identified her body.

"That must have been traumatic for you."

"At the time I was numb. But now it keeps coming back. I keep remembering little things, like how her feet looked hanging off that tray. I talked to her just before she died, and I noticed her feet in slippers. Now I keep putting those two pictures side by side, and it gives me the shakes." I didn't mention about the nail polish, but it was in my mind. Those blood red nails that hadn't been there before.

"You're a sensitive, vulnerable person. It's a shame you had to go through that."

His voice was warm and sympathetic. For a moment I envied Gloria. But maybe he saved his compassion for people he suspected were half off their rockers. I cleared my throat and told him about my visit to

Espey. Then I described my Leo Acker theory and how I'd given it to O'Dell. That surprised him.

"You really believe this Leo Acker is behind Rebecca's and Susie's deaths?"

"Well, I suppose it's farfetched. But serial killers are pretty farfetched themselves."

"Toni, how much do you actually know about serial killers?"

"Okay, I admit it's only what I see in the movies. But that's true of most people."

"Have you done any reading about the psychopathic mind?"

"No."

"Would you like to?"

"Sure, but I have trouble sounding out a recipe, much less a psychology book."

"Oh, yes, I'd forgotten." He didn't say anything for a minute. "I may have mentioned that I've written a book on the criminal mind. I was going to recommend it to you, but it's technical. With your dyslexia, you'd probably find it heavy going."

"I'd like to try, anyway."

"Then I'll drop a copy over to you."

"That's really nice of you, Doctor Simpler."

"Please, call me Jeff."

I felt a little funny calling him by his first name when he was married. But that was silly. I already called Gloria by her first name. "Thanks, Jeff."

"You're welcome, and Toni ..."

"Yes?"

"Watch your step."

* * *

I laughed at myself for being such a wuss, but talking to Jeff made me feel a whole lot better. It's like I used to feel when I was a little girl sitting on my daddy's lap. Those were the days when I thought he was God. For the flicker of a second I wished I could go back to those days. But they were gone forever, and anyway I didn't really want them back. I just wanted to get through this night. If I could do that, then O'Dell would nail Acker tomorrow and my worries would be over.

Actually, the rest of the afternoon and evening weren't so bad. I worked on a few sewing projects I'd piled up and then ironed while I watched the news. After I treated myself to canned minestrone and one of my weaknesses in life, a pecan twirl, I vegged out in front of the TV with an old Esther Williams flick. I love Esther Williams. They really knew how to throw a party in those days.

By the time the movie ended I was feeling pretty brave. I was also tired. After a long, hot soak in the tub, I climbed into bed and dropped right off to slumberville.

There's a rare and horrible experience you can have when you're very deeply asleep. A tiny surface part of you notices that something is terribly wrong and that you must wake up immediately. You can't. You try and try, but you just can't do it. It's as if you're at the bottom of a black ocean with planets of water pressing you down into the ooze. You thrash and struggle, trying to fight your way up through it. But it's too heavy, and you're made of lead, and the surface is just too far. Yet you know you absolutely must get free. Because to stay asleep a minute longer will be death.

That's how it was for me. As I fought, I heard this

keening noise in the far distance. It was like a warning siren. Yet it had a human quality, a terrible sadness and an even more terrible dread. All the time it was above me, urging me up, up through the sluggish layers of my unconsciousness.

When I got closer to the surface I realized I was listening to a young woman's screams, and my heart froze. I saw Rebecca's face then. It floated upside down in the water over my head. Her hair streamed back from her pallid features, and her eyes were dark holes. Yet something stared out of them at me, and I knew it was a warning.

Coated with cold sweat, I jerked awake. A metallic crash rolled at me from the living room. I jackknifed into a sitting position. Gasping, my heart pounding so hard it hurt my ribs, I stared into the darkness and listened. I strained to hear footsteps, but I heard nothing. As the ominous silence flexed and rippled around me, I remembered the hammer under my pillow. Uncoiling my icy fists, I snaked my arm behind my back and reached for it. Even as my fingers closed about the wooden handle, I pictured it battering in my skull.

Sitting in bed like this, I felt like a tethered goat. If there was a killer in my apartment, he'd know exactly where to find me. I inched my legs over the side and stood up. The bedsprings gave a little squeal, and I almost dropped the hammer. Normally I'm strong and fairly well coordinated. Now I felt like a marionette with cut strings. I was afraid to make a move for fear of stumbling over my feet. My breathing sounded like an overworked furnace wheezing through a clogged grate. Was something standing on the other side of the door listening to it and licking its chops?

That sent me tiptoeing around the bed with the hammer thrust out in front of me. I flattened myself on one side of the door and waited. What would I do if someone pushed it open? Would I bash him over the head and ask questions later? What if it were Damon or Randall? *C'mon, Toni, why would either of them come sneaking in here at this hour? That noise you heard was the cans rolling away from the window.*

I couldn't stand it a second longer. I kicked the door open and rushed out into the living room with the hammer raised over my head. For several endless seconds I crouched, my eyes darting to every corner. The streetlights lit the room so I could see clearly. No one was there.

No one was in the kitchen, either. After checking there, I hurried back to the living room and stood in front of the window closest to the bedroom. I'd been right about the cans. They lay toppled on the floor. A cold breeze ran over my skin like a chilly hand. I reached out gingerly. High on the windowpane a square of glass was missing.

I glanced at the floor. A scrap of something that looked like a rag caught my eye and I picked it up. For half a minute I stood there fingering it, not registering what it really was. Then I realized. It was the lace panties that had been missing from my bureau drawer when I'd found the bug. They were stained with something that looked like dried blood.

Half gagging and with my heart practically jumping out of my chest, I flattened my nose on the glass that was still in place and peered out. I was just in time to see the rear lights of a black Volvo disappear down the deserted street.

11

You can bet my first move after finding those panties was to call the police. A cop car came squealing up, and a black rookie named Lieutenant Grimsby took my statement. When I mentioned Rebecca and Susie and showed the bloodstained underwear to Grimsby, who looked fresh out of high school, he goggled at me. He promised that he'd make sure Detective O'Dell was informed of my break-in as soon as he came on duty.

That left two hours until dawn. No way could I go back to bed. After tacking a piece of cardboard over the broken windowpane, I circled the living room like an eggbeater. I was trying to think and make plans. Eight o'clock sharp I called Aronchick, yelled my head off, and demanded he get my window replaced pronto. When he agreed to that, I insisted he get wrought-iron grates installed over the window frames. The grates took a lot more pressure. But he was badly shaken by Susie's murder following so closely on Rebecca's and finally agreed. That gave me some satisfaction, but not a whole lot.

Twice I called the police to see if O'Dell was around. No such luck. At ten I phoned the gun store in Fells Point and asked if my registration had come in. Bad news there, too.

"You told me ten days. It's been more than that."

"Let me check the file. Let's see, Antoinette Credella. Yeah, I think I remember you. Little girl with a lot of browny-red hair, right?"

"I'm a grown woman, and my hair is dark auburn."

"Yeah, okay. Listen, it's not here. You're right, though. It should be in by now."

"Then why isn't it?"

"Got me. You know of anything that might hold it up?"

"Like what?" I started breathing carefully.

"A prior conviction?"

"Okay, I was on trial a few years back, but I was acquitted."

The tone of his voice changed, became more familiar. "That's probably it, then. Sometimes when the cops don't think a certain person should have a firearm, they'll hold up the registration."

"Even when that person is legally entitled?"

"If they can't deny you legally, they can at least give you a hassle. Get my drift?"

"Got it," I said between my teeth.

After I hung up, I stood pressed against the refrigerator with my fists clenched and an iron spike stabbing into my gut. I pictured the broken window in the living room. Now there was nothing but cardboard between me and whoever prowled my block leaving me nasty little presents. I'd feel better after Aronchick had the grates installed. But I'd still want a gun. I remembered what Mrs. Kelso had called my apartment: "the gates of hell." If I was going to spend another night in this place, I needed to be able to protect myself.

On the other hand, maybe I didn't. I took a deep breath and released it slowly. What if O'Dell hadn't been available at the station because he was tracking down Acker? Suppose he'd already got the goods on Acker and the guy was out of commission? Possibly I was going into panic mode for nothing.

As if in answer to my prayer, my buzzer rang. When I went to the window nearest the porch, I saw O'Dell standing there with the collar of his trench coat rumpled around his neck. His ears were red from the wind, and he looked no friendlier than he had before. Regardless, he was a welcome sight. Eagerly I let him in.

"You heard what happened?"

"About your break-in? I got the message. I also read the report. Busy night." He crossed the room and peered at my window. "That cardboard is an invitation to every crook who sees it."

"It's cold out today, and my landlord promised to have a glazier over here by noon."

"Fast work."

"Not fast enough for me. As you might imagine, I'm feeling just a tad anxious about all this. Have you talked to Acker?"

"I checked him out for you."

"And?"

He straightened. "Acker's not a suspect in Susie Zillig's murder or in Rebecca Kelso's, either."

"What?" Talk about getting the rug pulled from under you. "Have you checked his alibis for those dates?"

"Airtight. Acker was working late both nights. A dozen customers saw him."

"What does he do, strip in an all-male revue?"

"As a matter of fact, he's a bouncer on the Block."

"The Block? You're kidding. I can't believe Acker is working with strippers. He's a rapist, for God's sake."

"His parole officer says he's doing well there. The owner hasn't filed a single complaint. Besides, Acker's a reformed rapist. Before he was released he went through a rape rehabilitation program."

"Rape rehabilitation? What does that mean? Did they castrate him?"

O'Dell gave me an arrested look. "This is the U.S. of A., remember, we don't do things like that. From what I hear, rape rehabilitation involves education and group therapy. Then there's some sort of experimental drug. Anyhow, I don't have grounds to haul Acker in on. According to his boss and his parole officer, he's been a model citizen."

I felt crushed. I'd really convinced myself that Acker was behind all this horror and that O'Dell would nab him and solve my problems. Now I was nowhere again. Worse than nowhere. I was a target, and I felt so scared I wanted to strike out.

"What about the bug and the nail polish on my underwear?"

"So far we don't have anything on the bug. The polish

on the panties and on Susie Zillig's toes is a match."

"A match?" I lifted my head. "Then you have something to go on?"

"Not really. It's a common brand sold in just about every big drugstore. Impossible to trace."

"What about the panties I found this morning?"

"They've been turned over to the lab. They're checking the stain, but I haven't heard anything yet."

So where did that leave me? Being stalked by a maniac who liked to make sure his victims looked ready to party before he cut them up? Rage choked me.

"So, what are you going to do about this break-in?" I pointed at the spot where cardboard blocked the light from the street.

"I'll look it over, check for prints. Your neighbors may have seen or heard something."

"What if none of them did?"

"Then it's going to be very tough to track down the perpetrator."

"Even when the perpetrator has already raped and murdered at least two women and has starred me on his list of top ten for most promising next victim?"

O'Dell's eyes narrowed on me. "Do you know something more you're not telling me?"

"Like what?"

"Look, Ms. Credella, these are the facts. You live in a building where two other women have been murdered. Lots of people get murdered in Baltimore. So, that could just be coincidence."

"You're saying it's a coincidence that some nut is harassing me like this? I don't believe what I'm hearing!"

"Let me finish, please. Last night someone broke your window and left a pair of your panties on the floor. It could be a killer. But until we get an analysis on the stain, it could also be a friendly neighborhood pervert, someone looking to steal your TV, or an ex-boyfriend. Statistically, the latter is most likely."

"I don't have an ex-boyfriend."

"What about the guy upstairs?"

"Damon? He's not my boyfriend."

"The two of you looked pretty cozy to me."

I gritted my teeth. "Damon is not the one who broke my window. The person who did was Rebecca Kelso's and Susie Zillig's killer, and he'll be back. I need protection."

"If you believe that, maybe it would be smart for you to get out of here."

"And go where?"

"To a friend's. To your parents. Wherever you'll feel safer."

I glared up at his unsympathetic mug. He had eyes that changed color. Now they were bright green. "Why should I have to move? A person ought to feel safe where she lives, and that includes a woman living alone. We citizens of Baltimore hire you to protect us, isn't that right? I pay the taxes that go into your salary just like everyone else."

O'Dell jammed his big hands deep into his raincoat pockets. "I'll see what I can do. District has already been alerted. I'll make sure they give this place special attention. But, frankly, don't get your hopes up you're going to get a twenty-four-hour bodyguard. This is Baltimore in the recession nineties. The city budget is tighter than curls on a poodle, and violence is going on all around us."

"Are you saying you can't offer me any protection?"

"Look, Ms. Credella, do you have any idea how many—"

My normally pleasant contralto voice turned into a screech. "Don't 'Look, Ms. Credella' me. I don't believe you can't. I think you just won't. It's because of Nick, isn't it?"

"Nick?"

"My husband. It's because I shot my husband and he was a cop. I know how you guys think. Every one of you hates my guts. You're probably delighted I'm having this kind of trouble. Jesus! You won't protect me, and you've held up my gun registration so I can't defend myself."

To give O'Dell his due, he looked genuinely astonished. "Hey, cool off. I don't know what you're talking about."

"Sure you do." I flung open the door and motioned him out as if I were Queen Elizabeth giving a page the boot. "You're hoping I get my throat cut like Susie. Well, don't count on it. If you won't defend me, I'll do it myself."

As I hustled him out, he tried arguing back. But I slammed the door on him. After he'd stomped to his car and roared off, I dialed Randall and told him about the gun registration.

"Don't be so paranoid, Toni. It's probably just a bureaucratic slowdown."

"It's deliberate. No matter what's holding things up, I need that gun. I'm entitled to it and I want it."

He sighed. "I'll see what I can do."

"Thanks."

"Don't thank me yet. I'm not so sure I'm doing you a favor. You don't even know how to handle a firearm."

"I managed to kill someone with a thirty-eight."

"That was pure bad luck. If you're determined to own a handgun, you'd better learn what to do with it."

"Yeah, I guess you're right." I swallowed. My life was getting complicated all over again. And it was happening too fast. "Any suggestions who I should get to teach me?"

"I'll teach you."

"You?"

"Don't be so surprised. I was runner-up in the state handgun championships a few years back."

"You were?"

Randall laughed. "You sound as if I just told you I was born on Krypton. Did you think I only knew how to cook and fill my closet with clothes? To survive these days a gay black person has to be versatile. Listen, I've got a meeting, but I'll get back to you before the day is out."

"Thanks. I appreciate that."

"In the meantime, be careful."

"Whatever you say."

"Hold that thought."

I spent the afternoon welcoming first the glass man and then, miracle of miracles, the wrought-iron grate man. After they both did their work I heaved a big sigh of relief—even though the grates did mess up the view outside and make me feel like an inmate at the zoo. When the last of the installers left, I couldn't stand being cooped up in my apartment a minute longer.

The afternoon was still sunny, so I rode my bike over to the Hopkins campus. To my surprise, I found they were holding the Hopkins Spring Fair. With so much going on, I hadn't even realized it was that time. As I strolled among the craft booths sipping a lemonade in a big styrene cup, I thought of Rebecca and Susie. A year ago they'd worked together at one of these booths. Now they were worm food.

"Hi there."

I was studying a pair of earrings on a black velvet display stand when I heard the familiar voice. I turned and found Don Parham standing just behind me. He wore jeans and a ragged sweater, and the expression in his eyes was wary but not unfriendly.

"Oh, hi."

"How've you been?"

What was I supposed to say? Not wanting to ruin what was left of the sunny afternoon, I said, "Fine. You?"

"Okay, I guess." He kept looking me over. "Christine Kelso told me about your visit with her."

"Oh?" Now I was wary.

"She took quite a liking to you. Says you remind her of Rebecca."

"How could I? We're nothing alike."

"I don't know. Anyhow, she'd like to see you again. She asked me to invite you to come out and ride Rebecca's horse."

"I liked her, too, and I appreciate the invitation. But I don't know how to ride. I told her that."

"I could teach you. She's lonely. I was wrong to warn you off going to see her. Talking to you seems to have done her good, and I think it would do her good to see you again. How about it? Shall we set a date?"

"I don't know. Maybe." I was really taken aback by this and very flattered.

He took a little book out of his back pocket. "Let's see. How about a week from next Sunday?"

"Uh, yeah, I guess."

"Good. Then it's a date. Now, how about letting me buy you some fried dough?"

I spent the next hour wandering around the fair with Don Parham. It was a pretty schizophrenic experience. For even while I was being charmed by him, I was also wondering if I'd dismissed him as a murder suspect too easily. I kept looking down at his hands for signs of nail polish. There weren't any, but socializing with Rebecca's old boyfriend made me feel freaky. When he invited me to have dinner with him, I made an excuse to beg off and biked home as if the devil were after me.

Five minutes after I walked in my door, Randall called. "You ought to be able to pick that gun up Monday."

"You mean you've shaken the registration loose?"

"I made a couple of calls. It's all set."

"Oh, Randall, that's wonderful. Nothing beats having a tough lawyer on your side."

"If only I really thought so."

After we ended the conversation, I headed for the bathroom and a long, hot soak in the tub. Through all this long and weird day I hadn't forgotten the party for

my mother out at Sandy's. The time had come to pre-
pare myself to feel like celebrating.

I really did want to shove my troubles in a box so I
could put on a happy face for my mother. I mean,
scared as I was about having an untimely and entirely
too colorful death, I could imagine how great she
must feel to be getting this reprieve from the doctors.
It would be mean to spoil it for her. Yet I wasn't exactly
looking forward to an evening with Al Pennak. Spending time penned up with someone who's dreaming of
watching you get eaten alive by alligators isn't exactly
a morale booster.

After I climbed from the tub I picked out a dress I
thought Mom might like to see me wearing—little
yellow flowers and a Peter Pan collar. I brushed my
hair and put on lipstick—coral blush. Six o'clock
sharp my father's Lincoln coasted up in front of the
house. Smiling at me from the passenger seat, my
mother seemed like a new woman. She wore her
favorite lace collar secured with a cameo that she'd
inherited from her mother. I'd only seen her take it
from its hallowed spot in her jewel box once before
in my life. Mom looked positively pretty. Even her
bun seemed to ride a little higher on the nape of her
neck.

Pop, as usual, looked debonair and sounded dour.

"I don't like this neighborhood, Toni. Too close to
North Avenue, where it's all drugs and guns. I saw on
TV where they just found a nurse murdered in Druid
Hill."

"The neighborhood's all right," I mumbled as I
clenched my fists. "Mostly all students and retired old
ladies."

"Toni's doing okay for herself, Paolo," my mother spoke up. "See how pretty and healthy she looks?"

"Pretty is as pretty does."

"Thanks for the vote of confidence, Pop. Mom, you're looking pretty terrific yourself. *Sei bèlla!*" I leaned over and gave her cheek a kiss.

Al and my sister have a three-bedroom rancher in the planned community of Columbia. It's a lot different from the city. As Sandy repeatedly points out, the air is cleaner. Everyone has a nice little backyard and a driveway to park their car off the street, and racial relations are harmonious.

Call me a nut, but all those aluminum-covered houses sitting like holes in their doughnut of freshly mowed grass leave me cold. Of course, I know that doesn't make sense. I mean, here I am scared I'm going to get my throat cut by a serial killer while my sister's worst fear is that her baby-sitter will sneak her boyfriend over after the kids are in bed.

Once Mom and Pop were settled in the living room with Al and my demon nephews for entertainment, Sandy yanked me into the kitchen. Eyes blazing, she pinned me against the stove.

"What's this Al tells me about another person getting murdered in your apartment building?"

"Hey, nothing escapes the eagle eye of that hubby of yours, does it?"

"Stop mouthing off and tell me what's going on!"

"You need help with the lasagna?" Mom came in around the corner.

Sandy and I both jerked as though we had a guilty secret. Sandy said, "Go back and sit down, Mom. Relax for a change. This is your night to take it easy."

Ignoring her, my mother homed in on the oven door and peered in through the glass. "The sauce is bubbling. Another five minutes and it'll be ready. I see you already set the table in the dining room with your best dishes. Looks so pretty. You got a salad needs tossing?"

"Everything's all fixed in the refrigerator, Mom. You don't need to worry about a thing." Sandy took our mother by the shoulders and pried her away from the stove. "Al has a bottle of champagne for you. Let's get him to open it up so we can have a toast to the healthiest lady in Baltimore."

"Who are you talking about?"

"You, Mom, I'm talking about you! You're queen for the day here."

"What about the garlic bread? You need to put the garlic bread in."

Sandy pushed behind Mom as if she were the little choo-choo engine that could. "Toni will take care of that, won't you, Toni?"

"Sure thing." I gave Mom's thin cheek a peck, and she threw her arms around my neck.

"Oh, Toni, it does my heart good to see you here back with the family like this."

"C'mon, Mom, out of the kitchen. Out, out!" Sandy leaned over and whispered in my ear, "We'll talk later."

Alone, I stuck the bread in the oven and tried to figure a way to avoid my sister's promised crossexamination. During dinner it was easy. Between Al and Pop talking in loud voices about crime and the rotten economy, and the kids getting into food fights, the attention was definitely not centered on me. While

Mom and Sandy tried to reason Billy out of a tantrum because Alex had stolen his Gumby, I looked around the dining room.

To be honest, not only do I seriously question my sister's selection in husbands, I also don't like her decorating style. My parents' place is filled with inherited furniture from the fifties lined up against dark, cardboard-looking paneling. Walking into their living room is instant depression. Sandy's house runs to Sears & Roebuck modern. She'd glued marbleized mirror squares to the wall opposite me. All through dinner I kept catching my streaky image and grimacing at it.

Yet not so long ago Sandy and I admired exactly the same things. As kids we were always together, giggling about stuff in our bedroom, telling each other everything. When she started dating, she'd come home and give me the complete play-by-play with no reservations. It was as if I were her younger mirror image. Now, look at us. We might as well live on different planets. I understand how it happened, yet it still bewilders me. Maybe the way your life turns out really doesn't depend on you at all. Maybe, like they say, it's all a crapshoot. I don't like thinking this way, though. I want to believe I have some say.

"Into the bedroom," Sandy said after we'd cleared the table.

"Let me finish cleaning up in here. You go sit down in the living room with the folks and take it easy."

"No dice, Toni. I want a word with you." She hustled me down the hall and into her and Al's bedroom.

"Aren't you afraid Mom or Pop will come busting in?"

"Al will keep them busy. He's got a zillion snaps of the kids to wave around. Don't try weaseling out of this. I want to know what's going on."

"Okay." I sat down on the bed. "Do you really like this orange-and-brown spread, Sandy?"

"What do you mean, do I like it? I bought it, didn't I?" She scowled. "What's this about finding the girl who lives above you dead in Druid Hill?"

"That's it. They found her dead in Druid Hill."

"For God's sake, are you trying to kill our mother?"

"What's our mother got to do with this?"

"She's just come back from the dead herself. She's all excited about pulling the family back together, and here you are messing around with guns and murder."

"Guns?"

"Al said you're still trying to buy one."

"He did, did he?" I glared at the door. All evening my brother-in-law and I had been ignoring each other. Now I wondered if Al was the reason why I'd had to commission Randall to pry my registration out of the bureaucracy in blue. Oh, I wouldn't put it past him. "Tell your thickheaded husband to keep his nose out of my business."

"Tell him yourself. He's driving you home tonight."

"What?"

"Don't give me that look, Toni. Going nuclear isn't going to do you one bit of good. He's driving you home and checking out that apartment of yours before he leaves you alone there. I can't ask Pop to do it. It would kill him and Mom to find out how you've got yourself in trouble all over again."

Once Sandy's made up her mind to something, arguing is a waste of breath. That's why later that evening I found myself locked up with Al in his Camaro.

For the first twenty minutes we rode along in barbed silence. Al drove with one arm and stared straight ahead through the windshield. I made myself as small as possible on the passenger seat. Finally I decided to break the invisible barrier.

"There's a favor you could do me."

His head jerked around, and he looked at me as if I were a talking Chihuahua and he wasn't sure whether to listen to it or drown it. "Oh, yeah? What's that?"

"You could keep going on Martin Luther King and take me through Druid Hill Park."

"At this hour? What for?"

"I'd like to see the spot where Susie Zillig was killed."

"What makes you think I know it?"

"Do you?"

He glowered and then snorted. "Okay, Toni, I'll take you past, but I'm not getting out to prowl around and look for clues. I get enough of that stuff when I'm on duty." He swung the car to the right on 395 and headed out on MLK Boulevard.

"You're being unnaturally nice, Al. It's making me nervous."

"Don't give me that mouth. I promised your sister I'd see you got home safe, and I'll do it. That doesn't mean I'm happy to be your chauffeur."

"Obviously. I guess Sandy must have come down pretty hard."

"She's tearing her hair about you. It's only natural after I gave her the lowdown on where you live. You're the baby in the family and she's the big sister, so she feels responsible. Why the hell don't you give us all a break and move to the suburbs where it's safer?"

"I don't like the suburbs. Even if I did, I couldn't live there without a car, and it wouldn't be easy for me to pass a driver's test."

"Oh, yeah," he said as if remembering an obscure fact. "Sometimes you seem enough like a normal person that I forget about the reading thing."

"Oh, thanks. You say the sweetest things. Anyhow, the 'burbs aren't all that safe. Even in Columbia women get raped and murdered and banks get robbed."

"So far nobody's been stuffed into a trunk for their wallet."

Al was referring to a recent crime spree. Just a few weeks after a guy got out of prison, he started holding up well-dressed men in a downtown parking garage and stuffing them into trunks. He'd killed one of them.

"Hey, I've got that figured for an entrepreneurial opportunity," I retorted. "All I need is someone with a little imagination to bankroll me."

"What are you talking about?"

"Car trunk survival kits. You know—a freeze-dried sandwich, a thermos of wine, maybe a can opener or a miniacetylene torch."

"Hardy-har. No matter how bad it is, you've gotta make a joke."

He swung the Camaro onto Druid Park Drive. As we cruised past the lake, its dark skin glittered in the moonlight like black patent leather. It looked cold, beautiful, and deadly. I pictured that same silvery moonlight playing over Susie's naked dead body and clenched my fists. Truth is, I'd been trying not to think about her too much these past couple of days. Seeing her body in that morgue was just too vivid and painful. But I knew I couldn't avoid trying to figure out what had happened to her any longer.

The park is large and, word is, dangerous at night. Neighborhoods riddled with drugs border it. Susie isn't the only dead person who's turned up in Druid Hill. Al cruised along the curving drives and didn't touch the brake until he approached the zoo's reptile house on the right. He pointed to the left where a stand of trees grew close to the road in a sort of dell. "Corpse was found in there."

"Who found it?"

"Gang of kids, probably looking for a place to shoot up."

"They reported it?"

"Not exactly. They were scattering like bats out of hell when a cruiser spotted them and nabbed a couple."

I could imagine they would have been terrified and hysterical. It would be a shock to go into the woods for an innocent little drug deal and stumble over a naked dead woman. For Susie's body had been found naked. I remembered that from the morgue.

"How do you happen to know all this?"

"It's my district. Word gets around. This Susie Zillig living in the same building as Rebecca Kelso makes her murder kind of a big deal."

"Any sign they're going to catch who did it?"

"Not so far, though I know they're working hard on it. Trouble is, whoever the creep is, he's clever."

"What do you mean, clever?"

"He's smart about not leaving evidence. When he worked this Susie over, he stripped her naked. But he must have been wearing gloves, or maybe a whole plastic bodysuit. Anyhow, he didn't leave prints or hairs."

"You're saying that happened here in the park?"

"I doubt it, but I don't know where he did it. It's not my case."

"Al, how exactly was Susie murdered? I mean, I know she was raped and her throat was slit, but—"

He shot me a quick glance. "Word is, he didn't kill her quick. You know, tied her up and played with her. Then slit her throat while he was coming inside her."

Al gunned the accelerator and we were out of there. I sat back on the seat and looked at the gentle hills sweeping past and then down at the lake. I felt sick and cold. My fingers locked and twisted in my lap, and I pressed my thighs together as if my insides might spill out between them. "Since you know so much about Susie's case," I said in an unnaturally high voice, "do you happen to know the detective investigating it?"

"O'Dell? Sure. Funny duck."

"How do you mean?"

"Just a real funny guy. A loner, you know. Keeps to himself. He's like a pit bull when he gets a case, so my guess is one of these days he'll solve this. I wouldn't want to cross him, that's for sure."

O'Dell probably would solve it eventually, I thought. But eventually wasn't soon enough for me. I wanted the monster who'd done these things caught now.

Back at my place, Al found a spot across the street and killed the engine.

"Thanks for the ride."

"I'm not done yet. I gotta come in and check around to see no bogeymen are hiding in your bathroom."

"That's really not necessary."

"Tell Sandy. Come on, let's get this over with. I don't like it any better than you do."

I opened the passenger door before Al could open it for me, though I had no reason to think he was into chivalry. We crossed Charles, and I let him into my place.

"So this is the butcher shop," he commented. "Real homey." He glanced over at the grates on the windows. "Good idea. At least Dracula will have to turn into a bat before he flies in." His gaze fell on Rebecca's plastic bug, which now sat out on top of my TV. "Is that your idea of decoration?"

"It's a conversation piece. Does it look familiar?"

"We don't have roaches in Columbia."

"I mean, have you ever seen anything like it?"

"No, and I'd better not."

I dropped onto the couch and rested my hands on my knees while Al did a quick search of the premises. "Nobody home but us husband killers," he said when he came back out into the living room.

"I wondered when you'd get around to that. You really have it in for me, don't you? You'd probably like it if I got my head chopped off by an ax murderer."

"You just never were good at chitchat. Take it easy. Like I said, the guy who carved up the previous tenants uses knives, not axes."

"You sound certain they were both murdered by the same person."

"I don't know details, but I heard the MO was similar. If the guy gets you, you'll be in the hands of a pro."

"Thanks for the reassurance. I'm curious. Did it ever occur to you I might be telling the truth about how Nick got shot?"

Al's face went red. "Nick didn't *get* shot. You pulled the trigger, baby. And if you mean that bit about how Nick abused you, why should I believe it? Nick and I were buddies way back. He was the closest thing to a brother I had. Why should I believe you, just because he's not around to speak for himself?"

"What is it you think happened that night, then? Do you honestly believe I killed my husband in cold blood?"

"I'll tell you what I think, Toni. You always did have a mouth. I think you and Nick were arguing over something all right. I don't know—maybe you overloaded the charge cards, or maybe he didn't come home for dinner on time. I think things got hot and you grabbed his gun. Maybe you just wanted to wave it around. Then it went off."

I took a minute to digest that. It was close to the truth, actually, except the argument had been much more violent than Al would ever accept. "You believe I shot him by mistake, then?"

"Yeah, I guess so. But anyone who makes mistakes like that should be locked up where they can't make another."

"Now, let me see if I've got this right. Your opinion is because I shot Nick by mistake I should go to prison?"

Al's nostrils fluttered rapidly in and out. "I sure wouldn't allow you anywhere near a gun again."

"Are you responsible for holding up the paperwork on my gun registration?"

"I don't know what you're talking about."

"Al, given this situation, women being murdered right and left where I live, I need to protect myself. The cops aren't going to do it. Believe me, I asked."

Al shrugged, everything about him broadcasting that he didn't give a shit about my problems. "Times are tough. No one but the governor gets a twenty-four-hour bodyguard."

"All right, so I need a gun, and Monday I'm buying one."

"Maybe you've got a point, and I can't stop you. But you'd better learn how it works, so it doesn't go off by accident again."

"Randall is going to teach me how to use it."

"That pansy?" Al snorted. "Some teacher."

"He's good at everything he does. I'm sure he's an excellent teacher."

"I'll bet. Probably uses sequined bullets. You know who you should get to teach you?"

"Who?"

"O'Dell. Before he made detective he was on the sniper squad. They say he never missed."

I was searching for a reply when the phone rang.

"Probably Sandy checking up on me," Al said. "I'd better be going."

I figured the same, so I shouted, "Have a happy day!" and waited until he was out the door before I picked up the receiver. The voice on the other end of the line caught me totally unprepared. "I'm coming to get you, Toni," it whispered. "Not tonight, not tomorrow. But soon. I'm going to fuck you while I cut your throat, and then I'm going to wash my hands in your warm blood."

12

After I *slammed* the receiver onto its cradle, I sprinted to the door to call Al back. Too late. The Camaro had roared off. Back inside, I dialed Randall. I expected at least an answering machine, but the phone rang twenty times without a pickup.

I considered going upstairs to Damon. Pride kept me from that. I took several deep breaths, wrapped my arms across my chest, and walked the perimeter of my apartment. I had new locks on the door, grates on the windows. The place was practically a fortress. Besides, hadn't the creepy, whispery voice said he wouldn't be coming to get me tonight?

Despite this doubtful guarantee, you can bet I didn't get to sleep early. I sat up late waiting for the Volvo. When it didn't appear, I lay in bed speaking to Rebecca. "Are you there? Am I in danger? Are you sticking around here because you want to help me, or because you think I can help you? Sure, I'd like to catch this guy and stop him. God, I hate his guts!

Rebecca, I'm doing the best I can, but maybe you could be a little more helpful. I mean, if you'd just whisper a name or even a description—color of hair, eyes—it would be real handy."

Rebecca didn't answer. In fact, I had no sense of her being around. Since I usually felt her presence before or after something bad, I told myself to relax. Surely if I were in immediate danger, she'd give me a nod. After that I don't remember much, so I must have gone to sleep. Around three o'clock I woke up and looked out my living room window. I saw an unfamiliar sedan parked in front of the building. It didn't have the bulky outlines of a Volvo, so I went back to bed and slept until just before dawn.

I've wondered why it was always Rebecca I felt around me and not Susie. I mean, Susie had confided in me, and I'd argued with her just before she died. You'd think she'd be a stronger presence than a woman I'd never laid eyes on. Yet it was Rebecca I always thought of and whose tormented image haunted me. Except Susie was on my mind when I woke up the next morning.

I wolfed down a bowlful of cold cereal and changed into cycling gear. Outside, I wheeled my bike to the sidewalk and paused. The car I'd noticed in the middle of the night still sat there. It was a rusty yellow Pinto that had to be almost as old as me. Someone was inside it.

Gingerly I peered through the grimy glass. O'Dell sat with his head propped between the seat and the driver's door and his eyes closed. As I stared, his brown lashes snapped up like window blinds and he stared back.

"Why are you here?" I mouthed.

He leaned forward and cranked the window down an inch. "What are you doing up at this hour?"

"I get my question answered first."

"What was it? I didn't hear."

"What are you doing in front of my apartment? Did you sleep in your car?"

"Isn't that obvious?" He ran a hand over the pointy black stubble peppering his chin. "Christ, what a way to spend a Saturday night. Listen, step into my parlor, will you? I'm getting a crick in my neck."

I hesitated and then propped my bike against a tree and opened the Pinto's door. It felt frail from a combination of rust and metal fatigue. Inside, his seat covers were a plastic brown-and-white weave that struck a chord from my childhood. They were ripped around the welting, and tufts of grayish stuffing showed through. In one spot on the bare metal floor I could see daylight. Notebooks, newspapers, boxes, and clothes piled the backseat so high that I wondered how he could check traffic out his rear window.

"Impressive set of wheels you've got here."

"They take me where I want to go. When I'm on duty I drive an unmarked from the fleet."

"Why did you want to camp out in front of my place on your off-duty hours?"

"You did say something about wanting protection."

I could hardly believe my ears. "You parked out here on your own time to watch over me?"

He shrugged. "I had nothing better to do."

That must mean the poor guy's personal life was even more dreary than mine. I would have expressed sympathy except I knew from his clamped jaw and the glint in his eyes that it wouldn't be welcome. "Well, thanks. I wish I'd known I had a knight-errant out there. Last night I had kind of a bad experience." I told him about my obscene phone call.

"Is that why you're up so early? Going to run away from home on your bike?" He didn't smile.

"I thought I'd pedal over to Druid Hill. My brother-in-law showed me where they found Susie's body. I thought I'd have a look in daylight."

"Why?"

"I don't know. I just want to." Because I felt guilty and responsible, that's why. I kept wondering if my visit to Espey had anything to do with Susie's murder.

"If you're thinking you can find a clue in the grass, forget it. Forensics picked the place clean."

"I'm not looking for clues," I lied. That had really been in the back of my mind.

O'Dell sandpapered his hand on his chin again. "Okay, put the bike someplace safe. I'll take you. Just let me stop at a fast-food on the way and grab a cup of caffeine."

He pulled into a McDonald's on North and went in for coffee and, undoubtedly, a visit to the men's room. I suppose after his noble stint in this wreck of a car I should have invited him to my place for breakfast. But I didn't want to get social. Attractive or not, I found the guy a little scary. There was something so shut-down-for-action about him. He had a way of looking at me I didn't like. It was as if I were a fly some kid had dewinged and left floundering around in a bowlful of water and he were an observer in sixth-grade science class. I told myself not to be so paranoid. It couldn't be as bad as that if he'd spent the night guarding me.

He came out holding two cups, and I noticed how he was dressed. Jeans, T-shirt, and an orange-and-black Orioles jacket. The outfit looked a lot better on him than the rumpled suit and stained raincoat he wore during business hours. Since he was on the late shift, he must have changed clothes and driven over to my place right after he'd gone off duty. Hey, I was flattered.

He slid into the car and handed me one of the cups without comment.

"Thanks."

"Nothing."

Gulping hot coffee from his free hand, he peeled out onto North. Five minutes later the Pinto shuddered to a stop in front of the patch of trees Al had shown me. I'd emptied my cup and sat all folded together like a fan. Now that we were here, I didn't want to get out.

"Did you know that a guy named Olmsted designed this park?" I said.

O'Dell stared at me.

"Yeah, about a hundred years ago he was pretty famous. Designed Central Park in New York and even had a hand in Yosemite. He had a vision about what parks should be. He called them 'the green lung of the city,' a place to rest and refresh the eye."

"I guess he didn't picture them as dumps for nude bodies."

"Nope."

"I thought you couldn't read. How do you know about Olmsted?"

Now I stared at him. "Who told you about my dyslexia?"

"Your brother-in-law."

"Thank you, Al Pennak." Should I inform O'Dell that blabbermouth Al had called him a "funny duck" and given me lots of details about Susie's death that were probably considered top secret? "Well, I'll never win any spelling bees, but I can read now, sort of. I have to admit I didn't read about Olmsted. I saw a TV show about him on PBS."

I pushed open the Pinto's door, jammed my icy hands deep into my jacket pocket, and walked up the small grassy rise to the little V of woods. Spring rode the breeze. Under my Reeboks the damp earth sprang back like elastic. Baby green laced the tall beeches and peeped from the undergrowth.

O'Dell pointed at a trampled patch of half-rotted leaves. "There."

I pictured Susie, her body sprawled, her eyes open, blood covering her mouth. "It was chilly that night. Not exactly comfortable for an open-air rape in the park." My voice sounded unnaturally high.

"He didn't do it here."

"He didn't?" I remembered that what Al had said indicated it had been done elsewhere.

"Everything points to the killer just dumping the body. The murder itself probably happened some-place warm and comfortable. And it must have been somebody she knew and trusted. From everything we've learned about this girl, she was not a gullible lady. Unless she was forcibly abducted, she wouldn't have gone with just any guy off the street who gave her a come-on."

"No, never."

"She was last seen on the shuttle between Hopkins

and a parking lot west of Fells Point. She never took her car out of the lot."

"So it could have been someone she met on the shuttle or in the lot?"

"Or someone she'd made an appointment with, or maybe some guy off the street who bopped her on the head and stuck her in his trunk. It was dark when she got off that shuttle, and there weren't many people on it. It's a big lot, and the area is deserted at that time of night. Her car was parked at the back where it wouldn't have been difficult to assault her after dark."

"I suppose you've checked out the people on the shuttle?"

"We've interviewed the parking lot attendants and everyone on the shuttle. A couple people remember seeing her get off alone. After that, nothing."

A scene composed itself in my mind. Susie heads toward her car. She's tired, and her head is down. Maybe she's brooding about her argument with me earlier in the day, cursing me for visiting Espey. Just as she bends over to stick her key in the door, a dark figure rises up next to her and hits her over the head. She sags into his arms, and he pushes her into his car. She wakes up naked in the basement of a house somewhere, or maybe it's a garage. Probably she's tied and gagged so she can't move or scream. But she can see, and what she sees is him standing there with a knife and an evil grin.

I suppose I'd pictured myself scrounging around among the trees looking for some sort of clue. Now I didn't want to have anything more to do with this place. "I guess you guys did a pretty thorough search down there."

"No leaf unturned."

"You didn't find anything?"

"Footprints. Since the earth's been soft for a couple weeks now and the place was trampled by the kids who discovered the body, no way of telling for sure if the prints were the killer's."

I hesitated, needing to ask but not wanting to. "Do you think Susie suffered much?"

"You want me to say that she didn't."

I knew my question had been stupid, but certainly— that was what I wanted to hear.

"Sorry, lying isn't one of my vices. I think she suffered."

"The way she was murdered, was it similar to what happened to Rebecca?"

"Similar. A knife was used in the same way. Both women were raped. Unfortunately, semen samples from Rebecca's rape were from a nonsecreter."

"What's that?"

"It just means they didn't tell us much. Susie's samples aren't back yet. Other forensic information seems to indicate the same perpetrator. The nail polish was a new touch. There was nothing like that with Rebecca. If it is the same guy, he's getting more creative as he goes along."

A red tide of hate for her killer almost blinded me. For a moment I stood blinking, my brain buzzing, my chest rising and falling too fast. "This place is giving me the creeps. Let's get out of here."

O'Dell dropped me back at my place. In the entry I heard footsteps on the stairs and glanced up. A cute blonde with a bouncy ponytail came tripping down. She wore a pink warm-up suit and no makeup. Her lips had that swollen look of someone who's just been thoroughly kissed.

"Oh, hi."

"Hi there."

"I guess you must be Damon's new neighbor."

"That's me. Name's Toni Credella."

"I'm Lynley."

"Glad to meet you, Lynley. Any friend of Damon's is a friend of mind."

Her pink mouth formed a surprised O. "Well, bye."

"Bye."

I gazed as she slipped out and skipped down to a sporty little blue car. Good old Damon. I was glad to see he wasn't doing anything foolish like pining away over me. After I'd locked and bolted my door, I stripped and took a scalding shower. When every part of me had been scrubbed raw and I'd changed into jeans and an old T-shirt, I did t'ai chi for about an hour.

That finished, I still had most of the afternoon to get through.

On impulse, I dialed Jeff Simpler's number. I wanted that book of his and figured Randall might help me read the hard parts. When nobody answered, I threw the receiver back in its cradle. Frustrated, I paced around the kitchen a couple of times, then opened a can of minestrone and peeled a banana. It took me about ten minutes to eat lunch.

The next three hours stretched in front of me without landmarks. Not wanting to spend that time cooped in the apartment thinking about how Susie died, I unlocked my bike and headed out Falls Road to Mt. Washington. I figured if the Simplers weren't home, I'd leave a note on their door.

As I wheeled up their empty drive, I gave out a little moan. For me, even a simple task like composing a note about wanting the book was a major production. Nobody answered the doorbell, so I fished a ballpoint and a pad of paper out of my jacket pocket. I was just trying to figure out where to put the *i* in "friend" when Simpler's white Camry station wagon rolled up. There were two-by-fours strapped to the roof rack, and when Jeff Simpler got out he was carrying a big orange toolbox. He looked really surprised to see me, and all of a sudden I felt embarrassed for being such a pest.

"Hi."

"Hello there." He walked toward me very slowly. He was dressed in jeans and a chambray shirt. His short blond hair looked shaggier than usual, and I could see where he might benefit from a shower and a shave.

"Looks as if you've been working hard."

"I've been out at my father's place doing some plastering."

I glanced at his hands for signs of white stuff, but they, unlike the rest of him, were squeaky clean. "I'm sorry for showing up unannounced like this. I just came on an impulse. I thought I'd like to borrow that book you mentioned."

For a minute he looked confused. Then light dawned. *"The Pathology of Sexual Violence?* Why, of course. If you don't mind, let's go in the side door."

"Sure." I followed him around to the drive and into the kitchen. It looked a lot messier than when I'd seen it last. The dishes from what might have been last Friday's meal hadn't been put away.

"You've caught me with my housekeeping down.

Gloria is off visiting her mother, and I've been batching it the last couple of days."

"I'm really sorry for barging in unannounced like this. I guess you must think I'm a nuisance."

"I don't think that at all."

"How long will Gloria be away?"

"I'm not sure. She's unhappy about all the time I've had to spend fixing up my father's place, and we had a little spat. Typical newlywed misunderstanding." He grimaced.

"You guys are newlyweds? I thought you'd been married years."

"Oh, no. Barely six months. Look, if you don't mind waiting here, I'd like to change my clothes real quick. Then I'll get you the book."

"I can come back another time."

"No, no. Just take a minute." He pulled out a ladder-back chair and watched while I dropped onto its rush seat. Then he hurried off down the hall. A minute later I heard him running upstairs.

I really felt awkward. My glance swept the countertop, and it occurred to me that I could rinse off some of those dishes for him. But somehow I felt he wouldn't like that, so I just sat and waited. He was back fifteen minutes later. He wore a fresh shirt and khakis and carried a book that looked as if it probably tipped the scales at three pounds.

"A bit of a weighty tome, I'm afraid," he said as he set it in my lap.

"Wow. You wrote all that?"

"It took me five years of staying up nights and a lot of research, but, yes, I did."

He looked proud of himself, and as I opened the

dark red cover and flipped through some of the pages, I could see why. The print was small, and I didn't see much white space. My vision started to swim. How was I ever going to read something like this?

"How about a cup of coffee?"

"Oh, I don't want to put you out any more than I already—"

"C'mon. I could use one, and you look as if you could, too." He was already loading the coffeemaker. As we waited for it to perk, he tidied up. "Tell me what's been going on."

"Not much. I guess you probably know more about Susie Zillig's murder than I do, since you're connected with the police department."

"I've been busy with school, so they don't keep me that well informed. I do know that Gus O'Dell is handling the case."

"That's his name, Gus?"

"Short for Augustus."

Now that I'd heard it, the name seemed right. "I spent the morning with him, as a matter of fact."

"Oh?" The aroma of fresh-brewed coffee blessed the kitchen. Jeff filled two mugs and, after I declined milk, handed me one.

"What is this stuff? It smells great."

"Mocha hazelnut. When it comes to coffee, I indulge myself. What do you think of Detective O'Dell?"

I sipped the scrumptious coffee. "Well, he's not exactly Mister Congeniality, is he?"

Jeff laughed. "No, far from it." He hesitated, as if weighing whether or not to say something. Then he shrugged lightly. "He's an interesting guy. Are you aware he was a marine sniper?"

"I heard he was a sniper for the Baltimore police."

"That too. When he was promoted to detective, I reviewed his file. He's a classic case, a paradigm of the antisocial loner. Both parents alcoholics who died young. He was farmed out to rural distant relatives who ignored him. Dropped out of school in eighth grade and spent most of his time in the woods alone hunting. He became an excellent shot. He admits himself that he likes the thrill of stalking game and then bagging it with a single shot. On his seventeenth birthday he walked into a marine recruiting station. Two years later he won the Wimbledon Cup."

"What's that?"

"A high-powered rifle competition. Winning it means you're the best, maybe even the best rifle sharpshooter in America."

"What does a marine sniper shoot at?"

"That I don't know. Rumor is he did a lot of top-secret Special Forces work in South America."

"You mean he assassinated people?"

Jeff considered. "I can tell you this. Once during a hostage situation in Baltimore I saw him use a high-powered rifle to put a bullet in a man's head, and he didn't blink an eye. Showed no remorse, either. If anything, it seemed to have made his day."

I tried to picture that. "Not that I belong to the O'Dell Fan Club or anything, but was the man he shot threatening someone else?"

"His ex-wife and his three-year-old son."

"Well, that makes sense, then. The police wouldn't have put a sharpshooter on the job if they hadn't believed it was necessary."

"Oh, yes, people like O'Dell make excellent law-enforcement officers. What were you doing with O'Dell today?"

While he listened intently, I put his book on the table and described our visit to the woods in Druid Hill.

"Doesn't sound as if it produced much," he commented when I'd finished.

"No. Just the heebie-jeebies. I keep thinking how awful it must have been for her, how scared she must have been when she realized what was going to happen to her."

"There are things it's better not to think about, Toni."

"I know, but—I've got this guilty feeling."

"Guilty? Why? You didn't kill Susie."

"That's just it. I'm not so sure. I keep wondering if my going to see Espey could have anything to do with it?"

Jeff shook his head. "That's not possible. Espey's still in prison, where he's been for the last twenty years. Toni, you're too willing to see things as your fault. Just accept that there are evil people out there who do evil things. It's absurd for you to feel guilty when the person who actually murdered Susie probably doesn't."

"How do you know he doesn't?"

"Because I've spent time studying violent psychopaths and know a thing or two about them." Jeff pulled the book across the table, flipped it open, ran his thumb down a page, and began to read. " 'Developmental hallmarks consistently set off the psychopathic personality. Such characters tend to be antisocial, yet with an overwhelming desire to manipulate and control others. They operate in the present moment, with little regard to future consequences. Though they may be very clever, with well-developed senses of humor, their sense of right and wrong does not extend to the treatment of others, but applies only to their own well-being and personal gratification in the most pragmatic sense.'"

"So this killer probably isn't having nightmares about the women he's tortured and murdered?"

"Probably not any more than a hunter does about the rabbits he's bagged for tonight's stew. In fact, he's probably following the case with great interest. It wouldn't surprise me if he considers himself to be much smarter than the police and is enjoying baffling them. Hell, he might even be one of them."

I felt my eyebrows rise. "Actually, O'Dell sounds a lot like that description of a violent psychopath you just read."

Jeff laughed ruefully. "You'd be surprised how many sociopaths one finds on both sides of the law. One pathological personality chasing another, so to speak."

"Maybe it takes one to know one."

"Maybe, except the kind of personality we're speaking of doesn't really 'know' others in the sense the average person like you or I might mean. He's incapable of empathizing. Not that he isn't intelligent. These people are often diabolically clever. But their cleverness is all a charade. They're like actors, smiling, charming, flattering in order to manipulate an audience for their own gratification."

"Aren't we all like that?" I asked. Part of me was toying with the bizarre idea of O'Dell actually being the killer he was pretending to chase. On the other hand, I hadn't seen O'Dell smile yet. If he wanted to manipulate people, he could do with a few charm lessons. Besides, would a psychopath who considered nobody important but himself have sat in a car all night to make sure of my safety?

"We all manipulate to an extent," Jeff was saying. "But most of us are able to keep it in check and to feel a real sense of connection with our fellow beings, at least on occasion. A psychopath doesn't. The only connection he wants is to feel superior to them and to have power over them. And of course, the ultimate power is the power of life and death."

"But these crimes aren't just murders. This guy rapes, too, and his victims are all women."

"Ah, yes, sex. Sex and power. Try as we may to separate the two, we never really can." He cocked his head. "I don't have to tell you that, do I, Toni?"

I stiffened. "How do you mean?"

"I mean you suffered through a violent marriage. You must have some of your own ideas about sex and power."

"Yes." I rubbed my hands together. Normally this was not something I discussed. But Simpler was trained to help people with emotional problems. Maybe he could shed some light on my messed-up inner workings. "Sex scares me. It's so complicated. No matter how hard I try, I never really understand everything that's going on with it and with me. Not completely."

"Except with your lizard brain."

"What?"

"The part of you that's purely instinctual knew that

when your husband made love to you it wasn't all hearts and flowers, didn't it, Toni?"

"I guess so. I guess I always knew it was exciting partly because of his aggression and my submission, but I didn't want to admit it to myself. I wanted to believe in the kind of love on the valentine cards."

"I'm concerned about you, and I am a therapist, so I'm going to ask. Have you had lovers since?"

"Since my husband died?" Jeff was looking at me so intently. He seemed to really care. I'd been wanting to talk about my experience with Damon. If Randall were around, I might have told him. But now Jeff had asked point-blank and appeared really to want to help.

"One, an artist who lives on the top floor of my building."

"Has that been a healing experience?"

"We only did it once, and I don't intend to repeat."

"Why not? Was he such a bad lover?"

"He was okay. It's me who has the problem. I'm just not ready for intimacy yet. It still scares me." I looked into his light blue eyes, which were as clear as mountain lakes and didn't seem to condemn or to judge. Then I opened my mouth and said something that probably surprised me more than it did him. "You know what scares me most about pulling the trigger on Nick?"

"No, do you want to tell me?"

"Yes, I guess I do. Sometimes I'm afraid that I didn't shoot him because I was terrified of his violence the way I claimed during my trial. Sometimes I'm afraid that was just a convenient excuse and that I really shot him for making mincemeat out of my girlish fantasies about hearts and flowers. Pretty sicko, huh?"

"Toni, our fantasies about love are our most precious possession." He reached out and touched my cold hand. I was shivering. "You have to forgive yourself. Everyone else has. But that won't mean a thing until you do, too."

It wasn't true that everyone else had forgiven me. Al hadn't, for one. And I wasn't too sure about Pop, either. But I appreciated what Simpler had said. He was trying to be kind, and kindness always makes me feel like bursting into tears, like some dumb little kid at a Lassie movie. Only in this case, I was the bitch with the problem. Awkwardly, I thanked him. Then, clutching his book, I got up and backed out of his kitchen. "I gotta get back home," I told him. "I have a friend waiting for me."

That was a polite lie. No friend waited for me at home. When I walked into the apartment, it was as still as a forgotten closet. Warm, though. One thing I'll say for Aronchick, he didn't stint on heat.

Forcing myself to consider practical matters, I retrieved the cash I had stuffed into a pocket sewn into the bottom of my laundry bag. I've never been one to put money in the bank. With my reading difficulties it's a pain to deal with the paperwork, and I'm never flush enough to get greedy about collecting interest. On the scary scale, right now the state of my finances was right up there with everything else in my life. After I paid for this gun I intended picking up on Monday, I'd be down to my last twenty bucks. Good thing I was about to start a job with an hourly wage. For that, at least, I had to be grateful to loverboy Damon.

I called Mom and asked how she was doing. She's

never been one to talk much on the phone, or to talk much at all, for that matter. After an awkward four or five minutes in which I assured her I was happy, healthy, and wise, we said ciao. Then I dialed Sandy. She and Al weren't home. Probably out living it up at the local mall. After that, I spread peanut butter on four crackers and settled down with Simpler's book. I couldn't have been more than a couple of pages into it when I developed the headache that ate Baltimore.

Okay, so trying to figure out all those long words sent my tiny brain into spasms. The subject wasn't brightening my afternoon, either. Really, I wondered how Simpler had had the stomach to write at such length about minds more twisted than rotini. How had he managed to avoid going into a major depression himself?

I flipped to the table of contents. The chapter headings included interviews with sexually violent prisoners. I'd registered the page number on that and started trying to find it when I noticed something peculiar going on with my body. Goose bumps covered my arms, and the room felt like the outside of an igloo in an ice storm.

I checked the hall thermostat. It read 72. I went to my bedroom to get a sweater. The temperature in there felt perfectly normal. Back out in the living room it was like walking into a deep freeze. I stood shivering and stroking my forearms. The tiny hairs on them stood upright, and I knew the same was true on the back of my neck and all over my body. I looked all around me, and though I saw no one, I felt sure I wasn't alone. "Rebecca?" I said softly.

Instead of answering, whoever was playing with the

atmosphere dropped the temperature even lower. With a panicky half turn in the air, I dashed for the kitchen and dialed Randall.

"Sure you can spend the night," he said. "In fact, your timing is excellent. I'm just back from driving Jonathan to the airport. He won't be back until Friday, so we'll have the place to ourselves."

Joy and relief. Right now I'd accept an invitation to Death Valley in August to get out of here. If I could stay with Randall, I knew I'd be all right.

"I'll fix us something fabulous for dinner," he promised. "How does crab-stuffed flounder and a bottle of Domaine de Joy, 1990, sound?"

"Oh, Randall, anything, anything. I can't wait."

"Don't ride that silly bicycle of yours. Sit tight and I'll come get you, okay?"

"Okay."

I hate to admit this, but when I hung up, tears were rolling down my face. I must have stood there gulping and gasping for a good ten minutes. Finally I pulled myself together and started throwing clothes into my knapsack. "Sorry, Rebecca," I whispered as I grabbed my jacket and galloped out the door. "Whatever you're trying to tell me, I'm too scared to hear it."

13

Monday morning Randall insisted on dropping me off at work. As we rolled up Falls Road in his Mercedes, we got jealous looks from people on the sidewalk.

"I feel like the queen out viewing the lowly knaves in the slums."

"So, enjoy it. I always do."

"How can I enjoy it when I'm probably lowlier than they are?"

"You worry too much about details, Toni." He pulled up across from Smith's building. "Or maybe you don't worry enough. Good luck on the job."

I stepped onto the curb, then grinned and waved as the Mercedes sped off. Sunday night Randall and I had stayed warm and comfy in his designer minipalace. He'd made popcorn and we'd wolfed it down while we'd watched an old Thin Man movie on his VCR. It's truly amazing how much liquor that slinky couple tossed down in between tossing off witty repartee.

After the movie Randall had opened a bottle of Bergerac, and we'd stayed up drinking wine and gossiping. I told him about Augustus O'Dell.

"He actually sat outside your house all night? This man sounds intriguing. Attractive?"

I sipped and considered. "Maybe. In a weird, antisocial, Clint Eastwood sort of way."

"Ah, once again the magnetic draw of the misfit. You're interested in him, aren't you?"

"What?" I drew myself up and looked outraged. "Why would I be interested in another cop? And one who's made a career of shooting people in the head, to boot?"

"I don't know, kiddo. You tell me."

I'd responded by changing the subject and then thinking about it all night while I lay in splendor on Jonathan's Sheridan sheets. O'Dell didn't interest me the way Randall had suggested, I'd told myself. I was just curious about him. Maybe he fascinated me the same way a fox would fascinate a rabbit. On second thought, I hadn't liked that analogy. I remembered what Jeff Simpler had said about a psychopath having no more conscience about killing women than a hunter would have about bagging bunnies for dinner. I was the rabbit O'Dell was supposedly protecting.

Now on the first day of my job I dismissed such thoughts from my mind and headed upstairs to Smith's studio. It couldn't possibly be as wonderful as I remembered, I warned myself. It couldn't possibly be all gold and sunshine and soaring whitewashed ceilings. But it was. Bill, with his warm eyes and piano-key smile, greeted me with courtesy and charm.

That's not to say he didn't work me hard. I spent the morning learning how to make and apply gesso. It's a mixture of chalk and rabbit-skin glue used to fill wood before the actual gilding can begin. It's amazing how many artistic processes depend on rabbit-skin glue. Every time you walk through an art gallery, offer up a little prayer for all the bunnies who bit the dust to make the wonders on the walls possible. What was this rabbit thing, anyway? I couldn't seem to get away from the critters.

"How ya doin'?" Bill asked in his soft drawl.

I was spreading gesso on a nineteenth-century American picture frame. "Okay, I hope."

"Looks fine. You have a light hand. What do you think about it?"

"What do I think?"

"You believe you're going to like the work?"

"I love it." I turned to look up at him. "I'm grateful that you're giving me a chance despite . . ."

"Despite what?"

"Well, it's not as if I'm that well qualified."

"You got what it takes—a good eye, a good hand, a good heart."

Smith told me he didn't believe in slavedriver hours, so I got off work at three. That gave me time to catch a couple of buses and buy my gun before the shop closed.

"What's wrong, babe?" Randall juggled a load of groceries in one arm while he unlocked his door.

After he'd let us both into his apartment, I took my purchase out of its brown paper sack and held it up. "A Taurus 83 revolver. Two hundred and forty-nine dollars and sixty-nine cents. That leaves me twenty bucks until my first paycheck, and I don't get that for another two weeks."

"Hey, never wave a firearm around." Randall took the pistol out of my hand and walked on through to the kitchen. After he'd dumped the groceries on his tile counter, he flipped open the chamber on the Taurus to make sure it didn't contain any bullets and then hefted it.

"Nothing fancy, but looks businesslike."

"Looks too businesslike. Now that I've gone and bought the thing, it scares me."

"Given that this is the same type of handgun that killed your husband, I'm not surprised."

"Randall, you really think it's wrong of me to want a gun so I can protect myself?"

He looked at me thoughtfully, then crooked his forefinger. "Follow me, *liebchen*."

He headed down the hall, and I trailed after. I've only been in Randall's bedroom a couple of times—once to do his curtains and once when he wanted my opinion on an Italian chandelier he'd just acquired at one of the Howard Street antique shops. On both occasions I'd been dazed. For sheer wanton luxury and a florid display of pattern, the room could only be described as the Sun King meets Laura Ashley. One of its prize pieces is a ten-foot French-style linen press. Now, Randall turned an antique key in one of its curved inlaid doors and stood back. I caught the smell of oil and metal.

"My God, you must have half a dozen pistols there."

"Five. A Smith and Wesson combat Magnum, a Smith and Wesson masterpiece, a Ruger Redhawk, and two Colt revolvers."

"What are you doing with all these six-shooters? I thought you were a man of peace?"

"They're not all six-shooters, and as a matter of fact, I belong to the NRA."

"You?"

"You can't compete in certain handgun matches if you don't pay dues to the organization."

"But you were so dead set against my buying a gun."

"With your record, I still think it's a bad idea. If you shot someone a second time, even though clearly in self-defense, it would still look bad. But I have to admit, hearing what's happening in your life, I'm beginning to come around to your point of view. Better you should look suspicious than you should look good in your coffin."

"Well, thanks for that much." He shut the door on the linen press. "Do you ever carry a weapon with you?"

"If I'm going to be out late at night."

"Is that legal?"

"To carry a concealed weapon? Sure, if you have the right kind of permit."

"But is it safe, I mean, to walk around with a gun in your pocket?"

"First, it's not in my pocket. It's in a holster. Second, it's safe because I know how to handle firearms. That's the difference between us, Toni. I know how to treat a handgun and you don't. Time you learned. Tomorrow I'll pick you up after work and take you to a shooting range. Okay?"

"Okay."

* * *

Three-fifteen the next afternoon Randall's Mercedes breezed up to the curb, and I climbed in. "You look like the Marlboro Man wows a Paris fashion show." He wore a spiffy hip-length peccary suede jacket over a tailored washed-denim shirt and slacks. Hand-tooled cowboy boots, the kind that cost three or four hundred dollars, encased his feet. Perched casually on his head was a brown-and-gold billed NRA cap.

"I always try to look the part. Something to keep in mind, Toni. Costume is everything." He glanced scornfully at my jeans and threadbare corduroy blazer. "I wish, just once, you'd let me dress you."

"Maybe someday. Where are we headed?"

"A shooting range on Richie Highway. A lot of Baltimore cops use it."

My head whirled around. "I'm not exactly anxious to run into Baltimore cops, Randall."

"This is a weekday afternoon. The place will probably be deserted."

"I hope so."

An hour later we were inside a concrete-block warehouse with a curved tin roof. The interior had been divided into lanes almost like a bowling alley. Only they were for bullets, not bowling balls. I was glad to see that, as Randall had promised, it was virtually deserted. After he flashed his ID to the man at the gate, we set up on the far right-hand lane.

Randall handed me a set of foam earplugs and a pair of bulky plastic earphones and suggested I use both. "Eardrums are nothing to play with." Then he began opening boxes.

"I thought you were going to teach me how to use my gun."

"I am."

"Why have you brought along all those extras?"

"I want you to understand what guns are all about. They're just tools. But like all other tools, you have to understand them to use them correctly."

He lectured me about the difference between revolvers, semiautomatics, and automatics. He went on about gyroscopic action, flight of path, caliber, and smokeless powder. The man was obviously a frustrated college professor. Finally I got to load and then aim and fire my brand-new thirty-eight.

I had never loaded a gun before. The gun I'd killed Nick with had already been loaded. At the time all I'd known about revolvers was what I'd seen in cowboy movies. That hadn't seemed real. This, however, felt vividly real. Strange sensation to slip the bullets into those little black holes and to think that each was capable of ripping the life from somebody. I could aim it at anyone in this building and pull the trigger, and that person would be, at the least, injured. One of the bullets fell from my fingers and onto the floor. Randall picked it up.

"Your hands are shaking now, and you're just loading the gun. How are you going to hold it steady enough to aim at a target?"

"I don't know." My voice was barely a whisper. I felt a slight change in the atmosphere and glanced up. Gus O'Dell was walking down the aisle toward us. He carried a large brown plastic toolbox and wore jeans and a ragged gray sweatshirt with U.S. MARINES on the front. The gaze he flicked over Randall and me was unreadable and about as warm as the ice cap at the North Pole.

When he was within twenty yards, I called out, "Fancy meeting you here."

"I try to get in a little practice at least once a week. Don't think I've ever seen you here before, have I?"

Self-consciously, I waggled my head. "First time. I've bought a gun, and now I have to learn how to use it. This is my friend Randall Howarth. He's teaching me."

The two shook hands warily, each eyeing the other in that assessing way men have. I watched closely, looking for some sign that O'Dell had figured out Randall was gay. Somehow I knew he had, but not by anything he said or did.

O'Dell turned back to me. "You aren't staying at your apartment in Charles Village."

"No. I decided to move in with Randall for a few days."

"You might have informed me. I spent half the night in front of your place before I figured it out."

I gawked. "I'm sorry. I didn't think—"

He answered curtly. "Doesn't matter. I'd like your new address and phone number before you leave here, though. Just in case I should need to contact you." He nodded at Randall and then back at me. "Good luck."

"Thanks."

He strode off and took up a position a couple of lanes down. I turned back to Randall, who was watching me curiously. "So, that's O'Dell."

"Yes. So?"

"Nothing, my sweet, nothing at all. I do think it's time we dragged our wandering attention back to the business at hand. Before we leave, I'd like to see you load and fire at a target. I'm going to show you the Weaver stance."

"What's that?"

"A way to wrap both your hands around the trigger guard and handgrip. Now, watch me and mimic."

I had to give Randall credit. He was a good teacher and incredibly patient. He was also an excellent shot. Before he had me fire at the round bull's-eye target hanging at the end of the lane, he put several slugs in it himself.

"Hey, look at that," I crowed. "You're a regular dead-eye Dick. I wouldn't want to meet you in a dark alley."

"Sweetie pie, if you met me in a dark alley, you'd be perfectly safe. I can't say the same for your friend O'Dell over there."

We both turned and looked at O'Dell's lane. He was firing at a target shaped like a man. O'Dell wore ear-phones, and all we could see was his profile and rock-steady right-angled arm. I had a clear view of the target. Every one of his bullets made neat little holes in the center of the head.

"I've seen him here before," Randall remarked. "Always alone, always quiet, efficient as hell, and never misses. Now, how about you? Let's see what you can do."

I took up the stance and grip Randall had shown me and sighted at the round target. But I have to tell you, I was having a very hard time holding my hand steady. The feel of the revolver's steel backstrap against my palm, the sensation of my forefinger curled around a trigger, it was all bringing back terrible memories and worse feelings.

I told myself this was silly. I'd just cleaned out my wallet because I was convinced I needed this weapon. The least I could do was learn how to use it. I squeezed the trigger.

"Did I hit anything?"

"I believe there's a bullet hole about a foot to the

left of the black target area. You might do better if you kept your eyes open, Toni."

"Think so?"

"Why don't you give it a try?"

After that first shot it got easier. With Randall talking me through every step, I loaded and fired several rounds. Finally I began to hit the target where I was supposed to.

"You have good hands and a good eye. It's just a matter of practice," Randall said soothingly.

"I don't know. It feels so dangerous, so easy to have an accident."

"You aren't going to have any accidents. Now, there's one thing more I want you to do before we leave."

"What's that?"

"Fire at a target with a human outline."

"Oh, Randall—"

"All the cops use them."

"I'm not a cop."

"If you're going to do it, do it. You're talking protection, and this could make a big difference."

When I finally nodded, Randall walked to a control panel to arrange the change. I glanced over at O'Dell. He was blazing away at a fresh silhouette. Shooting at human shapes certainly didn't appear to bother him.

It bothered me, though. More even than I'd realized it was going to. The new target came down. With icicle fingers I reloaded my gun. When I lifted it to try to take up a shooting stance, my vision blurred. The outline of a man wavered before me, and I saw Nick. I felt as if my whole body were freezing solid. "Randall," I croaked, "I don't think I can do this."

"It's just paper, honey. Aim and fire."

"No, I don't think I can. I feel sort of sick." As if it were nuclear, I laid the loaded gun down on the railing, barrel facing out of harm's way.

Randall took the bullets out of it and then put his arm around my shoulder. I was shaking so bad he could feel it.

"Don't worry about this, sweetheart."

"I'm sorry."

"I figured it might happen, but I also figured you should give it a try."

"Does it mean if I had to defend myself against an attacker, I wouldn't be able to?"

"It just means you're still carrying around a lot of emotional baggage."

"Maybe what I need is a shrink, not a gun."

"Could be."

I thought of Simpler and then glanced over at O'Dell again. Instead of going on contributing to the paper shortage, he was watching Randall and me. He must have seen my miserable little exhibition. I felt myself go hot all over.

"Randall . . ."

"What, doll?"

"Let's get out of here."

"My very thought."

Outside in Randall's Mercedes I curled up into a ball of misery. The quiet purr of his car felt so soothing that it put me into suspended animation. I didn't notice that he'd pulled off the road until he'd killed the engine.

"We can't be home already."

"Look around you, my dear. We're at a roadside oasis, a twentieth-century guiding light, Friendly's."

Sure enough, the ice-cream parlor's red neon sign

flickered before me in the dusk. "I can't believe that a snobby supergourmet like you would be willing to defile his tonsils with a Friendly's hamburger."

"Hamburger, definitely not. Hot-fudge sundae with a cherry on top, definitely *oui*. C'mon. We both deserve a little sweetness in our lives."

Hot fudge turned out to be exactly the right prescription for my humiliation and uncertainty. On the way home Randall stopped at a video store. He picked up *Casablanca*, and we spent the evening watching it, drinking Fitou de Mont Tauch and stuffing ourselves with various goodies concocted from his overflowing refrigerator.

That put me in such a mellow mood that he was able to talk me into another round at his gun club the next afternoon after work.

"Practice makes perfect, sweetheart."

"If you say so, Randall."

In fact, our second session together went a lot better than the first. Randall didn't try making me shoot at a human silhouette.

"Not bad," he praised as we pulled out of the parking lot. "You may even have the makings of a marksman."

"Markswoman."

"Oh, yes, indeed. Sorry." He shot me a sideways glance. "Did it help not having an audience?"

"What do you mean?"

"Your pal O'Dell wasn't there to watch this time."

"He's not my pal, and he never watched last time."

"Oh, yes, he did. I saw him sneak glances our way. He's interested in you."

"Well, I hope so. I'm another potential victim in Aronchick's house of horrors. I hope he's interested enough to try to catch the killer before he adds me to his trophy wall."

"It's not just that. Unless my antennae are way off signal, it's the man-woman thing as well."

"You've got to be kidding."

"Now why is that?"

"He just seems like such a tough, unfriendly guy."

"Banked fires. Now tell old Uncle Randall the truth. Are you interested back?"

I considered that. "Maybe. But it doesn't matter. I'd never get involved with someone like O'Dell. The last thing I need in my life is another cop."

"I'm glad to hear you say that."

"Why?"

"Because I agree you don't need another violence-prone boyfriend who might not appreciate you. What you need is someone sexy but sympathetic, kindhearted but able to take care of his woman."

I had to laugh. "In other words, I need someone like you, only straight."

"Exactly."

"What if no such wondrous creature exists?"

"They say if you look, you find. What was it about Nick that attracted you, Toni? Was he like O'Dell?" Suddenly Randall's voice had lost all its usual humor. His eyes were kind, but curious.

"In some ways. Not in others. He was much better looking. When I first saw him I thought he was gorgeous. Tall, black curly hair, big muscles. He was plenty tough, but he wasn't a loner. He liked to hang out with the guys and do guy-type things. Pool halls, bars, bowling alleys—that sort of stuff. It was a challenge to me in a way."

"What was?"

"That he was so macho. I flaunted myself at him. Anything to get his attention."

"Well, you got it."

"Sure did."

Randall sighed. "Toni, I'm sorry. I can see I shouldn't have brought the subject up."

"You didn't bring it up. I think about it all the time. That's one of my big troubles. Even with all that's going on, I can't get it out of my mind. In fact, the odd thing is lately I've been thinking more about Nick than ever."

When we got back to the apartment, we were both feeling morose. I waited in silence while Randall turned the key in the lock. "Maybe dinner out tonight," he said after we walked in.

"I can't afford dinner out."

"I don't want to hear another word from you about money. I will be glad to pay for you. I know a little Szechuan place in Federal Hill."

"Randall, I already owe you more than—"

The phone rang, and Randall strode away to get it in the kitchen. A moment later he poked his head out the door. "It's for you."

I tried to think who knew I was here. O'Dell, Sandy, and my boss were the only ones I'd told.

"Ms. Credella?"

"Yes."

"O'Dell here."

"I recognized your voice." He sounded tired, yet uptight over something.

"I'm afraid I have some bad news for you."

I tensed, waiting.

"Your neighbor, Damon Wilkes, has been shot."

14

The next day after work I went to see Damon. They had moved him from emergency into a regular three-bed room.

"It's a good thing you could manage to dial nine-one-one," I said. Across from his bed, I perched on one of those chrome-and-Naugahyde chairs that hospitals go in for. I guess germs are less likely to nest in them.

Damon shot me a cocky grin. "Lucky me. I took the hit near my cordless telephone. Technology saved my ass."

I gazed at his bandaged head. "The bullet got you in the temple?"

"Grazed, baby, just grazed. If it had come any closer I wouldn't be sitting here talking about it."

I rubbed my cold hands together. "When did this happen?"

"Don't know. It was dark out. I was standing in front of my easel, working on a painting I'm getting ready for Balticon. Then, crack, wham, kaboom. Next thing I know I'm lying on the floor in the popularly acclaimed pool of blood."

"Oh, Damon, that's so awful. I'm really sorry."

"Why? It's not your fault. Jeez, I'm actually beginning to develop some sympathy for Aronchick. He must feel like the landlord with the property from hell."

"Probably." I laughed. "I'm glad that bullet didn't come any closer and that you haven't lost your sense of humor."

"That's me, laugh until you die."

I nodded, feeling admiration at the way he was tossing this off. Damon had class, I thought. His own brand, maybe, but it was still class. "Listen, when you get right down to it, what else is there but to laugh until you die?"

"That's what I like, a little philosophy with my misery. To tell you the truth, I'm really surprised." He raised a tentative finger to his head wound and then let his hand drop back onto the sheet. "I never thought I was in any danger. I figured the kook who was knocking off Aronchick's tenants only had it in for women. Not to sound sexist, but that did give me a sense of security. O'Dell says the attack on me puts a whole new complexion on the case."

"He does?"

"Yeah, maybe it's not just women this killer hates. Maybe it's Aronchick, or the house. O'Dell's out digging up the history on the property right now."

"Oh?" I looked at Damon doubtfully. Somehow I didn't buy any of that. When I'd told Damon I was sorry, I'd really meant it as an apology. The guilty feeling he'd been shot because of me nagged at the back of my mind. Of course, that made no sense, so I kept it to myself.

His smile warmed. "Hey, thanks for coming to see me and for these." He waved the pair of science-fiction books I'd brought him.

"While you're here you'll probably be too busy fending off your gaggle of groupies to read them. I met Lynley, by the way. Pretty girl."

"Yeah, she's a sweet kid." He looked at me closely. "Great body."

"Great," I agreed.

"She works for it. Teaches aerobics at the DAC. When did you meet her?"

"I walked in just as she was coming down from your place, so we made nice and introduced ourselves."

"Must have been a classic scene." Damon's eyes twinkled, and I grinned. He stuck a finger out and pressed through my jacket at my breastbone. "Cross my heart, I wouldn't have invited her over if I hadn't figured I wasn't going to make it with you again. Was I right about that?"

"Yeah, I think you were."

Suddenly the twinkle left. "Why, Toni?"

"It was a mistake. I'm just not ready."

"Was I that terrible?" He looked really concerned.

"You weren't terrible. It's me with the problem, Damon, not you."

"It's been three years since your husband died, and you're not getting any younger."

"I know that."

He leaned back and closed his eyes. I noticed that against the wrinkled white of his hospital gown, his face looked washed-out and slightly jaundiced. I seemed to see more gray in his curls than I had before, but that had to be my imagination. His hair couldn't have lost color overnight, could it? Just how old was he? I suddenly wondered. I had been thinking of him as close to my age. But forty was probably more like it. Forty and still playing with toy monsters and animated Barbie dolls like Lynley. He was clever and he had charm and style, but maybe for me that was all he had.

His eyes popped open, and I felt guilty for my thoughts. "I hate hearing myself say this, but can we at least be friends?" he asked peevishly.

"Sure."

"You mean that?"

"I mean that."

"Good thing I got that in," he said, "because I can tell from the way you just squirmed around that you're getting ready to leave."

"It's late, and I don't like being out after dark these days. Damon, before I go, is there anything I can do for you?"

"Yes. You could stop by my place and bring me some clothes. It'll be a lot easier to plan my escape from this wounded ward with something to cover my ass besides a backless hospital gown."

"True."

"Oh, and while you're at it, you remember that drawing I did of you?"

"I nodded."

"Well, why don't you take it? A little good-bye present, since I'm moving. I matted it a couple nights ago. It's sitting with a stack of other stuff on the table next to my easel."

"Thanks, I'd like that."

Damon's gaze had wandered to a spot behind my head. I turned and saw O'Dell standing there. It must have gotten windy outside. There was color in his lean cheeks, and his dark hair was mussed. If pressed, I would have reluctantly admitted that on him mussed hair looked quite attractive.

"Hello, Ms. Credella."

"Hello, Detective O'Dell."

"I hope I'm not disturbing anything, but I need to ask Mr. Wilkes a few more questions."

"Of course. I was just leaving."

"If you'll wait, I'll be glad to give you a ride home."

Normally I jump at a ride, but I didn't want O'Dell doing me any more favors. "No thanks. I'll catch a bus."

On the sidewalk outside the University of Maryland Hospital, I jammed my hands in my pockets and walked briskly down Baltimore Street to Charles. A cold breeze whipped up my coat sleeves and cut through my jeans. Crowds of people hurried from work all around me, yet I felt vulnerable in a way I never had before. I cast anxious looks up at the windows over the storefronts. Many looked vacant. How tough would it be to hide in one of those deserted rooms and pick off passersby with a rifle?

Who had shot Damon, and why? Was that person stalking me even now? I shot an apprehensive look over my shoulder and walked faster. It could be anyone, a kid who worked in the grocery store where I shopped, a guy who lived in one of the apartments two houses down. More than likely it was a stranger, but what if it was someone I knew?

At one time I'd even entertained the idea that it might be Damon, after all. In some ways he fit Jeff Simpler's psychopath profile. He was a loner who liked playing God so much, he'd created and marketed his own set of universes. He had a wicked sense of humor and no noticeable morals. Now that he'd been shot, though, that let him out—unless he'd somehow managed to shoot himself to allay suspicion.

When I'd met Don Parham, I'd decided he couldn't be guilty. But what made me think I was that good at judging character? Then there was O'Dell. Not that I suspected him of murdering people in his off-hours. But he, too, fitted the psychopath profile a little too close for comfort. For all I knew Jeff Simpler did, too. Maybe a lot more men did than I'd ever thought. Maybe the world was a lot more dangerous a place than I'd ever imagined. Suddenly I felt like a goldfish swimming in a tank full of hungry sharks.

At the bus stop on Charles I checked my change. After spending nearly fifteen bucks on Damon's books, I had just over five left to last me the rest of the week until I saw my first paycheck.

Usually I'm pretty tough about the panhandlers that plague downtown. But a woman stood on the corner with a little kid no more than four. They both looked pale and cold. "Change, could you give us some change," she whispered over and over. People hurried past her with their heads down and their collars turned up against the wind. I caught the hurt, bewildered expression in the kid's eyes and fished out the five dollars. After I stuffed it in her hand, I hurried past with my head down, too. A bus wheezed up to the stop, but I didn't pay any attention. From now on I'd be walking or riding my bike.

Four more blocks down, on the corner of Franklin, I heard my name. O'Dell peered out of a nondescript sedan. "Want a ride?"

"Thanks, but it's hardly worth it. I'm almost at Mt. Vernon." I thought again. Why cut off my nose to spite my face? "There's a favor you could do me."

"Such as?" He looked wary.

"Damon asked me to pick up some stuff at his place. It'd be great if you could take me there and then drop me at Randall's."

"Okay."

I got in and he pulled away from the curb. "This is a big improvement over your other wheels."

"Less character, but the city pays the bills. What are you picking up for Damon?" He shot me a quick glance.

"Clothes."

"You two seemed very chummy there in the hospital room."

"We're just friends."

"You have a lot of men friends?"

"Just two, really." Three if you counted Simpler. Jonathan I didn't regard as a friend. He just tolerated me for Randall's sake. Maybe Ron Smith would become one, but probably not. He was my boss, and I don't know if you can ever really be pals with a boss.

"What about girlfriends? Do you have a lot of those?"

"Susie Zillig was a girlfriend." Even as I made the claim, I knew it wasn't true. Susie and I weren't what anybody would call close. The few young women I'd regarded as friends in the days when I was Mrs. Nick Rosica had turned away from me. Now, aside from Sandy, the only female I felt close to was Rebecca Kelso. And she was nothing but a sad and frightened ghost. I wasn't exactly the popularity kid.

"Tell me," I said as we cruised past Twenty-fifth, "have you had any luck tracking down that bug?"

O'Dell shook his head. "Near as we can come, it was manufactured by a novelty firm that's been out of business for decades. What records there may have been about who their customers were are all lost."

"Before she was killed, Rebecca got one, too."

O'Dell ground his gears. "How do you know that?"

"Her mother told me."

"Mrs. Kelso? She never said anything about it to us."

"Until I showed her mine, she'd forgotten about it."

"When was this?"

"I went out there a few days back."

With two swift cranks of the wheel, O'Dell parallel parked in a tight spot near my Charles Village apartment. "You get around, don't you?" he commented as he climbed out from behind the driver's wheel.

"Try to." So, I'd done my duty and told him everything about the bug, I thought as he came around to the passenger door. I knew I should tell him that I had Mrs. Kelso's bug. But if O'Dell couldn't trace one, he wouldn't be able to trace its twin. So what was the harm in my hanging on to it a little longer?

"It's a good thing I caught you," O'Dell remarked a few minutes later as we climbed the stairs to Damon's place. "Since this is a crime scene, you're not supposed to go inside unless I give the okay."

I was glad to be with O'Dell, too. Past the yellow tape covering the apartment's door, the kitchen looked untouched. However, walking into the living room was like stepping onto a murder mystery stage set. All the props were in place, broken glass from the large dormer window, blood staining the floor, the overturned easel with a ruined painting of a gargoyle folded over itself.

We stood taking it all in.

"Wilkes must have made a pretty target, outlined in front of this window," O'Dell mused.

I remembered how I'd watched O'Dell pump bullets into a man-shaped target back at the shooting range.

I asked, "Is there any chance Damon could have shot himself?"

He cast me a sharp glance. "That was an idea I had until I saw the slug. It came from a high-powered rifle."

"Was the sniper across the street on the roof?"

"From the angle, it looks as if he took the shot from the street, most likely from a parked car."

Curiously, I returned O'Dell's scrutiny. "Taking potshots at people with high-powered rifles is your personal favorite, isn't it?"

"Once upon a time. I'm not on the Quick Response team anymore."

"Why did you quit?"

He turned away and walked over to the window. "I got a little too old for hanging off roofs popping at crazies through windows. It's a young man's game."

"The real question in my mind is why did you ever

start?" Of course, I had no business asking. I was just too curious not to.

He whirled around to face me. "Why do you think? You think I'm so turned on by the sight of blood I can't go a day without it?"

He looked more than a little hot under the collar. Apparently he could be perturbed.

"Did I say that?"

"You didn't have to. Funny how attitudes change, isn't it?" He began striding back and forth. "Time was when guys like Davy Crockett and Daniel Boone were American heroes. Yet, essentially, all they ever did was walk around shooting everything that moved."

"That's how you see yourself? Davy Crockett for the nineties?"

He stuffed his hands in his pockets. "That's how I saw myself when I was a kid spending every day in the woods. I was there, by the way, hunting squirrels so my Uncle Denton wouldn't beat the hell out of me for looking cross-eyed at him."

I blinked, taking that in. "Your uncle beat you?"

O'Dell smiled humorlessly, showing his teeth. "Whenever he had a drink too many, and that was every hour on the hour. But after I started bagging game and bringing it home to put in the pot, he laid off. That's not an answer to your question, is it?"

"Listen, I'm sorry. I had no business—"

"Wait, I've got a better answer for you." His hand came out of his pocket and he pointed a long forefinger. "When I walked into a marine recruiting office I was a seventeen-year-old high school dropout with no skills and less education. Hitting a target with a bullet was the only thing I could do that anyone else considered worth a damn. I wanted to take pride in something, so I took pride in that."

"Rightfully so, I guess. From what I saw of you at the pistol range, you're very good."

"Not like the guy who put Mister Wilkes here in the hospital." O'Dell's smile grew sharper. "If I'd been the one to shoot at Mister Wilkes, he'd be in the morgue, not flirting with his lady friends in the hospital."

I believed him. But it didn't exactly make me warm up to him. "I'm going to collect Damon's things, okay?"

"Sure," O'Dell said coldly. "Take your time. I'll go have a smoke out in the hall."

"Smoking is bad for you."

"You're just full of amazing information, aren't you?"

I watched him stride out and then, anxious to be out of there, set to work. It didn't take me long to scoop up a pair of jeans and a sweatshirt out of Damon's drawer and stuff them into a plastic grocery bag. After I'd added socks, jockeys, and a pair of sneakers, I went back out to the main room to hunt for my portrait. I checked the spot where Damon had said it'd be, but there was no sign of it on the table next to the easel. I'd been looking forward to having that drawing, so I felt a stab of disappointment.

Even though I was in a hurry to get out of there, I checked back in Damon's bedroom. Aside from the pictures on the walls, there wasn't much in that room. Quickly I dropped it as a hiding place. I was riffling through the stacks of matted drawings and paintings in the living room when O'Dell came back in.

"What are you looking for?"

I explained, and he shook his head. "Early this morning I was with forensics when they went through this place. If there had been a drawing of you, I would have seen it."

"Damon told me he'd matted it, but maybe he was mistaken. Maybe it's still in that notebook."

"What notebook?"

I glanced around and spotted it on a shelf behind the fallen easel. "There. It's got a sketch of me and a couple of Rebecca Kelso, too."

O'Dell reached up and plucked down the notebook. "Let's have a look."

I stood next to him while he riffled through. My portrait would have been toward the back. But the drawings of Rebecca were close to the front. I kept waiting for them to appear. When they didn't, I couldn't believe my eyes. I asked O'Dell to search through them all again. After he did, there couldn't be any doubt. They were gone. And this time I remembered there had been a sketch of Susie. Damon had pictured her locked in a block of ice and being dragged down a frozen river by a huge, shaggy polar bear. That drawing was missing as well.

"This is creepy."

"You're thinking that whoever shot Damon stole them?"

"Of course I'm thinking that."

O'Dell shook his head. "Unlikely. Since late last night only authorized personnel have been in here."

"Then those drawings must have been taken before. Damon's place would be easy to break into. Half the time he doesn't even bother locking up."

"I can guess what's on your mind, but I'd like to

hear you say it. Why would a thief steal those pictures and nothing else?"

"How should I know?" I reconsidered and didn't care much for what popped into my head. "Well, how about this? Whoever is doing these things is crazy. Maybe he wanted those sketches for trophies. Maybe he even wanted to throw darts at them."

When O'Dell didn't answer, I demanded, "Have you got any other theories?"

"None that make sense."

"Damon said you were going to look up the history of this house. Did you?"

"I spent the morning getting all the facts I could find."

"And?"

He gave a gusty sigh. "Nothing much. Before Rebecca Kelso's, no one committed a spectacular murder here. At least, none that got on the record."

I'd known that was a wild goose chase the minute Damon mentioned it. Now I turned away. "I've got everything I need here. Do you mind if I stop in my place for a minute? I could use a change of clothes myself."

O'Dell had slipped the notebook into a plastic bag and tucked it under his arm. "Be my guest."

Unlike Damon's aerie, my apartment was a stronghold. Since I'd been away so long, it even took me a couple of minutes to remember how to unlock it. While O'Dell waited in his car, I went inside and stood for a minute in the doorway with all my antennae out. The place had the stale, airless feeling of abandonment. I felt certain no one had been here since I'd left.

In the bedroom, I scooped some fresh underwear

out of my drawer and then grabbed a sweater and a couple of blouses. Who knew, maybe Jonathan would decide he liked it in Colorado and stay there. I knew I couldn't plan on being Randall's permanent roommate. But I sure wouldn't object if he let me stay on for another week. After that, I just didn't know.

I rolled all my stuff into a bundle and walked back out to the living room. As I put my hand on the doorknob, my eye fell on the plastic bug atop my TV set. It had stopped looking so menacing to me. I'd even begun to think of it as a sort of bizarre mascot and named it Herbie. On impulse, I crossed over and stuffed it in with my other things.

About ten seconds later I felt the change. The temperature in the living room started dropping like an anchor. I stood there several seconds, my hair reaching for the ceiling while I took in the new vibes. Much as I wanted to bolt for the door the way I had last time, I knew I had to stick around to see what happened next. "Rebecca?" I whispered.

No answer, just that gray and chilly breath from someplace I didn't want to know about, someplace that didn't have a zip code in Baltimore. I'm not sure what made me look outside. Maybe my friendly neighborhood ghost whispered the order in my head. "It's heeerrrre."

I hurried over to the window just in time to see it cruise past ever so slowly—the scary black Volvo that had begun to haunt my dreams. I barreled outside. After rattling down the steps, I skidded across the tiny square of lawn and onto the sidewalk past O'Dell's parked car. He'd been leaning back with his eyes closed. Now his head snapped up. Determined to get a look at the Volvo's plate, I tore past.

It was already too late. The car had sped up and rounded the corner. The brief glimpse I'd caught of the license told me only one rather peculiar thing. I stood at the end of the block with my hands on my hips while I tried to make sense of it.

O'Dell's car rolled up beside me. He shouted, "What was that all about?"

"That car has been circling my place for weeks now. I wanted to take a look at its license plate."

"Get in."

"It's gone, and I haven't locked my door."

"Get in."

I did as ordered, and we roared off and swerved around the corner, tires squealing. O'Dell accelerated to warp speed and took his sedan flying up and down all the cross streets that make a grid of the Charles Village area. We saw no sign of the black Volvo, but I got a lesson in rocket maneuvers.

Finally, much to my relief, we rolled back up in front of my apartment. "What do you do for fun when you're not playing with guns, set land speed records?" I demanded.

"I thought you wanted to catch that Volvo."

"I did, but not at the risk of winding up in a hospital bed next to Damon's. Besides, we didn't find it."

"Worth a try. Did you see anything on the license at all?"

I hesitated.

"So you did. What?"

"A handicapped symbol."

He stared at me.

"You know, one of those little line drawings of a

person in a wheelchair that let you park in spaces other people would kill for."

He looked highly unamused. "Yes, I do believe I've seen them before and would recognize one if I saw it again. Maybe you'd better explain what this is all about."

I wasn't sure I wanted to share my private fantasy about the Volvo of Evil with O'Dell. Yet I realized I had to tell him something. So I told him the truth. I even described how I was sure Rebecca's ghost wanted to warn me about the Volvo.

While I gabbled on trying to make all this sound reasonable, he just gazed at me in silence. It was damned unnerving, and my voice finally faltered.

"I guess this all sounds pretty crazy to you."

"I've heard crazier."

Sure, I thought. In his career he'd probably had to deal with whole platoons of raving lunatics.

"Why do I get the feeling you don't take my fears about this pesky automobile seriously?"

"How seriously do you take them yourself, now that you've seen that handicapped symbol on the plate?"

I had to admit it made the whole cockamamie theory even more ridiculous. Whoever had climbed through my window and whoever had dragged Susie's body to Druid Hill had had to be fairly athletic. My window was twelve feet off the ground, and Susie had been a tall, strong girl. It couldn't have been all that easy to kill her. As that thought scattered images of horror through my mind, I drew into the corner between the door and the passenger seat.

"Okay," O'Dell said, "I'll call the DMV tomorrow and run a check. There's bound to be more than one Volvo with a handicapped plate, though."

"It was a black Volvo."

"You can't be sure of that. You only saw it at night, right?"

"Right," I admitted reluctantly.

"It might have been charcoal gray, or midnight blue, or bottle green, or even oxblood red."

"My, you certainly have a way with words."

"My ex-wife sold cosmetics. She never describes colors with less than three syllables."

I cocked my head. "So, you were married."

"Briefly."

That was all he intended saying about it, and that was all I intended asking. As he drove me back to Randall's, however, I shot his sharp-edged profile a couple of curious glances. I wondered what the wife had been like and why the marriage had failed. I didn't waste energy speculating, however. Too many more important questions pressed on my mind. Like, why had Damon been shot, and why had his drawings of me, Rebecca, and Susie been stolen? In particular, why did a killer want me in a lineup of recently murdered women? Could he be drawing an X-marks-the-spot between my eyes even now? Was he the driver behind the wheel of the Volvo? And what, if anything, did the handicapped sticker mean?

I rubbed the groove between my eyebrows and made up my mind about tomorrow's after-work project. "I think I'll go see Leo Acker tomorrow," I said.

"What?"

"I know you think he isn't a suspect. Okay, maybe he isn't. I want to talk to him anyway."

"Why?"

"I won't be able to think of anything else until I've talked to him and convinced myself that he isn't connected with all this."

"You're one bullheaded woman, aren't you?"

"Heifer-headed." I didn't want to say I was cow-headed.

O'Dell gave me a sideways glance. "The man is not a recent graduate of Miss Manners Charm School."

"That much I can probably figure out for myself."

"He won't talk to you if you go by yourself. I'll go with you."

"Why?"

"Maybe I'm worried about you."

"I don't get it. I thought you said Leo Acker couldn't be the killer."

"He can't be."

"So then why are you worried?" Of course, I'd been worried about me all along.

He tapped the steering wheel with his thumb. "Toni, you remember those panties you gave Lieutenant Grimsby?"

"Of course I remember them."

"Well, that was blood staining them all right. The final tests aren't back yet, but there's a good chance the blood may have been Susie's."

15

Leo Acker worked at the Volcano Club. The Volcano seethes on what remains of the Block. In the old days, Baltimore had a classic sin strip. Girlie clubs flourished. Burlesque superstars like Lili St. Cyr played there, and Blaize Starr called it home. Now with downtown redevelopment nibbling away at all the sleaze, there's not much left of the old erogenous zone. Still, a few of the girlie clubs hold out. The Volcano is one of them.

Late the next afternoon O'Dell and I walked past stores selling dirty books, peep-show window displays, and a multiethnic gaggle of hookers. The white ones were frizzy peroxide blondes and the African-American ones sported elaborately gilded and sparkled hair worthy of Marie Antoinette in her prime. They all wore earrings down to their collarbones and neon stretch skirts an inch or two above their crotches. In my jeans, turtleneck T, and corduroy blazer I felt distinctly drab.

Next to me, O'Dell, with his Orioles jacket and jeans,

five-o'clock shadow, and lean and hungry demeanor could probably have passed for a potential customer.

"Hey, hiya, copper," one of the hookers sang out. "Anything I can do for ya?"

"You know those ladies?" I asked.

"Not as a client, but before I worked homicide I booked a couple of them."

"You must have made an impression."

"Who's your girlfriend?" another enterprising lady in the after-hours corner social group inquired sweetly. "Bet I can make your malted milk disappear before she can."

I hate to admit it, but I turned beet red.

O'Dell dropped an arm around my shoulder and steered me past. "Pay no attention. They're just colorful conversationalists."

"Sure."

"Actually, the one in the powder blue suede outfit wasn't a bad kid. She ran away from home when she was fourteen."

I looked back and spotted the girl he meant, a skinny blonde with a perky rear end and an insolent slouch.

"A couple years back I went to her place on a domestic violence call. She claimed her mother's boyfriend was slipping into her bed before breakfast. I arranged foster care for her with two different families. Never worked, though."

"Why not?"

"Who knows? She just couldn't make real life stick. So now she's back on the streets with a drug habit and a pimp who knocks her around."

I searched for a reply but didn't find one. Most people looking at that girl and me would say we were a world apart. But were we really so different? I glanced at

O'Dell. He'd picked up an earful on my history, of course. I saw that he'd had the same thought as me. The guy even looked embarrassed, which was a new development in our relationship.

"You know," I said, "this is only the third time I've ever been here."

"You grew up in Little Italy, didn't you? That's only a half-dozen blocks away."

"Yeah, but it's another world. At Saint Leo's the nuns taught us that nice girls would never go near a place like this. Still, a couple of times my sister and I managed to sneak over and gawk."

I didn't mention it to O'Dell, but I remembered an evening when Sandy and I went out with Nick and Al. They took us to the Block and walked us up and down—a prenuptial titillation ritual, I guess. We'd asked giggly questions, and they'd answered with manly condescension. Back then I'd never dreamed that one day I'd be strolling into one of the Block's sin bins to interview a rapist.

O'Dell and I stopped in front of the Volcano's blood red entrance. An artist with a testosterone-poisoned imagination had painted the door with flames and livened up its cracked stucco wall with gyrating girls wearing pasties and G-strings.

"Colorful," I commented, looking at the dancing girls' bazooms. They were wild explosions of flesh, breasts from some mad scientist's gel implant lab.

"That's show biz," O'Dell said.

I glanced up and saw the expression in his eyes. Amused.

Inside, the Volcano was still dormant. I had to stand for several seconds while my eyes adjusted to the gloom. A veil of cigarette smoke and stale beer hung in the entombed air. This couldn't be any worse than talking to Espey, I kept telling myself.

"Something I can help you get?"

A guy with tired eyes and graying, slicked-back hair slid off a bar stool. I wondered if he thought I was there to apply for a job on the bar's built-in runway. He looked me over as if he were trying to figure out whether what lay beneath my jeans and sweater might be worth a paying customer's while. Probably deciding not, he turned his attention to O'Dell. Despite the Orioles jacket, his expression turned respectful.

"The lady and I are here to see Leo Acker. Is he around?"

"Leo?" He called to the back of the place, where I could hear the clink of glasses and the swish of dishwater. "Hey, Leo, someone out here wants you."

Well, I wouldn't have gone that far, but I kept my mouth shut and waited. A squat, thick-shouldered man heaved out of the shadows. He wore baggy black pants and a white shirt and had graying brown hair cut in a bowl around his ears. He looked like someone you wouldn't want to bump up against walking down a deserted hall on the way to your apartment.

His flat, light-colored eyes skimmed me and then fixed on O'Dell. "Yeah?"

"I brought someone who wants to ask you a few questions, Leo."

"I'm on duty now."

The place was deserted. The show wouldn't start for hours.

"Your boss will give you a couple minutes. Or do I need to have a word with your parole officer?" O'Dell's voice was level, but I heard the subtle threat and so did Acker.

He looked toward the man on the bar stool, who shrugged and nodded. Acker pointed at an empty table in the corner. "Over there, okay?"

"Fine."

Once we were seated across from each other, O'Dell leaned back in his chair and made a curt hand gesture at me that said, "You insisted on getting yourself into this, so take over."

I breathed deep and plunged right in. After I explained who I was to Acker, I said, "I know you're out on parole from the state pen. I also know that you were cell mates with a man named Christopher Espey."

Acker had appeared wary before; now he looked hostile. "So what? You a reporter or something?" He shot O'Dell a resentful glare. "I'm not talking to any reporters."

My heartfelt assurances that I wasn't a journalist didn't relax Acker any. He sat hunched, peering out at O'Dell and me from the mound of his tensed shoulders like a suspicious snapping turtle. He was a solid lump of a man, sitting there eyeing me from his meaty face as if he'd like nothing better than to take me apart and leave the pieces in a plastic garbage bag.

Stumbling over my words because I was so nervous that my tongue kept getting in my way, I explained why I had gone to see Espey and then told him what had happened to Susie.

"O'Dell already bugged me about this," Acker exploded. "I'll tell you the same thing I already told him, okay? I got nothing to do with this, and I can prove it. I got alibis out to my wazoo."

"I'm not here to accuse you. I was a friend of Susie's, that's all."

"Hey, I'm not dumb. Something gave you and O'Dell here the idea I was connected with whoever iced her. Otherwise you wouldn't be here. Was it Espey telling stories? That little shit would do or say anything."

"No. Espey just mentioned that he'd discussed what he'd done to Susie and that other little girl with you."

"I don't need this." Acker scraped back and jumped out of his chair so savagely that it tipped over. Ignoring it, he stomped over to the bar.

O'Dell followed. He, Acker, and the man on the stool, obviously Acker's boss, talked in low, snarly voices. Every other minute they shot pointed looks at me. A couple of other guys capped bar stools now. They looked at me, too. The beery atmosphere in the place was poisoned with macho aggression, and I wanted nothing more than to head for the door. But I wasn't going to make a fool of myself in front of O'Dell. Besides, I hadn't got my nerve up to do this just to turn chicken and run away. I had to know if this guy was connected in any way with Rebecca and Susie's murders. Besides, he was the only idea I had.

Finally Acker came back with O'Dell at his elbow. "What is it you want?" Acker said, subdued now but still resentful.

"Honest, just to ask you a couple questions."

"Okay, but I don't want anything messing up my parole. I'm living clean."

"This isn't going to affect your parole." O'Dell picked up the fallen chair and pointed at the seat. After a taut couple of seconds, Acker dropped onto it.

Just then a redhead and a blonde breezed in. They wore three-inch heels, pasted-on jeans, and shoulder-duster earrings. One had on a waist-length leather jacket dyed to resemble denim. Under the makeup they both looked to be in their early twenties.

"Hi, guys." Their eyes widened slightly at me and O'Dell.

"'Lo, Patty," the boss said from the bar stool. "You two are early, aren't you?"

"Just dropping off some costumes. Don't let it worry you."

They strutted past, all the men's eyes following, including O'Dell's. When the young women disappeared, O'Dell said, "The talent?"

"Yeah. They're tonight's Easter bunnies. The smaller one, Denise, you should see her action in a grass skirt."

I felt irritated. For a minute there O'Dell and Acker had sounded almost buddy-buddy. "I'm having a little trouble with this," I said.

They both gave me a surprised look. "What trouble?"

I aimed my remarks at Acker. "You were in for rape, weren't you?"

"Yeah, so?"

"So, I mean, if you really want to straighten yourself out, this seems like sort of a funny place for you to be working—like an alcoholic earning his living as a wine taster. Wouldn't you be better off in a different atmosphere?"

"Like what?"

"I don't know—a gas station, a hardware store—"

"Pumping gas wouldn't be my bag. Look, lady, it's not so easy for guys like me to get jobs."

"Yeah, I know, but—"

"Happens Eddie over there, that's the manager, he's my cousin. That's why he gave me a break."

"Oh, I see, but—"

"Look"—he glanced at O'Dell and then back to me—
"I know I've got a problem, okay? But now it's licked. I'm
not going to jump any of the girls who work here."

"Why not?" O'Dell asked, sounding quite interested.

"Girls like Patty and Denise who've been around,
they're not my type. I liked young ones, innocent."

I remembered that Espey said Acker had "done" a
Girl Scout.

"Besides," Acker was going on, "I'm never going to
bother anybody again."

"Detective O'Dell mentioned to me that you'd been
through a rape rehabilitation program," I said. I didn't
believe in rape rehabilitation, but I was curious to
hear what he would say about it.

"Yeah, counseling, group therapy. But it's the
medicine that's going to do the trick."

"Medicine?"

Again Acker shot a wary glance at O'Dell. I realized
it was O'Dell he was trying to impress with all this talk
of rehabilitation, not me. "I volunteered for Depo-
Provera. I got no sex drive anymore. The girls working
this place could shake their boobies at me all day and
I wouldn't blink."

I must admit, that did make me feel a little better.
If the guy was taking antisex hormones, he must really
want to reform. Either that or he really wanted to
convince a parole board to let him out.

"Look," he said, "this is a big waste of time. I had
nothing to do with this Susie's murder, and there's no
way you or anyone else can pin it on me."

"But you understand the psychology," I persisted.

"What?" He looked taken aback.

"I mean, since you've raped people, you understand what makes these guys tick."

"Maybe, a little."

O'Dell sat up and looked at me in surprise. I guess he hadn't been expecting that I'd come out with anything quite like this.

"Do guys like you have it in for the women who put you away?"

"How do you mean?" Acker looked at me with extreme suspicion, and so did O'Dell. I knew I was poking under a very slimy rock and that something with really nasty breath could come out blowing fire. Nevertheless, I persevered.

"I mean, a woman who outsmarted you, or got away from you, or identified you in a lineup and testified against you—would a guy like you want to get her back if he could?"

"You're talking revenge? Yeah, maybe. That's natural, isn't it?"

I didn't think anything about these guys was natural but decided not to sidetrack my line of questioning by mentioning this large and glaring fact. "Would you want to get her back even if there's been a twenty-year gap between the time she'd outsmarted you and the time you were able to do something about it?"

"Listen, guys in stir can have very long memories. But if it's Espey and your girlfriend you're harping on, forget it. First off, he's still locked up. Second, he's too much of a chicken shit to look for revenge."

"Could someone else want to look for it in his place?"

"Like who?"

"Someone who'd heard his story and liked the idea of bagging the ones who got away."

"Lady, if you mean me, you've got it all wrong. Sure, Espey told me about the kids he lured into his van with a puppy dog and how one testified against him later. But I didn't have anything to do with this Susie Zillig's murder, and I can prove it."

"He's right," O'Dell butted in. "Believe me, I checked it backward and sideways."

"Who did Espey tell his story to besides you?" I asked Acker. Somehow I just couldn't let this notion go. Maybe that was because I wasn't smart enough to come up with a better one.

"Lots of people."

"Such as?"

"All his relatives and friends, if he had any. Other guys in stir. Shrinks."

"Psychologists?"

"Yeah, psychologists. They're always coming around to put us under the microscope. There was even a guy doing a book who came around."

I thought of Simpler's book. "Are you talking about Doctor Jeffrey Simpler, by any chance?"

"Could be. I'm not sure of the name."

Simpler's book was sitting back at Randall's on the marble-topped nightstand next to Jonathan's bed. Several times I'd dipped into it. But it was heavy going, and I hadn't made much headway. Tonight I'd try again. If Jeff Simpler had interviewed both Espey and Acker, he might have written something that would be helpful. He might even remember something. Hell, for all I knew he might even be the murderer himself.

"I gotta get back to work," Acker groused.

O'Dell looked at me, and I nodded. We all stood

up. O'Dell didn't offer to shake hands with Acker, and neither did I.

Back out on the street O'Dell said, "I can't decide whether you're gutsy or just plain stupid."

"Maybe both."

He started walking very fast, his hands jammed into his pockets, his face tight. "I shouldn't have let you do that."

"What do you mean, 'let'? I'm over twenty-one. You can't stop me from walking into a place like that any time I please."

"You shouldn't need stopping. You should have the sense to know better than to pull such a damn fool stunt. A woman with your looks bringing herself to the attention of a creep like Acker—" He gave his head a rough shake. "The things you asked him! Aren't you afraid he'll get to brooding about them and decide to pay you his twisted idea of a social call?"

Glancing sideways at O'Dell as I tried to keep up with him, I saw he was truly pissed. It puzzled me. I mean, I could see where he might not have enjoyed the last half hour too much. But it had been his idea that he needed to join the party, not mine. "Acker's on a drug that takes away his sex drive."

"Wise up. It's not just his sex drive that makes him dangerous. Rape is a crime of violence, of hatred. Besides, taking Depo-Provera is voluntary, and it has bad side effects. He could go off it any time."

I hunched up my shoulders and looked down at my feet. O'Dell's long legs were striding along fast enough that I was almost running not to get left behind. "Of course Acker scares me. Guys like that, bottling so much hatred and violence, they terrify me."

"Shit! The guy's a walking bomb. Why did you mix it up with him in there? God, I'll never understand women."

"You have a lot of women friends who like to interview parolees on the Block?"

"No, thank God. You're a first." He stopped short, and I almost lost my balance slamming into him. "Why are you doing this? What's in it for you?" he demanded as he steadied me.

I stared up into the strained lines of his face. "I don't know. I just feel I have to."

"You and Susie Zillig were that good friends?"

It wasn't Susie I was doing this for, but Rebecca and, in a strange way, Nick and me. How could I explain that to a man like O'Dell when I couldn't explain it to myself?

"Yes," I lied. "Anyhow, I feel I owe her something. Listen, would you be willing to do me another favor?"

"Jesus," he shouted at me, "now what have you got in mind?"

"Could you find out if the testimony of one of Acker's victims was responsible for putting him behind bars? And if it was, could you find out what happened to that woman?"

Instead of answering, he started walking again. For a couple of minutes he strode along in ominous silence while I trotted after. "You mean like if she's still around?" he finally asked.

"Yeah, like that."

"Once you get hold of a crazy notion, you hold on like an alligator with lockjaw, don't you?"

"I wasn't always that way. I used to be sweet and submissive, but it didn't get me far in life. Will you do it?"

He sighed, then shook himself the same way I'd

seen a polar bear shake water out of his coat at the zoo, a kind of ready-for-action signal. "Sure I'll do it. Why not? It isn't as if I have a better way to spend all my spare time."

I laughed, and then he broke down and chuckled, too. Half a block farther down, he stopped in front of Fuddruckers. "Have you eaten yet?"

"No."

"Me neither, and I'm starved. Mind if I buy us both a burger in here?"

Since I was hungry, too, and broke, I didn't give it more than three seconds' thought. I mean, a hamburger is no big social contract. "Okay."

It turned out to be a beer and a hamburger and then some double Dutch chocolate ice cream. But that was okay, too. We talked about neutral things, the weather, city politics, the recession. He didn't ask me about Nick, and I didn't ask him if he'd shot anybody between the eyes lately. Afterward he drove me home. Neither of us said much in the car until he pulled up in front of Randall's. Then he half turned so he could look at me directly.

Nervous because I'd sensed the change in the atmosphere between us, I spoke before he had the chance. "Well, thanks for dinner." I put my hand on the door handle.

"Before you go in, Toni, is there any chance I could take you out?"

"You mean like a date?"

"Yeah, a date."

I laughed at his expression. The word obviously didn't taste so good in his mouth, and I knew how he felt. We were both too cantankerous to think of ourselves as date material.

Then something in his eyes made me get serious while I thought it over. I couldn't lie to myself that I wasn't tempted to give him a green light. Bells had been ringing for me ever since meeting this guy. Why? Was it because in a lot of ways he reminded me of Nick? O'Dell was a tough, macho cop with a violent streak. It didn't show on the surface, but I knew it had to be there or he wouldn't be in this line of work. It wasn't just because of how Simpler had talked about him. Even I could figure out that nice guys with gentle spirits do not become crack shots so they can kill people for a living. I shook my head. "It's not that I don't like you, but—"

"Thanks but no thanks? Is it because you're hung up on Damon?"

"That's not it. He and I really are just good friends. Look, I'll be straight with you. You've heard about my husband. I just don't think I want to get cozy with another policeman. I'm not ..." Tongue-tied, I finished up lamely. "I'm sorry."

An invisible mask had dropped down over O'Dell's face. "Don't worry about it. My ex-wife felt exactly the same way." He reached into his pocket and pulled out a card. "My home phone in case you want to get in touch after hours."

"Thanks."

"I don't mean in case you change your mind about the date. I mean in case you should need help."

"Gotcha. I appreciate that."

"Yeah, well, listen, good night and good luck. I'll wait to make sure you get in safely."

"Thanks."

"Welcome."

* * *

Inside, Randall had two pieces of news for me, one bad and one worrisome. "I got a call from your sister. She says your mother is fidgety about you. She tried phoning you at home but got no answer—naturally, since you're not living there for now. Sandy thinks you should give her a ring."

I nodded and turned away. Randall followed me. "Something wrong?"

"What could be wrong? Don't I have a perfect life?"

"Who rattled your cage, pumpkin? Did some lowlife hassle you on the bus?"

"I didn't take the bus. Detective O'Dell gave me a ride home."

"Did he feed you, too, or do you want some of the omelet I'm about to whip up?"

"Thanks, but we ate."

"Ah, wined and dined by the Sir Lancelot of the BPD. So, what happened to put that dour expression on your face? Did you find walnut shells in your baklava?"

I couldn't even imagine O'Dell partaking of a gooey, sweet dessert like baklava. "He asked me for a date."

"And?"

"And nothing. I said no."

Randall cocked his handsome head. "You don't look happy about it."

"Right now I'm just not a cheery person, Randall. A complication like O'Dell is the last thing I need. What's wrong? Now you look as if you're the one upset about something."

"Sandy isn't the only one who called. Jonathan checked in, too. He wants me to pick him up at the airport tomorrow. Afraid you're going to have to move out of his bedroom. But you can sleep on the couch in the living room as long as you want."

The couch in Randall's living room was a claw-footed Victorian number covered in red velvet. Only Camille would be comfortable sleeping on it. The curtain was about to drop on my interlude of safe haven with Randall. Tomorrow I'd have to move back in with Rebecca.

Alone in Jonathan's bedroom, I sagged onto his bed and put my head in my hands. My temples throbbed, and I felt slightly sick to my stomach. All the delicious fatty beef I'd consumed at Fuddruckers wasn't sitting so well on my stomach. I didn't want to think about O'Dell or the interview with Acker. But it wouldn't go away.

My eye fell on Simpler's book sitting next to the telephone on the bedside table. Big and fat and impenetrable, it challenged me. With a sigh, I fished my pad of phone numbers out of my purse and dialed him. If he'd interviewed Acker and Espey, I wanted to ask him a few questions. No one answered. So much for that. Next I dialed my mother. She picked up on the second ring.

"Credella's."

"Mom, it's Toni. You busy?"

"We've got a big crowd out in the dining room, but it doesn't matter. I want to talk to you, Toni."

"How are you doing?"

"I'm fine. The doctor says I don't have any problems. Hah, what does he know. Tomorrow I'll probably keel over, and the next day I'll be in my coffin. I don't want to talk about me, Toni. I'm an old woman."

"Mom, you're not—" There's nothing like growing up with a parent who's a positive thinker.

"My life is over," she continued. "But you're still young, with everything in front of you. It's you I worry about. How come I couldn't reach you at home last night? It was late when I called."

"I was with a friend."

"A beautiful young girl like you shouldn't be out so late. It's not good for your reputation."

I restrained myself from pointing out that preserving my spotless name wasn't really a major consideration in my life these days.

"Where are you now? Are you safe at home?"

"I'm at Randall's. He's fixing an omelet."

Small unhappy silence. Mom didn't approve of Randall, but she also had to know he wasn't threatening my virtue.

"Toni, is something wrong where you live?"

I pressed a hand to my chest. Damn. My mother almost never looked at a newspaper. By some fluke, had she seen a story about Susie or Damon? Or had Sandy said something? "What makes you ask, Mom?"

"I had another dream about you, a bad dream. Toni, when I think of it my heart closes up with fear."

"What was the dream?"

Her voice throttled down to a frightened whisper. "It was a bug, a big bug."

"A bug?"

"It was eating at your face, Toni. There was blood everywhere. When I woke up, I wanted to scream."

"A bug." My gaze went to Herbie, who crouched on the bureau opposite the sleigh bed. All of a sudden he didn't look so harmless anymore.

16

Another sleepless night, another frenzied morning. I rushed between the kitchen and the bedroom trying to get myself ready for work and for moving back into my apartment.

"You don't have to leave," Randall kept insisting. "Just because Jonathan's coming back . . ."

"Honest," I said as I poured myself a cup of brew from his sleek black Krups coffeemaker, "it's okay. Three's a crowd and all that."

"It's not okay. You're scared about going back to that place, and no wonder. If you don't want to stay here, why don't you move in with your folks?"

"Because the idea of that scares me even more. I'll be fine. Removing myself from your premises will be a breeze. It isn't as if I have a lot of packing to do." Everything I'd brought to Randall's, including Herbie, I'd been able to stuff into three plastic bags. That included my gun. I hadn't mentioned to Randall that I was taking it, and, happily, it hadn't occurred to him to ask. If he knew I planned to carry a concealed weapon in a plastic shopping bag, he'd have a fit. But how else was I going to get it home without putting him to a lot of extra trouble?

Randall stalked around his kitchen, straightening his Brooks Brothers tie, checking to make sure that his gold cuff links were positioned symmetrically on his snowy cuffs. Obviously he wasn't buying my devil-may-care pose. "If you won't find another place for yourself, I'll do it for you. I'll start looking tonight."

"Randall—"

He held up a hand. "Say no more. If I'm to get to the office on time, I'd better drop you off at work now."

I showed Herbie to Ron Smith later that morning. It never would have happened except that I had the bug with me in my bags of clothes—along with the gun. To get the bags out of the way, I'd stowed them under my workbench.

Ron, a man with infinite patience, was teaching me how to apply gold leaf to a picture frame. Playing around with gold is not a cheap pastime. However, it's not as expensive as you might think, either. The leaf comes in little sheets one–two-hundred-and-fifty-thousandth of an inch thick. These sheets are created by people called gold beaters. Now, that has to be a strange way to make a living. "How was your day, dear?" "Oh, just the usual, standing around hour after hour beating up on gold."

As you can imagine, applying this stuff requires a certain finesse. It's done with a gilder's knife: first you brush the knife across your forehead for the grease and to pick up a light charge from the skin; then, with a deft flick of the wrist, you let it glide onto the prepared surface you want to gild. It was the deft wrist action I couldn't quite get.

As Ron demonstrated this technique for the fifth time, his toe scrunched one of the bags I'd stuck under my worktable. "What's that?"

"Just some clothes."

He probed some more. "Feels like something hard and pointy."

I worried about the gun. "Oh, yeah, Herbie."

"Herbie?"

"It's this big plastic bug that someone left in my place as a sick joke."

"What kind of friends you got, girl?"

"The kind my mother warned me about. Want to see the bug?" It had occurred to me that Herbie might be a theatrical prop of some kind and that Ron, with his knowledge of things artistic, might know something about it. Anyhow, since I'd probably have to turn it over to O'Dell pretty soon, it was worth a shot.

"Now why would I want to see a thing like that?"

I already had it out of the bag. When Ron's eyes lit on the bug, they blinked and then stretched so wide that the whites ringed the iris. I'd showed Herbie to half a dozen people who hadn't had any idea what he was or where he might come from. One look and Ron declared, "Bet I know where that bug came from."

"You're kidding."

"Nope. It's an antique store in Fells Point. Strange little place."

"Where in Fells Point?"

"On Fleet just off Broadway. It's called Antique

Freak, if I remember right. He's got a bunch of bugs just like that."

A *whoosh* of excitement knocked my heartbeat into double time. "What did you mean when you said it was 'strange'?"

Ron winked. Mischief danced in his dark eyes. "Words fail me. You'll just have to go see for yourself."

I'd been debating whether I should really go back home to Charles Village or whether I should accept Randall's advice and ask my parents to take me in for a few days. This tipped the scale. After work I'd drop in on Mom and Pop. But first I'd go to Fells Point and check out Antique Freak.

By the time I got to Fleet late that afternoon, I was afraid the store might be closed. Lots of the shops on these narrow little streets open only at their owners' whim. No place else is quite like Fells Point. Before I started working regular hours, it was one of my favorite places to go for a late breakfast and some goofing off. After I'd picked up coffee and a Danish at the Broadway Market, I'd just walk around taking in the sights. I'd check out the fleet of tugs at rest in the harbor, observe the night's collection of trash sloshing up against the pilings, and feed the seagulls gabfesting around the garbage cans.

After I'd tossed my coffee cup, I'd stroll east and scope out the line of huge beer trucks that crowd the southern end of Broadway. Their mission, should they choose to accept it—and they always do—is to replenish the stock of the dozen bars along pub row, places like the Cat's Eye, the Admiral's Cup, the Horse You Came in on Saloon. An hour before noon the iron doors to their cellars are thrown open, and workers lounge on mountains of beer cases stacked on the sidewalk. The more energetic ones stand around their trucks smoking and gossiping.

Sometimes I'd hang around to see the character of the place change. The bars would fill up. The bag ladies and bums and arty types would come out and mingle with the tourists—maybe try to persuade some change out of them. In the old days Fells Point was one of the busiest seafaring centers in the colonies. Ships from all over the world traded here. I remember from something I heard in school that Frederick Douglass learned to read by walking the cobblestone streets along the docks and studying the names of whalers and China traders. Now Fells Point is the drinking capital of Baltimore. But it's still alive and kicking.

I almost passed right by Antique Freak before I realized my mistake. It didn't exactly specialize in Queen Anne and silver. Displayed in the jam-packed window was a full suit of armor with the balloon head of Bart Simpson peering out from behind the visor. A large plastic Santa, several glass tops of old gas station pumps, grimy Donald Duck and Mickey Mouse statues, and a six-foot Styrofoam representation of a caped vampire all vied for floor space.

The inside of the store was equally crowded and even stranger. It was dark, musty, and teemed with motley objects. You could walk from one end to the other only by threading a narrow path and keeping your arms pinned to your sides. Grinning Little Black Sambo cookie jars, chipped wooden yard ornaments, nudes that reclined at the base of brass lamps, decoys, cat clocks with eyes that rolled back and forth as they ticked, things that looked as if they'd been hiding in your crazy aunt's attic or had been found at the side of the road in one of those jumble sales jammed either side of the aisle.

I leaned my elbows on a long glass case and then blinked and stepped back as I saw what reclined inside it.

"Something I can do for you?"

A fairly normal-looking guy in jeans lounged up behind me. Nevertheless, since it had occurred to me that if he were connected with my bug, he might be the killer, I decided to engage him in cautious conversation before getting to the reason for my visit. "What's that?" I pointed down at the mummified creature in the case.

"Kap-dwa, *Homo gigantis*."

"You mean it's a giant?" When he nodded, I asked, "Is it real?" How stupid can you get? Of course it couldn't be real.

"Who knows. The Bible tells us giants once walked the earth. Here." He handed me a sheet of yellow paper. "Tells you all about him."

I pretended to scan the paper, but I knew it would take an hour of work before I'd be able to make head or tail of it. I folded it and stuck it in my jacket pocket for later study. "You're selling him?"

He nodded, deadpan. "For the right price. Interested?"

"Now what would I do with a ten-foot mummy in a glass case?"

"Make a hell of a coffee table."

"Yeah, a real conversation piece. This is quite a store you have here."

"My partner and I like it." So he had a partner.

Another candidate for killer? *Careful, Toni, don't go shooting your mouth off until you know what you're doing.* "Mind if I look around?"

"Be my guest." A couple came in, and he turned his attention to them.

I poked here and there, hoping to find something that resembled my bug. It didn't take me long. At the back of the store I was leaning over an old wicker baby carriage, trying to get a better look at a Victorian bronze statue behind it. I glanced down and then let out a little squeak and jumped back.

The carriage held a skull wearing a leather World War I pilot's helmet. Skeletal hands poked out from a blanket, and in the center of the baby blanket sat a plastic insect identical to Herbie. My head swung up, and I spotted another dangling from the ceiling. To my right a third perched in the velvet-skirted lap of a blue-eyed mannequin with long shaggy blond hair.

Nerves jumping, I walked back to where the proprietor sat perusing a horror comic. "That's an interesting arrangement you've got in the baby carriage back there."

"Glad you like it." He smiled sardonically. "My partner dreamed it up."

This partner of his was really beginning to intrigue me. "Imaginative fellow." I knew I was taking a chance, but what the hell— "Listen, I'm curious about the bugs. Where did you get them?"

"The bugs? Oh, yeah, came from an exterminator who had a place around here. I think he used them to demonstrate what his customers had running around in their houses."

The answer came so easy, it floored me. And it really was as obvious as the nose on my face. Why hadn't I thought of it myself? Yes, they were props. But not theatrical props—exterminator props.

"Do you know his name?"

"Uh, not offhand. I'd have to look in my records for that."

"Could you? It's real important."

He looked at me curiously. "Why? What's the big deal?"

"It's a personal matter, a very important one. I'd really appreciate it if you could give me the information."

"Okay, but I can't do it until later tonight. The records are in my computer, and that's at home. Leave your phone number and I'll call you, okay?"

I hesitated. I'd been toying with the idea of sacking out at my parents' place. But I didn't want to receive a call like this one at Credella's. Mom or Pop might pick up the phone, and they wouldn't rest until they'd pried all the details out of me. Then I'd never hear the end of it.

On the other hand, the only other phone number I could tell him was mine back at Charles Village. Ruefully I gave that. Like it or not, I'd just have to spend another cozy night with Rebecca, at least until I heard about this exterminator. After that maybe I could head for Little Italy or even to Randall's if I was really desperate.

By the time I walked back downtown and used my last quarters for bus fare, it was dark. The driver let me off on the corner, and I trudged down the sidewalk with a feeling of dread in the pit of my stomach.

Aronchick's building showed nary a light. Of course not. Susie's place was empty, and Damon was still in the hospital. I wasn't home yet, either. But soon I would be, and I'd be all alone.

As I unlocked the outside door, I considered breaking into the second and third floors and turning lights on to make the upstairs apartments appear occupied. But that was silly. If the person I was afraid of had killed Susie and shot Damon, he'd know they weren't there.

When the door swung open, I snaked my arm in and switched on the porch light. The hall was empty. Inside it, I unlocked my apartment door and pulled the same maneuver, switching on my living room light before I walked in. My heart thudded away like a wrecking ball, and my stomach was doing major flippety-flops. My living room appeared empty. Of course, a murderer could always be waiting in the bedroom or kitchen.

I have to stop coming home like this, I thought as I slipped inside and stood there staring around with saucer eyes. I dumped the contents of the plastic bag on the floor and took out the gun. Then I loaded it and held it in front of me while I searched through the apartment. Nothing. The place was clean.

Whew! I made sure the locks on the windows and door were tight and then removed the cartridges from the gun and left them in a little brass pile next to it on a table. After that I went back into the kitchen to scratch up some dinner.

I found only canned tomato soup and stale English muffins, which was fine. Really, Randall's gourmet repasts and nightly bottles of pricey wine were a little rich for my simple tastes. My jeans were tight enough so that I knew I'd put on a couple pounds. Besides, I'm one of those people who actually likes canned tomato soup.

I spooned it up in front of the TV while I watched the "MacNeil/Lehrer NewsHour." When it was over, I dialed Simpler's number again. Nobody answered. Then I washed up and sat waiting for the phone to ring. It didn't make a peep until almost nine-thirty.

"Ms. Credella?"

"Yes?"

"This is Bob Ricardo. You know, Antique Freak?"

"Yes, hi."

"Sorry to be calling so late. Something came up at the store and I didn't get home until just about an hour ago."

"No problem. Have you had a chance to check your files yet?"

"I'm sitting in front of the computer looking at them now."

"And?" I felt breathless. This could be it, the big clue.

"The exterminator had a place called Bugout over on Baltimore Street. He sold us the fake insects when he retired about four years ago. His name was Ivan Heiser."

Well, Ivan Heiser was nobody I'd ever heard of. Still, this might be a serious breakthrough. And if it wasn't, I now had other possibilities to pursue—like Bob's partner.

"I wonder if you could give me your partner's name and number. I'd like to talk to him."

"Well, his name is Bruce. But you can't talk to him unless you're willing to call Paris. That's where he's been for the last three months."

"Oh." So Ivan Heiser was my only option. I thanked Ricardo and hung up. After pacing up and down a couple of times, I dug my phone book out of the drawer under the counter and looked under the H's.

I was lucky at guessing the spelling. There were several Heisers and one Ivan Heiser. He lived at 4396 Indianola. I know Baltimore well enough that that street name rang a bell. With a sigh of resignation, I unearthed my map.

There are lots of things I'm terrible at, and one of the worst is deciphering maps. It must have taken three-quarters of an hour of squinting and groaning to figure out the exact location of Indianola. The street wasn't all that far from me. The realization put the tiny hairs on the back of my neck at attention.

I glanced at my digital watch and saw it was ten-thirty. Then I looked over at the black squares of the windows. For the first time that night I thought about the black Volvo. What if it came by tonight? What if it had a handicapped sticker because it belonged to Ivan Heiser? He had to be an old man, right? So what was a handicapped old man doing murdering and raping young women and taking potshots at Damon? That didn't make sense. But maybe I was overlooking something. Maybe Ivan had a demented nephew or a creepy roomer who borrowed his car and his bugs when he wasn't looking. Anyhow, there just might be a connection. And if the black Volvo came by tonight, I might have a chance of figuring it out.

However, despite my earlier delusions of grandeur, I was no heroine. I'd far rather someone else figured it out.

First I dialed Randall and got his answering

machine. He and Jonathan were probably out wining and dining. Damn, I really needed his advice. After I hung up, I chewed my thumbnail. The beep on Randall's machine had sounded long. That meant the tape on his machine had to be full of messages, and possibly some of them were for me. I redialed his number and pressed the code he'd given me to replay his messages. Sure enough, one of them was from O'Dell.

"This is Gus O'Dell calling at five forty-five P.M. I thought you'd be interested to know that I checked Acker's court records. The testimony of a woman named Janet Greenwich put Acker in jail. Three years ago Greenwich moved to Columbus, Ohio. When I checked with the police department there, I was informed that thirteen months ago Janet Greenwich was raped and murdered. The MO was the same as that for Rebecca and Susie. At that time, Acker was still in jail."

I don't know how long I stood there, transfixed. Finally I searched out O'Dell's card and dialed, first his office phone—he was off duty—then his home number. Another answering machine.

With disgust, I listened to his recorded voice and then slammed the receiver down on the cradle. The damn machines are taking over the world. I called the police department and demanded to speak to him. They told me he was off duty and not answering his beeper. I slammed the receiver down again.

Well, of course, this *was* Friday night. Probably when I'd turned him down Thursday, he'd driven back to the Block and made a date with one of those hookers. Good for him. She'd probably be better for his type of guy than an uptight broad like me ever would be. But what had he made of this new info on Acker and its tie-in to Espey and Susie Zillig's murder? A pattern was being established. It was just a matter of figuring out what it meant.

As a last resort, I dialed my sister's number. Ordinarily I'd never dream of asking Al Pennak for help. But I was desperate. A tinkly little-girl voice answered, and my insides sank like a soufflé.

"Pennak residence."

"I'd like to speak to Mr. or Mrs. Pennak, please."

"Sorry, they're out. This is the baby-sitter. Can I take a message?"

I weighed that and rechecked my watch. Getting close to eleven. "Yes, you can. Please write this down carefully. Ask Al to call his sister-in-law when he gets back. If I'm not home, I've gone to—" I gave her Ivan Heiser's address. "Tell Al I think this man might be connected with Rebecca Kelso and Susie Zillig. Okay?"

"Uh, yeah, sure." The baby-sitter sounded highly confused. Probably thought I was a crackpot. Maybe she had me right.

After I hung up, I stood squeezing my temples with the heels of my hands. It was almost as if I were afraid my skull might explode. I couldn't seem to get away from the scheme taking shape in my brain like the monster from Planet Nancy Drew. That didn't mean I liked it. No, not one bit!

In desperation, I redialed O'Dell. Damned answering machine again. As I listened to his recorded voice, I pictured him cavorting in bed with one of those bimbos. I wondered what he would be like naked and panting with lust. However, I didn't waste much mental energy on this, as I had more compelling matters to consider.

At the sound of the beep, I identified myself and explained about the bug. I told him what I planned to do and gave him Ivan Heiser's address. I hoped O'Dell had a long tape in his recorder and that he was either home listening now or would be home listening soon. Reluctantly I replaced the receiver and stood with my fists clenched at my sides. I wanted O'Dell to call back right away. He didn't. I took a big gulp of air. Did I really intend to do what I intended to do? I asked myself. The answer was yes, I really did.

The minutes were ticking by. For all I knew, the Volvo had already come and gone and this was an exercise in absurdity. Nevertheless, having decided, I moved quickly. I changed into sneakers, my black spandex riding pants, and a dark-colored jacket. My pocket flash went into that. Then I snapped a pouch around my waist and slipped a spray cylinder of Pro-Stun in one pocket and the unloaded gun and a dozen cartridges in the other. I left a light on in the living room and went out in the hall and unlocked my bike.

Walking the bike down the porch steps made me feel vulnerable and silly. What if the Volvo cruised by now? If he happened to have his rifle handy, he could pick me off as he flew past. No Volvo, so I had plenty of time to hide myself and the bike in the bushes at the side of the porch.

Now I really felt idiotic. As I shivered in the darkness, I reviewed all the possibilities and felt monumentally stupid. The Volvo had already come and gone. I was imagining the whole thing, anyway. It would never show up, and I'd stand here all night freezing—even though the night was still fairly warm.

What if Al or O'Dell called back now? I'd hear the

phone, but I'd never be able to get back inside to answer it in time. They'd go racing over to this Ivan Heiser's house and make fools of themselves because there was probably no connection between him and the Volvo anyway. They'd never forgive me. I felt even more idiotic. I was about to roll the bike out from behind the bushes and call the whole business quits when I saw it.

As it approached my block, the big, square car slowed and rolled forward at a snail's pace. I squinted through the shadows, trying to get a look at whoever was inside. But the interior of the car was an inky pit. I could make out only headlights and the boxy shape.

It was my Volvo all right. My car of death, my circling automotive shark, my bogeyman. Right now it was stalking me. I was going to turn things around and stalk it. Ignoring the frantic rat-a-tat of my heart, I tightened my grip on the handlebars of my bike and waited.

It took forever, but finally the Volvo cruised past and disappeared around the corner. The moment it was out of sight, I wheeled the bike onto the postage-stamp lawn and jumped aboard. I was so nervous and scared, I almost fell over. I righted myself, dug my heels into the scrubby grass, and pushed off.

I bounced the bike off the sidewalk and onto the street. Pedaling at a furious rate, I crossed Charles and headed toward the Johns Hopkins campus. I couldn't follow the Volvo without being seen, but I thought I knew where it was going, and I wanted to get there first.

Cutting through that and Wyman Park to Roland Avenue would give me a head start. The Volvo's driver would have to take a less direct route—especially if he intended circling my block a couple more times. Maybe he even planned to stop in for a visit. Maybe I was safer pedaling a bike through Baltimore's crime-ridden night streets than I was sitting home alone with nobody but Rebecca to stand up for me.

Consoling argument, but I didn't feel any too safe as I zoomed past Art Museum Drive and then caught a footpath that connected with Stony Run. Wyman Park was just an extension of Druid Hill Park. Bad stuff happens in both places these days, as Susie Zillig had found out.

The wind bit into my face. Grit pummeled my eyes so I could barely see. Somewhere to my right I heard dogs howl. There were stories going around about a pack of wild dogs in the park. I jumped a curb and almost crash-landed. If I fell going at this speed, I'd crack my head open. Then the dogs would smell blood and eat me alive. *Early this morning half a young woman's body was found—*

My legs pumped furiously and my heart banged against my rib cage as if it wanted to get out and fly away like one of those weather balloons.

Take it easy, Toni. Cool it. Don't make yourself crazy. You're not even in any real danger yet. You're just taking a little ride through Baltimore's scenic night spots. Yeah, sure.

As my bike stuttered over a speed bump, I nearly toppled again. Somehow I retrieved my balance and seconds later spilled out onto University Parkway. My thighs ached, but I was so pumped on adrenaline that I hardly noticed.

University Parkway turns into Roland Avenue. It was scary riding it at night. Though traffic had thinned, the occasional car still whizzed past and cut within inches of my unprotected body. It occurred to me I might encounter the Volvo on this street. Not a happy thought.

Next empty stretch I veered to the left and started cutting through side streets. That wasn't as fast, but I felt safer. Roland Park is a classy old neighborhood filled with winding, overgrown lanes. Its big houses are shingle or stucco. They are the kinds of houses where you would like to be invited for Christmas and where a rich, kindly grandmother who bakes cookies ought to live. Many perch atop hills or are set back behind tall trees and thick stands of rhododendron and mountain laurel.

I know all about rhododendron because when I was a kid my mother took me to the Cylburn Arboretum. The lush, purple flowers and the thick, leathery green leaves I saw there stunned me. Since then I've been very rhododendron-conscious, especially in spring. Back then I imagined that one day I would have a yard filled with them and a big, old rambling house in Roland Park, too. Now, of course, that's an idea I've abandoned.

Panting and breathless, I rounded the corner on Indianola. I braked and then cruised gingerly down the street, peering at house numbers and keeping an eye out for headlights. Roland Parkers aren't night owls—too busy getting eight hours' sleep so they can be fresh to drive the kids to private day school come seven A.M.

Except for an occasional upstairs window, the

street was dark. Cars were tucked away in garages or parked safely on driveways. House numbers were impossible to see. The only way I finally zeroed in on 4396 was because the house next to it had its porch light on. Just as I approached, whoever lived inside switched it off.

I was glad. Tonight darkness was my friend.

Ivan Heiser's place was a typical Roland Park shingled bungalow with a big screened-in front porch and dormer windows. A hedge of lilacs cut it off from the other houses. They were blooming, and as I wheeled my bike up to the edge of the drive, their seductive scent perfumed the damp night air. The smell was so divine, it made me want to cry. How could there be anything bad here in the midst of such sweetness? Certainly there was no sign of a Volvo in the empty drive.

So either I was completely loony tunes and the Volvo and this house weren't connected, or I had beaten my mystery car back here and should consider competing in the next Tour de France. On the off chance that the latter was the case, I hid my bike in a stand of evergreens across the street and waited.

I waited a long time. One car rolled down the street. It wasn't a Volvo, and it kept right on going past. I watched it pull into a driveway half a block down. After that, nothing.

Bedroom lights blinked off. A wind came up, and the night got chillier. A ragged cloud scudded across the thin wedge of moon. My legs ached and the insides of my thighs felt sore from all the bruising they'd taken during the ride. This is silly, I told myself. This whole thing was a wild goose chase. *You should just turn around and go home, Toni.*

All the while, I studied the black hulk of Ivan's house. When the moon escaped a cloud I could see that the yard looked unkempt. The bushes to either side were out of control. Not that I'm an expert, but compared to my sister's neatly trimmed property, this place was a hedge clipper's paradise. Where were Sandy and Al now? I wondered. Had they got my message? Had O'Dell got it? What if they all showed up here prepared to defend me? This could be seriously embarrassing.

Still, I lingered on. Despite my conviction that coming here had been stupid and waiting around dumber yet, I couldn't seem to tear myself away. Maybe I was afraid of riding back through the park. At last, however, I knew the time had come to do something. I wheeled my bike out onto the road. Instead of getting on, I walked it across the street and left it leaning against a lilac. I'd decided I'd just take a quick walk around the house and see if I could get a peek into one of the windows.

The windows in the front were shuttered tight. I kept walking until I found a basement window. It was too dark to see anything through it. Then I came to the side door. My brain knew I shouldn't touch it. My hand had its own ideas. It reached out, gripped the knob, and turned it. The door swung open.

I snatched a deep breath and then stepped in. I took out my pocket flash and swung the beam around. I was on a landing. One set of stairs led down to the basement, another went up. Gingerly I mounted the up side. It opened to a kitchen. A tiny red light burned to the left. I swung my flash and saw that a coffeemaker was on. I smelled a familiar aroma, but I didn't stop to analyze it. The beam of my flash had lit on the bulletin board over the tubular steel-and-Formica table. My picture was fixed to it, held in place with a nail through the forehead.

I gasped and then walked forward and stared. No question, it was the drawing Damon had made of me. So now I knew what had happened to it. I lifted my head. The house felt empty, but that didn't mean it really was. Mr. Art Lover could be sleeping upstairs. Or maybe he was hiding behind a corner waiting to grab me and pound a real nail in between my eyes.

I swiveled and hurried back the way I'd come. As I hit the small landing at the foot of the kitchen stairs, my flash picked up another drawing tacked to the wall. It was the one Damon had made of Susie. A reddish brown X had been painted over it. Dried blood?

My breath came out in a horrified *whoosh*. My pulse roared in my ear. Instead of going for the door, I took a step down to get a better look at the picture. The beam of my flash picked up another picture. It was Rebecca's.

I took another step down and then another. This Ivan guy had quite a portrait gallery. Not just women I knew, either. There were lots of pictures, photos taken from newspapers, snapshots, line drawings. Horrified but fascinated, I let my flash play over each one, all the time going step by step farther down into the basement. At the foot of the rough wooden staircase I played my beam around the dank darkness that surrounded me on three sides. Then I froze. My light had picked out the body of a naked woman.

17

She'd been laid out on what looked to be an old billiard table covered with some shiny material. Someone had stretched her arms to the sides and tied her hands and legs down with twine secured to metal clamps screwed into the corners of the table.

I wanted to bolt. I wanted to fly out of there and leap on my bike. But I couldn't until I'd checked to see if she was dead. All the time I'd been staring at her, she hadn't moved. Yet it was too dark to see well. What if she were still alive and I could help her?

Pressing an ice-cold hand against the cement-block wall to steady my quivering legs, I began inching down the steps. I told myself I should look around for a light switch. Yet I didn't. Part of me knew I had to find out exactly what was down there. Another part of me didn't want to see it.

When I got to the floor I stood with the beam of my flash directed at the pale body. It was the color and texture of soap. Intuitively I knew that was how it would feel, waxy and cold. The basement was refrigerator-cool, which, if she were dead and had been that way for any length of time, might account for my not smelling anything.

Holding the flash in front of me as if it were a weapon, I took a few steps forward. She was a young woman. Slim, well made. I moved the beam to her head. She had short, dark hair. Then I inhaled, and my breath gurgled in my constricted throat. It was Gloria Simpler.

"Gloria," I whispered harshly.

She didn't answer me. I skimmed the beam to her breasts. She wasn't breathing. Then I saw the blood. "Oh, God." I took several more shaky steps toward the table. Black plastic of the type that gardeners use under mulch beds covered it. To catch the blood? To make cleanup easier? There was a long gash across Gloria's throat. An obscene crust of blood caked her breasts and chest. There was congealed blood all over her legs and her crotch. Her pretty blue eyes were open, staring up sightlessly.

My hand jerked, and the beam of my flash caught a bit of fresh scarlet color. Her toenails. They had been painted bright red.

That was all I could take. I whirled around, my free hand flattened to my mouth. I had to get out of there. I had galloped halfway up the stairs when I heard it. The sound of an engine. A car had just pulled into the drive. I froze, my heart thudding like an overwound metronome. The Volvo. I knew it even though I had no window to look out of. And I knew who was driving it.

I raced the rest of the way up to the landing. It was

too late to go out the side door. He'd probably come in that way. From what I knew of him, he always came in the side door. And, oh damn! He'd probably already seen my bike. Stupid, stupid! Like a fool, I'd left it leaning against the lilac bushes next to the drive.

My brain thrashed like a fish in a net. The front door? Maybe, if I could find it fast enough, I could slip out that way while he was coming in the side.

As I was thinking this, I dashed through the kitchen and into what had to be the dining room. It was pitch black in there, and terror blinded me. As my flash bounced off unfamiliar shapes, I crashed into the dining room table. A chair fell over. I was huffing and puffing, the sound of it deafening in my ears. I jumped over the chair and headed through an arch.

Unfortunately, the house was not a center-hall design. I went directly into a living room jammed with a million pieces of old-fashioned furniture. Some were covered with sheets. A musty smell hung in the air—old fabric, old stuffing, Oriental rugs that had absorbed the dust of too many years. The skittering beam of my flash revealed a staircase on the far side. It must go to the bedrooms. I didn't want the bedrooms. I wanted out!

I spotted a little hall leading off between two big shuttered windows. The door. I rushed for it. After I slid to a stop in front of it, I stood with my hand on the knob, listening. When he comes in the side, I'll go out the front, my brain chanted. But I didn't hear the door on the side click. Everything was quiet. Too quiet.

He must have found my bike, I thought. He must

be waiting for me. At that point I remembered the gun and the Pro-Stun I'd stuck in my pouch. Unfortunately, the gun wasn't loaded. I'd been afraid to bounce around on a bike with a loaded gun. The bullets were in the pouch, but in the dark I was afraid to try loading when at any moment I might need my hands to open the door and fly out. I was convinced he must be waiting on the driveway near my bike or by the side door. If I was right, I could still make a dash for it.

Just for insurance, I swung my pouch around to the front and fished out the canister of Pro-Stun. Then I pushed the pouch back in place. After taking a deep breath and bracing myself to leap forward, I turned the knob and cautiously pulled the door open. It exploded inward, and Jeff Simpler locked a hand around my wrist. The Pro-Stun dropped from my hand and crashed on the floor.

"Hello, Toni," he said. "Welcome to my humble abode."

I yanked back, and he slapped me so viciously that I was knocked momentarily senseless. It felt hideously familiar, for Nick had hit me that way. While I struggled to clear my head, Simpler pinned me against him and then swiveled and set an elaborate system of dead bolts on the door. With clammy horror, I realized he'd used a key to lock it from the inside.

"You're not very smart, Toni," he said in a voice that hummed with excitement. "I knew you'd go for the front. I always go in the side door at Mt. Washington, so you thought you'd outsmart me, didn't you. Fat chance. I could outthink you so easily. I can outthink them all. Stupid, stupid, all of them stupid." He laughed gloatingly. "I knew I was going to get you. I knew you were meant for me. It was just a matter of time."

His voice scraped over me like a buzzsaw. Why had I ever imagined it was soothing? He flicked on a light, and I found myself staring up into his eyes. Blue, colder than polar ice, yet flaring with maniac fire. "So I didn't have to get you, after all. You came to me. You even opened the door and welcomed me in." Then, as he gazed down at me, I saw his mouth twist. He started to laugh again, evil and low.

It started a chain reaction in my gut. I kicked him in the shin, jabbed at his face with my free hand, and sank my teeth into his wrist. Somehow I tore loose and started to run back toward the dining room, hoping to make the side door. My feet stumbled over the canister and kicked it hopelessly out of my reach. Simpler seized my shoulders.

"You'll be sorry for that," he screeched into my ear as he spun me around. He punched me so hard that he sent me sprawling on the white-sheeted couch. I tasted blood in my mouth. My head was jammed up against a wooden armrest. The pouch around my middle jabbed into my backbone, reminding me of the gun it still held, for all the good it would do me unloaded.

"How did you find this place?" Simpler demanded. "Did Gloria tell you about my stepfather? I bet that's it. Gloria did a lot of stupid things."

I tried to push up, but Simpler hit me again and then clutched my shoulders and ground me down into the couch with his full weight. All the while he glared into my eyes. I hated looking at him. It was like staring at death. For now I saw in his eyes what I'd been too blind to see there before. Hatred, raw, gloating hatred. And this was a man I'd confided some of my most intimate secrets to, a man I'd thought wanted to help me.

"You can't get away," he said. "All the women who tried getting away made a big mistake. You saw Gloria down there, didn't you?"

When I didn't answer, he shook me until my teeth rattled and then slapped me twice across the mouth again. "Didn't you?" He grabbed my hair and yanked viciously.

"Yes, yes, I saw her," I cried.

"She tried to leave me," he whispered. "Not a good idea. Now she'll never leave anybody."

"You killed her."

"Oh, yes. Oh, yes. I certainly did."

"You killed them all. Susie. Rebecca."

"Oh, yes. More than that. Many more." He said it matter-of-factly, his gaze still glued to my face, studying me as if I were a prize experiment under a microscope. "I shot your lover, too. Unfortunately, he moved when I squeezed the trigger, and I didn't kill him. But he never had you again, did he? I wouldn't let him because you are mine. I'm the one who's going to get to do things to you." His hand tightened on my hair so cruelly that I was sure he meant to pull it all out by the roots. I squirmed in pain.

"There's blood on your mouth," he whispered, plainly fascinated by the sight.

I squeezed my lids shut, unable to bear the sight of those greedy, speculative eyes boring into me, crawling over my face with an almost physical touch.

"Is this the way Nick treated you?"

"Uhhh . . ."

"Answer me nicely." He yanked my head back at an angle so sharp, it made speaking impossible.

"Did you like it?" He pinched one of my breasts, twisting at the nipple until a scream tore from me. "I think you did. I think you're sorry you shot him because you liked it when he knocked you around. I think it made you feel sexy. Seeing you like this makes me feel sexy, Toni."

Then I felt his mouth on mine, grinding down, smearing the blood and tearing at the cut so it flowed faster. Suddenly I realized what had taken him so long to get here. He'd stopped someplace to eat a hamburger. I could taste it on him, smell the half-cooked meat still clinging to his teeth. A picture of cows in a slaughterhouse flashed behind my eyes. I saw the ax coming down, heard the screams, smelled the gore, saw the flaring blue Antarctic eyes of the executioner.

I felt Simpler's hands on my crotch, kneading and pulling, then tugging roughly at my waistband. The skintight spandex pants were difficult to tear. I fought. It was useless, of course. He was much too strong. But I had to put up a struggle. I used everything I had, my legs, my hips. No matter how much he hurt me, I wouldn't lie still like some passive dumb animal.

Then all at once his weight left me, and he dragged me off the couch by my wrists.

"I don't need to bother with this," he snarled.

"Uhhh—"

"I can fix it so you don't give me any trouble. That's how I do it. I have it all set up."

I opened my mouth to scream, and he backhanded me. "Try any more of that and I'll knock your teeth out. You won't be so pretty then. Men won't dream about you then. Now, why are you here? Did Gloria tell you Heiser was my stepfather? Or is it something else?"

I wanted to howl at him that he'd never get away with it. I'd left messages with half the city of Baltimore about this place. But my only hope now was that O'Dell or Al would show up before he killed me. Maybe if I told him I'd left a message with O'Dell, he'd just kill me right away. What did he have to lose?

On the other hand, I had to tell him something. "I traced the plastic bug," I managed to get out between my bleeding lips.

His pupils narrowed to needle points. "Oh, yes. The calling card I left in your bed. How did you like it? I wish I could have seen your face when you found it. I bet that was an amusing moment."

"How did you get into my apartment?"

"Why, with a key, of course. You shouldn't leave your keys around so casually when you go a-wall-papering. It's so easy to make an impression and get it copied. Now how did you trace the bug?" When I didn't reply, he shook me. "Tell me the truth, or I'll make you suffer. And I'm quite an expert at that."

When I told him that I'd found the bug's twin in an antique shop, his lips drew back from his teeth. "So the cheap old bastard sold some of them. He never told me, but I should have guessed. God, how I hated him!"

As he talked of his stepfather, he appeared distracted. Desperately I screamed as loud as I could and yanked back to break free. Simpler easily reasserted his hold on me and strangled my cry. Then he pressed my back against his body. With one hand gagging my mouth and the other arm locked across my midriff, pinning both my arms to my sides, he frog-marched me through the dining room toward the kitchen.

"I don't have to deal with this," he kept muttering. "There are better ways, much better ways. I used chloroform on Susie. Did you guess that? No, of course you didn't. Nobody knows, not even the police. She didn't realize what hit her until she woke up on my operating table."

With a horror so deep it left me almost numb, I realized he intended to take me to the basement. Once down there and staked out for crucifixion, I'd never get out alive.

In the kitchen, I glanced at the coffeemaker with its little red light and realized that the familiar odor I'd smelled had been Simpler's mocha-hazelnut coffee. Now, he dragged me past the coffeemaker and released my waist long enough to lean sideways to take a wicked-looking knife out of a butcher-block holder. With my suddenly unpinned arm, I flailed maniacally and by some miracle knocked the glass carafe full of hot coffee over both of us. Luckily, more of it landed on him than on me.

"Shit!" he cursed, and danced in front of me so I couldn't get past him to the side door.

Ignoring my burns, I swept the whole countertop with my stinging forearm. I caught up the butcher block of knives and hurled it at his chest. Whirling, I dashed back through the dining room. I knew I couldn't get the door unlocked. But there were windows in the living room.

Yelling as loudly as I could manage, I leaped over the fallen chair in the dining room and barreled into the living room. I swept up an end table and hurled it with all my strength. I had forgotten the wooden shutters covering the windows. The glass broke, but the barrier kept it and the end table from falling outside. A neighbor might hear the noise, but if he opened a curtain to peek out, he wouldn't see anything unusual.

"Bitch!"

Simpler was on top of me before I could throw anything else. Cursing, he lunged at me, and all at once we were both on the floor at the foot of the stairs. We rolled back and forth, me kicking and scratching, he digging his hands into my hair and banging my head hard against the oak base of the bottom step. "Damn you, damn you, damn you!" he kept chanting. "You'll never leave me. No one leaves me!" He seemed to want to knock all my brains out. Then his hands jerked down to my throat and he started to squeeze.

I had rolled on top of something hard and round. The Pro-Stun. His thumbs dug into my throat, cutting off all air, crushing my windpipe. As my hand finally came in contact with the smooth cylinder of pepper spray, I felt myself beginning to lose consciousness. I couldn't let it happen. Lose consciousness and I'd wake up tied down the way I'd seen Gloria. With the last bit of strength I could muster, I hefted the Pro-Stun and sprayed it directly into his face.

The second it hit him, he let out a terrible shriek and reared back, clawing at his eyes. We'd been so close that a bit of the cloud had affected me. Or maybe it was just the choking and the terror that was making my eyes water and burn. As I struggled to my feet, I pushed Simpler off. He was still flailing and tearing at his eyes, but I was afraid that even blinded he might grab me and rip me to pieces. I backed up the stairs and then turned and stumbled to the top, half dragging myself with the railing. There was pain all through my body, but I was so pumped on adrenaline that I hardly noticed it.

Maybe I could scream out the window of one of the bedrooms and get help, I was thinking as I opened the first door I saw. Maybe I'd even find a phone.

I slammed the door behind me, pushed the button to lock it, and then, gasping and choking, reached frantically for a light switch. The house was old enough to have overhead fixtures, so my fingers found a switch. When the light went on, I saw a bedroom done up in faded floral wallpaper. There was a maple four-poster with a white chenille spread in the corner next to the window. Opposite was a vanity table loaded with cosmetics. The air smelled musty, and dust covered everything. No phone in sight.

I lurched to the chair in front of the vanity and wedged it under the doorknob to keep him out as long as possible. Already I could hear him on the stairs.

"Get out of my mother's room, you bitch!" he screamed. "You have no right to go in there." His voice shook with rage. The doorknob rattled, and then the door panels thudded. "You get out of her room or you'll be sorry!"

I was trying to open one of the double windows that looked out on the street, but they were both painted shut or perhaps even nailed shut. Glancing back over my shoulder, I spotted a heavy-looking mirrored tray loaded with little glass bottles of nail polish. It wasn't until I'd smashed the tray through the left-hand window, bottles and all, that I noticed most all the polish was crimson.

"Help!" I shouted through the shattered glass.

"Help me!" Simpler's choking hadn't improved my voice. It came out lost and thin, not nearly loud enough. And though I screamed over and over, I didn't see any lights going on in nearby houses, either.

Behind me, the door rattled and vibrated. It sounded as if he were beating at the door with a battering ram. Luckily for me, it was an old door, solidly made. Then the noise stopped, and instead I heard my heart hammering my ribs and my breath rattling through my windpipe like a load of rocks. Tears streamed down my face, and my eyes burned like crazy. "Help me!" I screamed. "Simpler's trying to kill me. Help! Call nine-one-one! Help!" My voice seemed to disappear into the night, swallowed up by the void.

What was it with these people? Were they all on sleeping pills or dead drunk? Weren't there any nosy old busybodies across the street who lived to call the police? And where the hell were O'Dell and Al? Wasn't it about time for one of them to come riding out of the west?

A metallic scraping, clinking noise interrupted the ominous silence in the hall. "I'm going to get you, bitch!" he called through the crack next to the floor. "I'm prying off the damn door. And when I've got you, I'm going to skin you alive."

Somehow, I didn't think he meant that threat figuratively. That was it. I needed fresh air. Jagged shards of glass lined the window frame. I stuck my head out and looked down. It was too dark to see clearly, but I made out some sort of big bushes. Just my luck they'd probably be pyracantha. If I didn't break all my bones falling, I'd be blinded by two-inch thorns. In the drive I spotted the dark outline of the Volvo. Since he'd backed it in, I could even see the moon reflecting off the handicap license. Must have been his stepfather's, and judging from his remarks, their relationship hadn't been any too good.

Wishing I still had my flash, I craned my neck. A little peaked roof sat like a paper hat over the window. There was a chance that if I could climb out and get my footing on the window ledge, I could hoist myself out onto the lower part of the roof and then to the window gable. From there I could keep Simpler from following just by kicking at him. At least I hoped I could. Anyhow, surely someone would notice me screaming if I was hollering like a banshee up there.

I looked back and saw the door quivering under Simpler's battering and heard him muttering incoherently. Panting, lungs pumping like an overworked bellows, I snatched a pillow from the bed and used it to clear the window of broken glass. Under the circumstances, I did the best job I could. Still, as I grasped the sides of the wooden frame and put my leg over it, razor-sharp fragments dug into my palms and through my riding tights to the soft flesh of my thighs. It would have been nice if I'd had leather cycling gloves on. But I'd always been too cheap to bother with them. I promised myself that if I lived through this, I'd buy a ton.

I'm not unathletic, but I wouldn't describe myself as a gymnast, either. The tricky part was getting turned around without losing my grip and falling out. By the time I managed it, blood streamed down my wrists and forearms and my thighs were on fire with nasty little cuts. Bits of embedded glass peppered my flesh.

I was standing on the window frame with my hands reaching for the lower part of the gable while I used my right foot to try to get a purchase on the steeply pitched roofline. I heard the door to the bedroom crash inward. An instant earlier my arms and legs had been trembling so much, I'd wondered if I had the strength to pull myself over and up. Now stark terror turned me into Superwoman.

I surged out. Ignoring the old cedar shingles crumbling beneath my hands, I clung like a spider, all the while pulling myself while I walked my sneakered feet up the adjoining asphalt shingles slanting up from the edge of the cornice board. I was almost out of reach when Simpler poked his head out the window and grabbed for my ankle.

"You'll pay for this!" he shrieked. "You and my mother will both pay!"

What was it with his mother? some part of my brain wondered. I remembered Gloria telling me something about him losing her early in life. I kicked at his hand and called on every ounce of strength I had left to heave myself up and onto the gable.

For several seconds I just lay there, gasping like a traumatized fish. Then I peered over the edge. Simpler was staring up at me. Between the moonlight and the artificial light streaming out from the room, I could see his face. It was swollen from the pepper spray. His eyes had puffed into blood red slits. He looked like a demon from hell. "It's too late!" I shouted at him. "Now you can't get away with it anymore! Someone's bound to have noticed all this by now." I certainly hoped and prayed they had.

"It's not too late to kill you," he called back. Then his hideous red face disappeared.

Something about the way he said that renewed my chills. Frantically I pulled my legs up under me, pushed myself into a sitting position, and looked around. The gable where I'd found refuge stuck out from the front of the house like an eyebrow and joined at the peak with the main roof. There must be attic space. What if Simpler knew a way onto the roof from the attic? What if there were matching gables like this on the back of the roof and he could just use them as an exit and walk up and over?

All this time I'd given up any idea of using my gun. Downstairs there hadn't been time to load it. In the bedroom I'd been so stressed out I hadn't even considered it. But I could feel the weight of it still in the pouch at my waist. Where I'd taken out the Pro-Stun, the zipper hung half-open. With everything that had happened, it was amazing the gun hadn't fallen out. What about the bullets?

My hands shook so badly, it was tough to get the zipper open the rest of the way and take out the Taurus. With its butt clutched in one hand, I felt around the bottom of the pouch for the bullets. I'd packed enough to fill all the chambers. Now there were only two.

It was dark, and my eyes ran and burned so badly that I could hardly see. I was sniffing and sniveling like a six-year-old with a cold. I had given up on screaming and calling for help. It didn't seem to be doing any good, and my throat was now too sore to manage anything but a croak. A frigid night wind bit at my skin and sent my hair flying around my face so I was even more blinded. Somehow I managed to open the cylinder and poke one of the cartridges into a chamber.

The wail of a distant siren cut through the night, and I jerked. The second cartridge, which I'd had between my thumb and forefinger, slipped away and rattled off the edge of the gable. I heard it thunk softly somewhere in the bushes.

At that instant I felt a vibration on the roof above me. My heart leaped like a rocket blasting off to outer space, and I turned myself around so I faced the roof, almost losing my balance in the process. At the same time I clicked the cylinder shut on the Taurus and pulled back the hammer. Unfortunately, my fumbling fingers had spun the cylinder before it snapped into place.

The siren was getting closer, wailing like a banshee. But it wasn't close enough. In the moonlight I could see Simpler edging toward me along the rooftop. The moon and stars shone down on his blond head and glittered off the mammoth butcher knife he carried in his right hand.

"I've got a gun," I shouted through my sniffles and wheezes.

"I don't believe you."

I raised my hand and waved the gun so he would see it. "Stay away from me or I'll kill you."

He hesitated a moment, obviously surprised by the big, businesslike-looking Taurus. Then he started forward again, walking apelike but surefootedly on the ridgepole.

"Stay away from me, Simpler!"

"Oh, no, Toni. You and I were meant for each other. This was preordained. You're not going to get away. Nobody gets away!"

"Keep off!"

"I'm a psychologist, remember? I understand

people like you, women like you. You're a passive personality. Shooting Nick was a fluke. You'll never forgive yourself for it. You're weak and guilty, and you want to be punished. You need to be punished. If you're not punished, you'll be haunted all your life."

His voice had gone silky, insinuating. It crawled up my skin like some sort of horrible, many-legged insect. The hand with which I held the gun began trembling uncontrollably.

"I'll shoot you!" I threw out.

"Oh, no, you won't."

"I shot Nick, you bastard. It wasn't a fluke. I shot him because he was going to kill me."

"Yes, but you're sorry, aren't you? You know you shouldn't have done it."

I tried to take aim at him, but the barrel of the gun wavered like a flag in a high wind. Tears gushed out of my eyes and streamed into my nose and mouth. My hair flew around and whipped at my eyelids. Somewhere in the distance I became aware of noise. Cars screeched. People shouted. Lights began to flash on. I heard someone shouting my name and then Simpler's.

None of that mattered now, either to Simpler or to me. He didn't even spare a glance for the activity beneath us, and I couldn't.

The knife came up in his hand, and he began to slither down the side of the roof toward me. "I'm your executioner, Toni, your retribution. You're guilty, and you need to be punished."

I felt as if there were an unbearable pressure inside my chest and it was moving up to my head. When it got there, I would explode. The revolver wobbled and trembled. My trigger finger seemed to have lost all strength. I saw the gleam of the knife and felt the roof tremble as Simpler inched crablike toward me.

I managed to aim the barrel at his midsection and squeeze the trigger. Only a click. The bullet could be anywhere in the cylinder.

Grinning triumphantly, Simpler came closer. "No bullets in your gun, Toni? Stupid broad. It's no good if you forgot to load it."

I grasped the grip and the trigger with both my hands, steadied it, and pulled again. Another hollow click. I pulled again. *Click*.

As he rushed to close the distance between us, I started to squeeze the trigger one last time. I could see Simpler's face clearly, for a spotlight from the ground lit him up. His swollen, glaring eyes, his mouth twisted with hatred. Hatred not just for me, but for every living thing.

Crack. A spot appeared in the middle of his forehead. His face went blank. The knife he'd raised over me dropped from his hand and clattered on the shingles. Inches from where I crouched, he toppled and then slid with a horrible crashing rush. Then he slipped off the edge of the roof. Screams flew up, almost as if the whole world were terrified.

I turned and looked down where he'd disappeared and saw only darkness. Then I looked toward a flashing light and spotted O'Dell. He had a rifle in his hands, and he was crossing the street toward Simpler's body.

"Are you all right?" he called up.

"Just great," I replied shakily. "Just swell. Thanks."

Epilogue

Two weeks later O'Dell, Damon, Randall, Jonathan, and I all had dinner together at Randall's place. It was a royal feast. While we ate, we talked about what had happened.

O'Dell filled us in on some facts. Simpler's mother had run away when he was ten and left him in the care of his stepfather, Ivan Heiser. My guess is the old guy didn't treat him too well. The police now plan to look into how Heiser died. Maybe it wasn't just old age that put him in his coffin.

As for why Simpler started to murder women and just how many he'd murdered—the police don't know that yet, either. Did he start to interview serial killers because he wanted to consult with colleagues, or was it their accounts of their murders that set him off? Did the evil he was trying to understand reach out and understand him all too well?

They do have a record of how many serial killers he interviewed for his book. They also know that he was in Columbus, Ohio, for a professional meeting at the time Acker's victim, Janet Greenwich, was murdered.

How many killers did he talk to about the women who got away before he decided to start tracking down those women and settling the score himself? Eventually the police may find out. I doubt, however, they'll ever find out whether he killed Rebecca because he mistook her for Susie. I suspect that's what happened, but it's so awful I don't want to know it for sure.

I'm still living in Rebecca's apartment. But I don't expect to be there much longer. Mrs. Kelso has given me the $10,000 reward. I'm thinking of using it to buy rehab property somewhere near Mt. Vernon Square. I'm not in any big hurry, though. Rebecca and I are getting along just fine now. I've been back to Greenspring Valley to visit her mother. When Mrs. Kelso and I talk about Rebecca, it's as if I'm remembering a close friend. In fact, I dreamed about her last night. She wasn't crying anymore. I felt she was—if not at peace—at least at rest.

Oh, about Al. You know, he never did come to my rescue. Sure, the baby-sitter passed along the message. But he never told Sandy. He just figured I was pulling some kooky stunt. Luckily for me, O'Dell took seriously the message I left on his answering machine. I must say, I'm feeling a lot warmer toward Gus O'Dell these days. But when it comes to men like Gus, I've got to be careful. In lots of ways he's like Nick. I'm happy to say that in lots of others, he seems very different. Still, I've got to take things slow.

Oh, another thing. I'm glad it was Gus who shot Simpler and not me. At least, part of me is glad. But you know, there's another part that wishes I'd been the one to put that slug in him. I would've, too. When O'Dell got in his shot, I had the bullet in the chamber under my hammer.